Also by Kieran Scott

I Was a Non-Blonde Cheerleader
Brunettes Strike Back
A Non-Blonde Cheerleader in Love

a novel in five acts

kieran scott

G. P. PUTNAM'S SONS

G. P. PUTNAM'S SONS
A division of Penguin Young Readers Group.

Published by The Penguin Group.

Penguin Group (USA) Inc., 375 Hudson Street, New York, NY 10014, U.S.A. Penguin Group (Canada), 90 Eglinton Avenue East, Suite 700, Toronto, Ontario M4P 2Y3, Canada (a division of Pearson Penguin Canada Inc.). Penguin Books Ltd, 80 Strand, London WC2R 0RL, England. Penguin Ireland, 25 St. Stephen's Green, Dublin 2, Ireland (a division of Penguin Books Ltd.). Penguin Group (Australia), 250 Camberwell Road, Camberwell, Victoria 3124, Australia (a division of Pearson Australia Group Pty Ltd). Penguin Books India Pvt Ltd, 11 Community Centre, Panchsheel Park, New Delhi - 110 017, India. Penguin Group (NZ), 67 Apollo Drive, Rosedale, North Shore 0632, New Zealand (a division of Pearson New Zealand Ltd). Penguin Books (South Africa) (Pty) Ltd, 24 Sturdee Avenue, Rosebank, Johannesburg 2196, South Africa. Penguin Books Ltd, Registered Offices: 80 Strand, London WC2R 0RL, England.

Design by Ryan Thomann. Text set in Caslon.

Library of Congress Cataloging-in-Publication Data

Scott, Kieran, 1974– Geek magnet : a novel in five acts / Kieran Scott. p. cm.

Summary: Seventeen-year-old KJ Miller is determined to lose the label of "geek magnet" and get the guy of her dreams, all while stage managing the high school musical, with the help of the most popular girl in school. [1. Dating (Social customs)—Fiction. 2. Musicals—Fiction. 3. Theater—Fiction. 4. High schools—Fiction. 5. Schools—Fiction.] I. Title.

PZ7.S42643Ge 2008 [Fic]—dc22 2007028707

ISBN 978-0-399-24760-6

1 3 5 7 9 10 8 6 4 2

THIS ONE'S FOR ALL MY FRIENDS FROM PHHS, especially those who made my own *Grease* experience so very memorable that I could actually smell the auditorium while writing this book.

Special thanks to the following geeks, without whom there would be no *Geek Magnet*:

Jen Bonnell (super-smart editor geek), whose patience and insightful comments keep making me better

Sarah Burnes (enthusiastic agent geek), who believed in me even when this particular labor of love was too heavy for either of our athletic selves to lift

Lee Scott (loving mom geek), who looks at me like I'm an angel fallen to earth no matter how much I think I suck

Erin and Ian Scott (sister and brother geek), who got me through a lot of the familial tribulations which inspired parts of this book

Matthew Viola (adorable, hockey-loving, politico geek), the love of my life, who never stops reminding me that I am also his

AND

GREASE

(A Washington High School Drama Club Production)

•

LEAD CAST

KJ MILLER..........Geek Magnet (Stage Manager)

FRED FRONTZ..........Geek #1 (Doody)

GLENN MARLOWE..........Geek #2 (Lighting & Sound)

ANDY TERRERO..........Geek #3 (Assistant Stage Manager)

CAMERON RICHARDSON....Most Athletic, Most Popular, Nicest Smile, Best-looking (Audience Member)

TAMA GOLD..........Most Popular (Sandy)

ROBBIE DELANO..........Most Enigmatic, Most Musical (Danny)

STEPHANIE SHUMER..........Brainiest (Miss Lynch)

ASHLEY BROWN..........Most Likely to Star on Broadway (Rizzo)

CARRIE DANES..........Drama Twin #1 (Frenchy)

CORY DANES..........Drama Twin #2 (Jan)

MR. KATZ..........Drama teacher (Faculty Adviser)

CHRISTOPHER MILLER..........KJ's little brother

JILL MILLER..........KJ's mother

GREG MILLER..........KJ's father

ACT ONE, SCENE ONE

In which:

WE MEET THE GEEKS

OKAY, SO I WAS DIZZY WITH POWER. CAN YOU BLAME ME? IT WAS the first day of rehearsals for the spring musical, *Grease,* at Washington High and I, KJ Miller, was the stage manager. The woman in charge. The first junior ever to be granted this most prestigious position. So when I walked into the auditorium after the final bell that afternoon, I'll admit it: I sort of felt like I was surveying my territory. Those two hyper drama guys up on stage parrying with old, plastic French bread props? I was in charge of them. Tama Gold chatting illegally on her cell in the front row? I was in charge of her, too (though she'd never admit it). Theater diva Ashley Brown and her two sidekicks Cory and Carrie Danes (a.k.a. the Drama Twins), who were singing select songs from *Dreamgirls* at the piano? You guessed it. I was even in charge of Stephanie Shumer, my best friend in the entire world. But I had to be sensitive to her. She had *so* wanted the part of Rizzo, but Riz went to the indomitable Ashley, who had actually wanted to play Sandy. Meanwhile, Stephanie was stuck playing the principal, Miss Lynch. Ugh.

Before anyone could spot me, I took a long, deep breath

and let that very particular auditorium aroma fill my senses. It was like moldy, old stage curtain, mixed with dust and chased by Sour Apple Blow Pop. I loved that scent. It was the scent of the best part of the year.

Musical season. It was finally here. And it was the only time of year that a girl like me—a short, red-haired, flying-below-the-social-radar girl like me—could suddenly become one big blip on the radar screen. Basically, it was magic.

"All right, people!" I announced, my heart pounding with wild anticipation. "Let's—"

"KJ!"

So much for my moment. Fred Frontz, my neighbor and eternal stalker, materialized as if by magic. Not that it was that much of a surprise. Fred was everywhere, all the time.

"KJ! KJ! KJ!" Fred hustled over to me, his T-shirt riding up and exposing more and more of his wide, pale stomach with each step. His blond hair was plastered to his forehead with sweat, and his face was blotchy and red. Like always. Even on freezing cold mornings when I took pity on him walking to school alone and offered him a ride, he was always blotchy and red. "How cool is this? I still can't believe I'm gonna have a solo. Can you believe it? Me! With a solo!"

"Um, Fred? Your shirt's kind of . . ." I pointed at his Buddha belly. Fred yanked the shirt down and crossed his arms over his chest.

"Thanks," he said. "So listen. I got you something."

He reached into his overly large burlap backpack and came out with a Hostess cupcake, half mushed on one side. "To celebrate your first day."

"Thanks, Fred," I said, touched. Considering Fred's sugar

addiction, I knew that refraining from eating this must have taken gargantuan effort.

"She doesn't need that right now."

Andy Terrero, my assistant stage manager, stepped in and snatched away the snack. Andy was a health and science nut, so skinny he must have weighed less than I did. His brown hair stuck straight out from the crown of his head like he had a tiny propeller up there, and his glasses were constantly sliding down his nose. "Refined sugar just gives you a super-high high followed by a major crash. You don't want to crash on your first day, do you, KJ?"

Andy's brown eyes were wide with hope. So were Fred's blue ones. To take the cupcake or not to take the cupcake? That was the question. If I took it, I would crush Andy. If I didn't take it, I would crush Fred. And although it might seem like a teeny tiny thing to a normal person, it wasn't to them. They *would* be crushed. Just like that, I was going to have to let somebody down. My heart squeezed at the thought. Why me?

"You know what? I'm gonna save this for later," I said. I took the cupcake back from Andy and shoved it inside my messenger bag.

"Okay, but you *are* gonna eat it," Fred tried to confirm.

"But *after* rehearsal," Andy clarified, glancing at Fred. "Right?"

"You can't tell her when to eat something, Terrero," Fred complained.

"Do you realize how many preservatives are in that thing? You're basically giving her poison."

Okay. They were starting to make a scene.

"You guys? You know what? I really have to go, uh . . . get

everyone out of the dressing rooms before they, you know, stain . . . something!" I improvised, inching away. "I'll be back in a sec!"

"I can do that for you, KJ!" Andy shouted after me.

"It's okay! I got it!" I shouted back. I tore up the stairs and into the cool darkness of the wings. Deep breath. Okay. I was safe. Now all I had to do was—

Oh crap.

A sudden chill raced down my spine. I was not alone. I could feel it. And I knew exactly who was watching me. I had to get to safety, like, now. I turned on my heel and walked directly into the concave chest of Glenn Marlowe.

He took a slug of his Yoo-hoo, his Adam's apple bobbing above a curl of chest fuzz sticking out of the V-neck of his velour pullover. A chocolate moustache clung to his pathetic attempt at an actual moustache. Meet Glenn "All-Hands" Marlowe. The bane of my existence. If Fred and Andy were semi-irritating gnats, Glenn was one big-old, soul-sucking mosquito.

"Hey, KJ." He licked his teeth. "You're looking mighty . . . fetching this afternoon."

His eyes trailed down to my breasts. My stupid, mongo, mega-breasts. This whole thing was their fault, really. Glenn Marlowe had been stalking me for exactly six years—longer than Andy, but not as long as Fred—and I can remember the exact day it started. It was the first warm day of fifth grade—before I was even aware of the effect that boobs had on boys—when I'd worn that stupid white T-shirt that I hadn't realized I'd grown out of. Glenn had walked into homeroom right when I was stretching my arms over my head and his bug eyes had practically catapulted out of his head. He hadn't stopped looking at my chest since.

"Congrats on being stage manager," he told my left boob.

"Thanks, Glenn," I said. I tried to move past him. Like he had ever let *that* happen.

"What's the rush?" he asked, blocking my path. "I mean, look around. You. Me. The dark. What do you think the universe is trying to tell us?" He reached out and squeezed my upper arm. Hard. And suddenly I was not only boiling, but could hardly breathe.

Why couldn't he just leave me alone? And why couldn't I bring myself to tell him off? Tama Gold would have. She would have told him to back the f-word off and probably would have kicked him in the groin for good measure. But me? No. I was a good girl. Ask anyone. I was incapable of making people feel bad. Even if they were in the process of torturing me.

"Glenn? I really have to get the table read started. Why don't you go check on the sound system? That would be *such* a big help."

His lascivious grin widened. "Really know how to crack the whip, don't you, KJ? Well, don't worry. I like it."

Ew.

"I have to go."

I faked left, then dodged right, and somehow got around him. Maybe somebody on stage would save me. Please let Mr. Katz be here so we can start rehearsal. Or let Steph be here so we can run to the bathroom together. Something. Anything to get me away from—

"So, KJ, when are you gonna quit playing games and go out with me already?" Glenn asked.

The entire cast, whom Andy had gathered on the stage by now, fell silent.

"What?" Andy blurted, his clipboard dropping.

"You're gonna go out with *him*?" Fred asked.

A few people laughed. A few people whispered. I looked up at the pink light above us and willed it to fall on my head.

Welcome to my life. The life of a Geek Magnet.

I am the geek pied piper, drum major in the geek parade. Ever since I can remember, a steady stream of unsavory guys has been following me around like I was God's gift to geekdom and I have no idea why. Stephanie was always telling me that I shouldn't complain. That at least someone was crushing on me. And she had a point. She did. But at times like these, that logic really did nothing for me. I mean, *this* was what my days were like. Embarrassing ambushes, awkward conversations, horrible letdowns, me feeling like this evil, superficial person who couldn't see past face value. But it wasn't my fault. I would have gladly fallen in love with one of these guys. My life would have been so much easier. But I couldn't do it. My heart already belonged to another. And besides, these guys really did make it so damn hard. I mean, it wasn't like they were funny-cute dorks (no Andy Sandbergs here), or even semi-hot dorks (Jimmy Fallons don't actually exist). Each one of these guys had at least ten strikes. And I'd been through this so many times before that really, all I wanted was for that stupid light to fall and flatten me. I would have gladly taken one on the head if it would have gotten me out of this mortification.

"Glenn, I thought you were going to go check on the sound," I said finally.

"I will. As soon as you give me an answer."

He looked around at our audience gleefully. He was enjoying this. And so were they. Which meant no one was going to help me. Stephanie would have, but she hadn't arrived yet. I was going to have to kill her later.

"KJ? What's going on?" Fred said, his expression pathetic.

And suddenly, my heart skipped a beat. Epiphany!

"Glenn, you . . . you know I can't date anyone in the cast," I improvised. "I'm the stage manager. How would that look?"

Ha! Now I couldn't date Glenn or Andy *or* Fred! Three geeks down with one blow! Genius!

"I'm not in the cast. I'm in charge of AV," Glenn said, all proud.

Damn these geeks and their quick minds.

"Well, I'm still in charge of you," I said with a shrug. "And we all know how messy on-set romances can be. Sorry."

"Tough break, Marlowe," one of the ubiquitous drama guys said as he walked by. He slapped Glenn on the back at the exact same moment that Glenn was taking another slug from his Yoo-hoo bottle. There was a gross choking sound. His eyes widened. And suddenly, I was on the receiving end of a cool, refreshing chocolate shower.

The Drama Twins screeched. Nobody moved. I looked down at my new light blue sweater. A constellation of brown droplets. Everywhere. All the heat in my body rushed up my neck and into my face.

It's fine. It's fine. Do. Not. Panic.

"Are you okay, KJ? Are you okay?" Fred asked, loping over.

"I'm fine."

"Oh, God, KJ. Your sweater!" Glenn cried. He looked around the stage, searching for God knows what. "Here! Take this."

He pulled his velour shirt off over his head, momentarily exposing his prominent ribs before the white T-shirt underneath fell back into place.

"No! Take this!" Fred yanked his hooded sweatshirt off the back of a chair, knocking the chair over in the process.

All around us, people started to chuckle. My skin burned so hot it was going to incinerate my clothes. Then Glenn would really get a show to remember.

"I'm fine, you guys, really." I walked over to the pile of unclaimed scripts that were left on the stage, turning my back to them and willing them to go away. Couldn't they see they were embarrassing me?

"No. Really. I want you to have it," Glenn said, following me. "Please. Take it."

"No, take mine," Fred said.

"It's my fault. You want mine."

"I've got a cardigan!" Andy announced helpfully.

"No, you want mine, KJ. Don't you? KJ? KJ?"

I looked down at the stains on my new sweater as laughter filled my ears. I was going to cry. I was actually going to cry. So much for being dizzy with power. If anything, I was suffering a serious power outage.

Go away! Please just *go away*!

"Holy crap!" Robbie Delano, the tall, emo-cute, drummer/actor/class cutup who was playing Danny Zuko, looked up and shoved his chair back suddenly. He put his hand on Glenn's chest, effectively pushing him away from me. "Glenn, buddy, I think I see smoke in the AV booth."

"What?" Glenn's jaw dropped. He was gone in a flash. The air around me cooled slightly.

"Hey, Freddy. You wanna go over some lines?" Robbie crooked his arm around Fred's neck and basically yanked him away. "Andy! Where's my script, man? I thought you were on top of things around here. Chop chop."

Andy dropped to the pile of scripts at my feet to find it. Suddenly I could breathe again. I was still covered in chocolate, but Robbie Delano had saved me. Why? We'd barely ever spoken two words to each other. Robbie was one of those guys who functioned in his own little world, outside the crazy clique society of our school. Back in middle school he had been one of the jocks, one of the blessed ones, bff with Cameron Richardson, who ruled our class to this day. But somewhere along the line, all that had changed. Now Robbie was sports-team free and instead, played drums in the marching band, sang in the choir, and was always in the musicals. Yet he never hung out with the drama crowd or the band geeks or anyone else, really. He'd been in my class since kindergarten, but other than that, I knew next to nothing about him.

"*Thanks,*" I mouthed to him.

He smirked in response. "*No big.*"

My body heat returned to sub-nuclear levels. Okay, so I knew one thing about him. I now owed him one big, fat favor.

ACT ONE, SCENE TWO

In which:

WE MEET TAMA GOLD, CAMERON RICHARDSON, AND MY BOOBS

"KJ, IT LOOKS FINE," STEPHANIE TOLD ME, STARING AT MY CHEST IN the bathroom mirror. We were on a five-minute break from the table read so that Mr. Katz, the faculty adviser, could go out to his Subaru and chain-smoke Marlboros. "It totally fits."

I turned to the side and there they were in full glory. The mega-boobs. My face burned with irritation. The curse of being a redhead—my face flushed at the drop of a hat.

"It so does not," I said, crossing my arms over the hot pink hoodie she was attempting to lend me. I pressed my forearms down so hard it hurt. God, I hated those damn things. Sometimes I wondered if there was some breast fairy who came in the window every night, attached a tire pump to my chest area and went to work. "You are of a normal size. I am purely Himalayan."

"Well, what do you want to do? Wear a stained sweater for the rest of the day?" she asked, wrinkling her small upturned nose. Everything about Steph was small. Her feet, her boobs, her ears, her hands. With her blue eyes and curly brown hair she was like a walking, talking Precious Moments figurine. I, meanwhile, was deformed.

"All right, fine," I said finally, grabbing my bag. "Let's just go back."

"You're welcome!" Stephanie said with a hint of sarcasm. She's like a mom that way. Always making sure you're polite.

"Thank you!" I replied with a smile, matching her tone.

We walked out of the bathroom and headed for the lobby outside the auditorium.

"So Robbie Delano really saved you?" she asked.

"Yep. It was like he had some geek-repelling force field around him or something," I told her. "It was super cool."

"Huh. Well, by definition that would sort of make him a geek, too," she said thoughtfully.

"Uh oh, Science Girl has a new hypothesis," I joked.

Stephanie could make a scientific theory out of almost anything. She once did a whole project on how White Castle isn't as popular as Burger King, McDonald's and Wendy's because red, yellow and orange promote hunger, whereas blue and white promote inner peace. No, I'm not kidding.

"Well, think about it. With magnets, the positive force is attracted to the negative force. So let's say you're the negative force—"

"Why do I have to be the negative force?" I asked.

She rolled her eyes. "Okay, you're the positive force. The geeks are the negative force. The only thing that could repel them is another negative force. Therefore, Robbie is a geek!" she finished happily.

We had just stepped into the lobby, and about a dozen people stopped talking as Stephanie's last four words echoed throughout the room. Laughter quickly, inevitably, ensued. Stephanie looked like she was about to die.

"Omigod. Kill me now," she said.

I didn't answer. I couldn't. Because my Cameron Richardson radar was going berserk.

"Cameron Richardson," I whispered through my teeth, my heart pounding.

"What?" Steph asked. She was still distracted by her verbal vomit.

He was standing in the corner with Tama and some other guys from the basketball team, all sweaty from practice, cradling a ball and laughing at some joke his friend had made. I loved his laugh. It wasn't the usual popular-guy laugh. You know how they always laugh really loudly while looking around at their friends to make sure they're all still laughing, too, so they'll know when to stop? Like the second something stops being funny to one of them it must stop being funny to all of them. Not Cameron. He laughed like no one was watching him. And sometimes, when you thought he was finished laughing and he'd gone all quiet, he'd suddenly, spontaneously giggle out of nowhere to himself. Sometimes, in bio class, I'd catch him doing that. I loved him most in those moments.

Of course, *he'd* never caught *me* doing anything. I was pretty sure that Cameron had a special superpower that enabled him to see right through me.

"CameronRichardsonCameronRichardsonCameron Richardson," I muttered.

I was moving Steph through the lobby now, trying to look casual and cool as we passed by Cameron's little klatch of friends. His red-and-white Washington High cap was on backward and he lifted it up to scratch at his dark blond curls. My palms were sweating and I felt lightheaded, just like I always did when Cameron was around. The agony of him being right there and not being able to talk to him was a daily torturous bliss. Yet somehow, every day I woke up believing this would be the day. The day that he would see me walking into one of our shared classes and realize he had a major thing for short, shy, red-haired artists. He'd suddenly find his leggy, supermodel, Catholic-schoolgirl-of-the-month ridiculously boring, dump her on her perfect ass, and sweep me off my feet. It could happen. It just . . . hadn't yet.

Steph and I were just about through the doors to the auditorium when Tama Gold spoke.

"Hey, KJ. Come here a sec!" I froze. Stephanie tripped over my ankle and took a header into the auditorium. I was powerless to stop her. Everyone was watching me now. Including Cameron.

Those were the first words Tama had spoken to me all year. She used to talk to me all the time. Last year during the musical I had actually thought we were becoming friends. But the second the show was over, she went back to the beautiful people, back to acting like I didn't exist. I still felt stupid for thinking we could have been friends. I mean, Tama was the most blessed of the blessed. Two years ago she had waltzed right into this school as a transfer student, and before the first mystery meat of the year had been served, she had the popular crowd under her thumb. She was model gorgeous with blemishless cocoa skin, stunning green eyes and smooth brown curls that were never, ever out of place. Not to mention the legs. The height. The ability to wear a plastic garbage bag and make it look like haute couture. How could I have ever thought that a girl like that would waste her time on a girl like me?

Stephanie dusted herself off, shot me a quick look, and headed to the table to grab her script.

"KJ! Are you in there?" Tama trilled, earning a round of laughter from her friends.

I turned around. Cameron Richardson's eyes went directly to my breasts. Damn. I crossed my arms and held on tight. He blushed and looked away.

"What's up?" I asked Tama.

"Nothing. You never talk to me anymore," Tama teased with a pout. "I was so psyched when I heard you were going to be stage manager."

"You were?" I asked, approaching slowly.

The other guys, Tommy and Dustin, looked me up and down like they'd never seen me before. As if Tommy hadn't regularly peed in my pool back in grade school when we were briefly friends.

"Omigod! Totally," Tama said. "It's always good to have friends in high places."

She reached out her long, slim arm and wrapped it around my shoulders, tripping me closer. I hazarded a glance at Cameron. He looked right in my eyes this time, and smiled. No. Freaking. Way.

"You guys all know KJ, right?" Tama asked, presenting me like a child. As if I hadn't been going to school with them my whole life.

"S'up?" Dustin and Tommy said in unison, with the exact same nod.

"Hey, KJ," Cameron said, tossing his ball up and down. "How'd you do on the bio test?"

Wait a second. He knew I was in his bio class? He knew I existed?

"Good, uh, fine. You know. Got an A," I said.

What!? What!?

"You're such a little brain," Tama teased, knocking me with her elbow.

"KJ and I are the only juniors in our section of AP bio and she's pretty much the only one who ever gets A's," Cameron said.

This was unbelievable. Cameron Richardson noticed my grades? I was so floored, and so very, very red, I couldn't look any of them in the eye. I stared down at my blue plaid Converse and tugged at my hair.

"Dude. What's all over your hands?" Dustin asked, disgusted.

I held out my fingers. There were purple and red splotches of paint on a few of my fingertips and under my nails. From art class. Eighth period. I had forgotten to clean up in all my haste to get to the theater. I looked at Cameron and gulped. I bet money none of the girls he went out with was ever seen in public without a professional manicure.

"It's just paint. I had art," I said, shoving my hands under my arms.

"It's called soap and water. Ever heard of it?" Tommy joked.

He and Dustin slapped hands and cackled. I was starting to wish Tama had never invited me over here.

"That's real class, man," Cameron admonished. "Shut the hell up."

Hang on. Had Cameron just defended me? Okay, Tama inviting me over here was the best thing ever!

"Come on, kids! Let's make magic happen!" Mr. Katz announced, coming through the door behind us.

"Mr. Katz! Mr. Katz!" Tommy shouted mirthfully. "Is it too late to audition?"

Mr. Katz paused in the auditorium doorway, his Grateful Dead T-shirt bulging with his stomach from under his tweed jacket. He looked at Tommy curiously. The guys dropped their gym bags and balls and backed up.

"'Go, greased lightning, you're burning up the quarter mile,'" Dustin sang. Badly.

"'Greased lightning! Go, greased lightning!'" Cameron and Tommy chorused. They did a rough imitation of the dance from the movie. Horrible, really. But it was Cameron, and pretty much the cutest thing ever.

"A fine rendition, gents, but get out," Mr. Katz said wryly as he smoothed down his comb-over. "Ladies? Shall we?"

Tommy and Dustin took off for the gym at a jog, but Cameron hung back. "Don't worry about those guys," he said to me, grabbing up his basketball. "They can be real jackasses sometimes."

"Yeah. And the sky is blue," I said without thinking.

Cameron laughed. Laughed! At *my* joke!

"Good one. See ya in class," he said.

"Yeah. See ya."

I stood there and watched him go. I had to remember every single detail of this moment. What I was wearing. What he was wearing. The exact hue of the sunlight streaming through the windows. Every detail of the day Cameron had finally seen me. How was I going to function normally for the rest of the day? How was I going to function normally ever?

I took a deep, giddy breath and turned around. Tama was still there. And she was smiling in a way that made me feel like she knew every single one of my innermost secrets and found them all hilarious.

"What?" I said dumbly.

"Oh my God! You like him! You like Cameron Richardson!"

she squealed. "You naughty girl, you. Crushing on the big basketball star."

"I don't like him," I protested.

"No! Cage! I love it! You and Cameron is exactly the out-of-left-field idea this school needs," Tama said. "In fact, I am totally going to talk you up to him."

"Really?" There was no hiding my excitement.

"Totally!" She draped her arm over my shoulders again as she led me through the double doors. "Now, let's talk costumes. Blue is really my color, so I'm thinking Sandy's clothes should have blue as a theme. . . ."

She was still talking as we made our way down the aisle, but I didn't hear a word. All I could think about was Cameron. Cameron had smiled at me. He'd spoken to me. He'd defended me. And biggest miracle of all? Not one geek had interrupted us the whole, entire time. And now, Tama Gold, a member of his blessed inner circle, was going to "talk me up." In five minutes, my whole entire world had changed.

There was no denying it. The theater really was a magical place.

ACT ONE, SCENE THREE

In which:

WE MEET THE FAMILY, AND WAIT

"KATIE JEAN, WILL YOU PLEASE AT LEAST CHEW?" MY MOTHER snapped, exasperated. She dropped her fork with a clang and ran her hands over her short, dark hair.

I glanced at my little brother, Christopher. We were both thinking the same thing: Uh oh. Mom's tense. Chris doesn't talk much, but we can speak volumes with our eyes. I lowered my fork, chewed and swallowed. I took a gulp of my soda.

"Sorry. I just have a lot of homework to do," I told her.

I was lying. She knew I was lying. Even Christopher knew I was lying, and he was eight. I mean, I did have a lot of homework, but that wasn't the reason I wanted to finish fast. It was the empty chair across from my mom's at the square kitchen table. The perfect place setting with its napkin still folded and tucked away, waiting for someone to put it to use. Someone who was not there. Someone I wanted to see less and less with each click of the wooden kitchen clock.

But it was Monday. Monday was usually a safe day. Where was he?

"Well, it's still going to be there when you're finished. How about you don't choke yourself in the process?" my mother said, forcing a smile. She glanced at the clock and pressed her lips together before lifting her eyes. They were sad eyes. I felt angry just looking at them. "So how was your first day at the musical?"

I cleared my throat. "It was great. We did the table read. Robbie Delano was really funny as Danny, and Ashley was perfect, of course. Tama thinks, like, half her lines are too dorky, but it's all good."

"What about Freddy? He's in it again this year, right?" my mom asked.

My mom had loved Fred Frontz ever since he showed up on our doorstep with a homemade valentine for me in the second grade—a ritual that had been repeated every year since. He always acted like they were just friendly cards, but I knew they weren't, and every year when the doorbell rang on V-Day, I went to get it, terrified—petrified that this would be the year he finally got up the guts to ask me out. But my mom didn't get that. She just thought that Fred was "the sweetest boy."

"He was good," I said. "He's all tense about getting his lines right, of course."

"That sounds like Freddy," she said with a knowing chuckle.

We all heard a car turn onto our street and my mother's eyes darted to the kitchen window. It took about two seconds for all of us to recognize that the car was not his. I could feel my mother and brother de-clench.

"That's why I was late. He was all over me after rehearsal to run lines with him, so I went over there," I told her. "Otherwise he never would have let it go." My foot bounced up and down under the table. I should have put Fred off until after dinner. Then I'd be able to get out of here.

"That's nice. You're a good friend to him, KJ," my mother told me.

"Yeah, well," I said. Boy made it impossible not to be. He was like a big puppy dog, just begging for affection. I was incapable of saying no to him. Which was another reason to be terrified of the day he finally got up the guts to ask me out.

I took a bite of my chicken and tried to concentrate on chewing. Another car turned onto our block and sped by. The clock tick, tick, ticked. Christopher thudded his foot against one of the table legs, mimicking the beat. My mother picked up her napkin, crumpled it, and dropped it on top of her almost-full plate.

"Well, it looks like Dad's going to be late again," she said with a sigh.

Chris and I glanced at each other and jumped up from the table to clear it. My mother had just given us our get-out-of-jail-free card. If we could just get the table cleared (except for *his* plate) and get our butts up to our rooms before he came home, then we might not have to deal with him. It was already seven forty-five, and if my father walks through the door any time after seven thirty, there's no telling what kind of shape he's going to be in. It's always better to be out of sight and armed with an excuse to avoid him.

I scraped my plate over the garbage can, then my brother's, then my mom's. Chris swiped the table for crumbs, then scurried up the stairs. I loaded up the dishwasher and closed it, then quickly followed. When I glanced over my shoulder, my mom was leaning against the kitchen counter, staring out the window at the pitch-black front yard in a pose of grim resignation.

Mom doesn't have a second-floor room to go to. No matter what, she always has to deal with him. My heart went out to her, but that didn't stop me from taking the stairs two at a time, and shutting my door behind me.

ACT ONE, SCENE FOUR

In which:

WE MEET MY DAD

"I CAN'T BELIEVE I MISSED IT. HE ACTUALLY LAUGHED AT something you said!" Stephanie gushed on the phone that night. "Cameron Richardson thinks you're funny!"

I'd already told her the story ten times, but neither one of us had gotten bored of it yet. We'd spent the last five years of our lives talking about how this moment might happen when it finally happened, and now that it *had* happened, we were dissecting it hard core.

"He even said 'good one!' So he laughed *and* complimented me," I told her, spinning around and around in my desk chair. "This was the best day ever."

"Do you realize what this means?" Stephanie blurted.

That we're going to fall in love and live happily ever after? "What?"

"It means he doesn't actually have superpowers," Stephanie joked. "I'm kind of disappointed, to be honest. It would have been cool to know someone who had actually evolved into a superbeing that could see through genetic matter. I so would have liked to study him."

"You and the rest of the female population of Washington High," I said with a laugh.

An IM popped up on my screen. The time stamp said nine fifty-five. I stopped spinning. Was it that late already? And still no sign of dear old Dad. I waited for the stomach knot of dread to pass, then read the message. It was from Andy.

> **Terrero365:** do we need to do a props list or did you do it already? Because I can do it if you need me to or we could do it together. If you have time at lunch or before rehearsal or . . . what do you think?

I typed back.

> **KJrocks:** lunch works 4 me.

> **Terrero365:** kewl. I'll bring the soy chips I was telling you about!!!

Oh. Yay.

> **G_Marlowe:** the virtual me is holding the virtual you's hand.

I cringed and closed the new IM window. The best way to deal with Glenn's IMs was to ignore them.

> **Ready4Freddy:** hey kj!!!!! wanna ride 2 school 2gether? have a q 4 u.

I rolled my eyes. As soon as my away message left, they were all over my IM. I couldn't even get away from these guys when I was in the privacy of my own home. Now Fred wanted a ride in the morning. What if Cameron saw us get out of the car together and thought we were, like, dating? Still, what was

I going to say to Fred? He knew I had a car. He knew I had to drive past his house to get to school. I was trapped.

With a sigh, I typed back.

KJrocks: sure. c u then.

G_Marlowe: r u holding my hand?

I groaned and closed the window again.

"Do you think he'll talk to you again tomorrow?" Steph said in my ear.

"I don't know. I hope so," I said.

TamaRama: How over the top was Ashley today? You should get her to tone it down.

I blinked. Seriously? I had thought Ashley was just fine. Very tough-girl with a heart of gold.

KJrocks: u think?

TamaRama: Totally! But of course, it's your call. Don't let me dictate.

"You should wear your hair up. You look much more sophisticated with your hair up. Cameron likes sophisticated girls," Steph said.

"Totally." He had, after all, dated a senior last year when we were only sophomores.

G_Marlowe: HELLO? I KNOW YOU'RE ONLINE!

KJrocks: screw you, glenn. i don't have to answer you if i don't want to!!!

Of course, I deleted that the second I was finished typing it.

"What are you going to wear?" Steph asked.

"Omigod. I have no idea." I was about to log off and go through my wardrobe with her piece by piece when I heard the very specific roar of my dad's car engine turning onto our street. A rock formed in the space between my heart and my stomach, pressing against both.

"Steph, I gotta go. My dad's home," I said.

"Oh. Okay. Is everything all right?" she asked.

Stephanie was the only person on the planet who knew the whole truth and nothing but the truth about my dad. The only person I had ever trusted enough to share all the gory details with. Of course, she was over here all the time, too, so she'd witnessed enough mortifying behavior to fill ten journals, but she'd never uttered a word about it to anyone. That was a real best friend.

"Who knows? I'll see you tomorrow."

We hung up. Hand quaking, I reached for the mouse and closed all the IM windows, then logged off my e-mail. I needed complete silence. No distractions.

The front door opened, then slammed. My heart jumped. His footsteps on the kitchen linoleum were both heavy and dragging. Yep. He was wasted. Not that I was surprised. It was after ten, for God's sake.

My hands curled into fists. How the hell did he drive in that condition? I knew it was just from the bus station to our house, which was only a few miles, but you'd think that sooner or later he'd pass out at the wheel or something. Playing the odds, I mean. God, I wished he would. I really wished he would. Maybe if he were in traction in the hospital, he might actually wake up and realize he was a total addict.

Yeah, right. The man would stop drinking when he was dead.

"KJ! Christopher!" he shouted. I swallowed hard and looked at my door. Just leave me alone and pass out on the couch, why don't you?

"KJ! Christopher!" Louder this time. I shoved myself up from my chair and went out into the hallway. Chris was already standing there, his legs planted a foot apart. Scared.

"Did you leave your bike in the driveway again?" I hissed at him.

He shook his head, staring at the top of the steps.

"Chris!" I whispered.

"No!" he whispered. "I swear!"

I sighed. Took his hand. "Come on, then."

"Hey, Dad," I said warily.

He stood at the bottom of the stairs, his white shirt wrinkled with the sleeves rolled up. His blue eyes swam in their sockets and his face was red all over. His usually normal-sized nose looked swollen, and one lock of his brown hair hung over his forehead.

"Are you two gonna come down and say hello to me?" he said. "I've been at work all day trying to keep a roof over your heads, you know."

Christopher and I looked at each other. Like we hadn't heard this one before. We tromped down the stairs side by side. I reached up and hugged my dad. He. Totally. Reeked. What did he do? Roll around on the floor of the bar and let people pour drinks all over him?

"Hi, Dad," I said, holding my breath now.

"Hi, Dad," Christopher echoed.

"Hey, buddy," he said to Chris. He ran his big hand over Christopher's hair until it stuck straight up. Then he kissed the top of my head and squeezed me so tightly I almost coughed. God, it was gross being near him when he was like this.

I pulled away, looking at the floor. "I kind of have a lot of homework to do."

"Okay, hon," he said. "Let me know if you need any help."

Yeah. Sure. Because you'll still be awake in fifteen minutes. Not snoring on the couch with your head tipped back against the wall.

"Okay," I said.

I was back in my room so fast I could have been a member of the Justice League. I waited until Christopher had returned to his room as well, then closed the door and turned around, my fingernails cutting into my palms. Okay. It was over. The worst part of the day was over. And it hadn't even been that bad. No yelling and screaming over stupid stuff. No inexplicable, incoherent rages. But my heart was pounding like I'd just run cross-country in gym class, and I felt like I could scream.

There was a clean canvas on the easel by the wall. Perfect. Headphones. Angry metal CD. Thick brush. Red paint. Five seconds later, I was cranked in and starting to slash.

ACT ONE, SCENE FIVE

In which:

A PLAN IS HATCHED

"You don't want to eat that," Andy said at lunch the next day.

I paused with my french fry halfway to my mouth, a white-hot flash of anger searing through me. "I have a father at home, Andy. Thanks," I snapped.

"KJ!" Stephanie scolded me.

I paused as I chewed. Andy was wide-eyed—stunned. My heart turned. Thank you, Dad. Now you're turning me into a bitch.

"I'm sorry," I said quickly. "I'm just in a bad mood."

"It's okay. I know you must be tense about rehearsal today," Andy said, recovering quickly.

"Yeah. The first singing rehearsal." Sure. That was why I was tense.

"Should we do a song order? I think we should do a song order." Andy pulled out his tightly ruled notebook and rapidly tapped his mechanical pencil against it. "Unless you don't think we need one, in which case we could just wing it, but if you want to wing it, it may run over and—"

"No, no. A song order is good," I said, cutting him off before his ramble reached world-record length. Andy was notoriously indecisive when it came to anything other than organic food and recycling. "We should probably get through all the group numbers first, so people can go home, then wrap up with Sandy, Danny, Rizzo and Kenickie."

"Good call. Right." Andy pushed up the sleeves on his baggy gray sweater, then reached for his script and flipped through it. "Now, all the group numbers . . ."

He paused and started to make notes. Stephanie watched his hand as he formed his perfect, square letters, curling one of her hundreds of curls around her finger.

"You really take your job seriously, huh?" she said.

"Of course," Andy said. "What's the point of doing anything unless you're going to take it seriously?"

Just then Tommy and Dustin ran in, passing the inflatable CPR doll from health class back and forth between them, like they were playing a game of keep-away. Everyone in the cafeteria turned to watch and laugh until they got to their usual table near the windows, in the sun. Cameron trailed after them, shaking his head at their antics, and I sat up straight, heart pounding. Would he talk to me again? Should I say hello first, or would that look too pathetic? He was getting closer. Closer . . . His eyes flicked in our direction as he approached. This was it! Public cafeteria acknowledgment!

"Here's what I would do, but obviously you can change anything you want if you think, you know, it would be better some other way," Andy said, tearing a page from his notebook and holding it out to me.

Cameron blinked and kept walking. Moment over. *Geekus interruptus.*

"I'm sure it's fine, Andy. Thanks," I replied, slouching again.

"So, KJ, I have a few questions for you, if you, you know, don't mind." Andy produced a new, smaller notebook from his backpack.

"Questions? What do you mean?" I asked.

"What are your five favorite songs?" Andy asked, pen at the ready. I glanced at Stephanie. She gave me a look like *what the?*

"Uh . . . that's kind of hard to say."

"That's okay. You can think about it." Andy made a check mark in his notebook. "What about movies? What movies make you cry?"

"Um . . . I don't know. *The Notebook*? *A Walk to Remember*?"

I looked at Stephanie the whole time I was answering. Which was easy to do, since Andy never looked up from his notebook. Both Steph and I were very intrigued. Stephanie leaned forward to try to get a glimpse as Andy scribbled in his book.

"Okay, five top things to do on a Friday night."

"Andy. What the heck are you doing?" Stephanie asked finally.

"It's an experiment," Andy answered quickly, shielding his book from her view. "A scientific experiment. What makes guys and girls different? I've got a list of a hundred questions and I'm going to take a cross-section of the student body to try to determine the results."

"Is it for class?" Stephanie asked.

Andy's cheeks grew pink. "No. It's for, you know, personal, um . . . whatever."

Oh. My. God. This couldn't be what I thought it was, could it? Was Andy's quiz just a thinly veiled attempt to get to know me better? Looked like Geek Number Three was taking his stalking to a whole new level. A scientific one.

"Aren't you introducing a few too many variables there?" Stephanie asked, raising her eyebrows. "Shouldn't they be yes or no? Or at least multiple choice?"

Andy had no idea who he was dealing with here. If there was anyone at this school who knew how to properly conduct a science experiment, it was Steph. He opened his mouth to respond, but then just tucked his chin again. "Five favorite foods, KJ?"

My skin prickled with embarrassed heat. "Uh . . ."

"KJ! KJ! KJ!"

Suddenly Fred's stomach was right in my face, swathed in the bright red of his Flash T-shirt. Fred likes superhero T-shirts. The kind with just the logo of the superhero on the front. He thinks they're way cooler than ones that actually *say* "Batman" or "Superman" or what-have-you.

"Here. I got you a cookie."

He dropped one of the caf's large chocolate chip cookies on my tray, wrapped in wax paper.

"Thanks, Fr—"

"You don't want to eat that," Andy put in.

Fred ignored him. "Okay, listen," he said, spreading his arms wide, his fingers wide, his legs wide. "Which way does this line sound best? 'Hey, Kenickie, whatcha got in the bag? I'll trade ya half a sardine!'" he recited loudly. Very loudly.

I sank down in my chair. Stephanie pulled all her hair forward, hiding.

"Or . . . or . . . what about this: 'Hey! Kenickie! Whatcha got in the baaag? I'll trade you half a sardine!'" Fred drawled.

Everyone at the tables around us laughed. Dustin smacked Cameron's shoulder and pointed. I somehow sank even lower. Cameron was laughing. Laughing at me. I had *just* gotten him to talk to me and now this. Why was Fred doing this to me?

"Fred, I—"

"Or wait a minute, wait a minute. One more. 'Yo, Ken*ic*kie, whaddaya got in da *bag*? I'll trade ja half a sar*dine*!'" He threw on a heavy New York accent.

The entire cafeteria erupted in applause at the Mafioso version of Doody. Fred looked up as if he'd just realized there were other people in the room and raised his hand. "Thank you! Thank you!" he said, bowing his head modestly. "So? Which one? I thought the first one, but from the crowd response, maybe it's the third. Ya think? KJ?"

"Do it again, Freddy!" someone shouted.

"No!" Stephanie and I both threw our hands out.

"You're right, Fred. The first one. Definitely. Definitely the way to go," I assured him. "Doody isn't from the Bronx."

"Okay, cool! That's what I thought! Thanks, KJ. Thanks a lot!" Fred broke off half the cookie he'd given me, then turned and hurried away.

"I gotta go to the library," Andy said, standing. "I'll see you at rehearsal, I mean, unless you need me before then, and then you can just text me, but don't forget to think about the song question, okay?"

"Yeah. I'm on it," I said.

Stephanie and I stared at each other across the table, dumbfounded. There was just way too much stimulation at lunch sometimes.

"So, Andy's getting pretty serious, huh?" Stephanie asked.

"You don't think it's really an experiment?" I asked with false hope.

"No. Unfortunately, I don't."

Suddenly Andy's vacated chair was pulled out and Tama perched right on the edge of it. Jaws dropped all over the cafeteria. Apparently hell had just frozen over.

"This is never going to work," Tama said.

"What?" I asked.

"How am I supposed to get Cameron to like you if you're constantly surrounded by geeks?" she asked, lifting her hand.

"What?" Stephanie asked. Right. I'd forgotten to tell her about that whole Tama-talking-me-up-to-Cameron thing.

"Do you even know what just happened? Cameron was totally going to stop to talk to you, but he was thwarted by Inconvenient Truth Boy." Tama took a carrot stick off Stephanie's plate and crunched into it. Stephanie glared at her. She was not a fan of bad table manners. "Hey. Problem?"

Stephanie huffed and dragged her calculus book out of her bag.

"No way." I swallowed a not-quite-chewed chunk of food and almost gagged. "He was not going to stop here."

"Yes he was!" Tama said. "I saw him hesitate. The whole world saw it. Now tell me. Who would you rather talk to? Cameron Richardson or Andy Tererro?"

Um. No contest.

"You need to lose the losers. You need to start being mean." Tama pointed the remainder of the carrot stick at me. "Like, stat."

I felt a thrill of excitement. Sometimes, more than anything, all I wanted was the ability to tell Fred and Glenn and anyone else who had joined the geek parade over the years to just leave me alone. The problem was, I could never do it. The idea of hurting their feelings always made me squirm.

"I don't think so," I said, crumpling my napkin.

"Why not?" Tama asked.

"It's just . . . believe me, the thought *has* crossed my mind. I just don't have it in me," I confessed, feeling somehow immature. "I can't be mean."

"Yes you can," Stephanie put in.

"Excuse me?" I asked.

"You were just mean to Andy, like, five minutes ago," Stephanie said. She wasn't admonishing me. Just stating a fact. And, okay. She had a point. But that was only because I was pissed at my father. I couldn't control that.

"See? You can do it. You just have to learn to focus on what you want and do what needs to be done," Tama said. She dropped the carrot stick and broke off a piece of my half-a-cookie. "I'll even help you if you want. I've blown off a few dorks in my day."

"You will?" I was shocked. So was Stephanie, from the look on her face. "Why?"

"Because." Tama shrugged and wiped her hand on my napkin. "I don't know. I think we should hang out more, Cage. I feel bad that we don't. You're cool and I think you deserve to not have a posse of losers stalking you all over the place. I think we should do something about it."

Every inch of my skin tingled. All these years I'd been whining about my geek plight with no clue as to what I could do about it. But now, just like that, here was a girl with a plan.

"Trust me, Cage," Tama said conspiratorially. "The rewards will be worth the effort."

She glanced over her shoulder and I did the same. My eyes locked with Cameron Richardson's. My whole body turned to goo. He was watching us. Watching me.

And suddenly I was very, *very* intrigued.

ACT ONE, SCENE SIX

In which:

THERE ARE NEAR MISSES

"WE'LL START OUT EASY," TAMA TOLD ME AS WE WALKED INTO THE auditorium that afternoon. "Four small words: No. Stop. Go away."

I almost laughed. "No, stop, go away?"

"Simple. Direct. To the point," she said, clapping her hands together. She meant business. "The next time one of those dorks corners you, try any one of them out."

"Oookay," I said dubiously.

"Trust me, Cage. I know what I'm talking about," she said.

I left her at the piano where Mr. Katz was warming up the rest of the Pink Ladies, including Ashley, the Drama Twins and Jane Larsen, the senior who was playing Marty. The set crew was painting the Rydell High backdrop along the back curtain, and I dropped my bag on the floor and grabbed a brush. I still had some pent-up anger to expel from last night. This would do nicely. And I'd be right here if Mr. Katz needed me for anything.

After outlining several bricks on the school wall, I started to feel calm for the first time all day. While I was painting, my dad didn't exist. While I was painting, no one could touch me. I hummed along to "Freddy, My Love" until I felt someone watching me.

Damn. Not again.

I looked up, expecting to find Glenn drooling Yoo-hoo down my back, but it wasn't him. It was Robbie Delano, sitting on a stool a few feet away, blatantly staring at me. His script was rolled up in his hand, and his drumsticks were jutting out of his back pocket. I gave him a quizzical smile. He just kept staring. Almost like he was looking at me for the first time.

Oh no. This. Could not. Be happening.

I knew that look. I had performed many a letdown after seeing that look. I swear, "I like you as a friend" was going to be my motto in the yearbook. Was this why he had saved me from the geek brigade the other day? Because he liked me, too? Stephanie's scientific theories had proven correct yet again. Robbie *was* just like the rest of them. I almost couldn't wait to tell her. She so loved being proved right.

I quickly returned to my work. Maybe if I seemed engrossed he would leave me alone. But no. Out of the corner of my eye, I saw him move from the stool. He was coming over here. Oh, crap.

No, stop, go away. No, stop, go away. No, stop . . . who am I kidding?

His sneakers—white Converse that he had drawn black stripes across—stepped into my line of vision. He drummed out a quick rhythm on his thighs with his palms. I held my breath.

"You should consider a career in comics," he said. "You could totally do ink."

"No!" I blurted.

"Yeah, you could," he said. "You have such a steady hand."

Great. He totally missed the point. He thought I was being humble. He squatted next to me, still drumming away with his palms, and looked me in the eye.

"Stop!" I said, anguished.

"What? Oh. Sorry." He stopped drumming and laced his fingers together. "Occupational hazard."

Oh, God. This was not working! I thought Tama said it was simple!

"I've been watching you," he said.

Go away. Just say it! Just say, "Go away."

A concerned look crossed Robbie's face. "Are you okay?"

No, I wasn't okay. My breath was catching over and over again. I was starting to hyperventilate, and I hadn't even truly channeled my inner bitch yet. How did the popular girls do it? I saw them be mean to people every single day. Were their hearts actual blocks of ice?

"M'fine," I mumbled.

"Okay." He sat his butt down next to me and blew out a sigh. "I wanted to talk to you," he said, nervously avoiding my gaze. "It's probably totally obvious, but I have this sort of huge crush . . ."

No no no no no!

". . . on Tama," he finished.

Whiplash. "Huh?"

Robbie raised his eyebrows. "Oh. Well, then I guess it's not obvious. Solid. Anyway, I saw you guys talking the other day and I was thinking maybe you could, like, plant the seed."

"The seed?" I said.

"Yeah, you know. The Robbie seed. Drop my name, tell her how unequivocally cool I am. Farmer KJ, plant the seed. Then I come in and, you know, cultivate the seed. Water it, what-have-you. It's not the greatest metaphor, actually."

I grinned. I took a deep breath. He didn't like me. He liked Tama. I was so psyched to have avoided the awkward conversation bullet, I wanted to throw myself at his feet and tell him I'd do anything he asked.

"How can I tell her you're unequivocally cool when I hardly even know you?" I joked, all giddy with relief.

He raised his eyebrows. "Can't you just take my word for it?"

"I guess."

"I did also divert Glenn Marlowe's attentions that first day," he pointed out.

And Fred's and Andy's, I added silently.

"Or has that beneficence already been forgotten?" he asked.

"Oh no. Believe me. That one will be remembered for a long time."

But there was still one largish problem.

"Um, you do know she has a serious boyfriend, right?" I said.

His name was Leo. He drove a Ducati. He had supposedly graduated the year before, but rumor was that he hadn't actually finished school. Last year, during the musical, he always picked Tama up from rehearsal, and every time I saw them together, they were either making out or screaming at each other. They had a very volatile relationship.

"Biker dude? Of course. Everyone knows about biker dude." Robbie lightly hugged his knees and looked up at Tama, who stood upstage, haloed by the stage lights as she delivered her lines. "In my opinion, Tama Gold deserves better than biker dude. I mean, look at her."

Tama and the Pink Ladies were now blocking out one of their scenes with Mr. Katz. Somehow Tama looked even more gorgeous under the stage lights.

"She is a true original. She's popular, but she does her own thing, you know? Dresses how she wants, does the musical even though it's considered uncool in her crowd. I've even seen her study in study hall when all her little friends are texting each other about, like, who Hilary Duff is dating now or whatever. Who has that kind of confidence in high school? That kind of, like, 'I know who I am and I don't care if you like it' thing?"

You do, I thought. Robbie was the guy who had gotten up at last fall's talent show, sung an a capella version of John Lennon's "Imagine" and just sat down again. He hadn't even been on the program. He'd just snaked the spot between Ashley's Kelly Clarkson impression and the guys from the jazz band who had decided to try their hand at hair metal. No one could get away with that kind of behavior, but somehow, Robbie had. I would have gotten picked on mercilessly, but everyone just left him alone. It really was like he had a force field around him.

He was just as untouchable as Tama, but in a different way. Maybe these two crazy kids *could* make it work, I thought, glancing over at Tama again.

"I'll see what I can do," I told him.

Robbie smiled, revealing a pair of deep dimples I had never noticed before.

"Mr. Katz! I can't work like this!" Ashley announced suddenly. She slapped her script down in a huff, her blond ringlets shaking. Ashley was a tall, big-boned, solid girl with serious lungs. She raised her voice and you could hear her in the next county.

"Oh, *you* can't work like this? You're the one hogging the

stage like it's your own personal *American Idol* audition," Tama shot back.

"Uh-oh," I said.

Ashley kept her shrewd blue eyes on Katz. "She is *so* unprofessional. This kind of behavior would never fly at the Papermill."

"Never," Cory and Carrie echoed, crossing their arms over their chests in perfect unison. The Drama Twins were fraternal, not identical, with Carrie towering a good six inches over her sister, but they consulted on hair and wardrobe every day so that they always rocked the same kind of braid and similar, but usually different colored, outfits. They also had this freakish habit of mirroring each other. It was like they wished they had been born identical.

"Ladies!" Mr. Katz scolded. He whipped open his leather bag and started blindly searching it with his hand.

"Oh my God! How many times a day are you going to remind us that you did a Papermill Playhouse production?" Tama snapped. "What were you, milkmaid number three?"

I tried not to laugh. The Papermill was this well-respected regional theater in Jersey that Ashley had been auditioning for forever. Finally, this past winter, she had gotten to play one of the random daughters in *The Sound of Music*, and never let anyone forget it.

"How would you know? It's not like you came to see it! You are so not a supporter of the arts," Ashley retorted. "Why are you even here?"

"Cat fight! Cat fight! Cat fight!" the drama dudes started to chant.

Mr. Katz finally produced the Tums he'd been looking for, popped three of them and hung his head, at a loss.

"I better go," I told Robbie. "It's not a good sign when the Tums come out in the first week of rehearsals."

Robbie gave me a straight-backed salute as I shoved myself up from the floor. I smirked and jumped into the fray, just hoping I wouldn't get my eyes scratched out.

ACT ONE, SCENE SEVEN

In which:

I GIVE A GIRL A RIDE

"NOW, YOU NEED TO BE CLEAR WITH MS. LIN," MR. KATZ TOLD ME as we walked out of rehearsal. "If you don't tell her very specifically what you want, she'll just go off in her own direction and we'll have Tangerine Ladies instead of Pink Ladies."

"Tangerine ladies. That's a good one, Mr. Katz," Andy said.

"Got it." I made a note.

"All right, then. I'd better get going," Mr. Katz said. He glanced over his shoulder at Tama, who stood on the far side of the wide room, barking into her cell phone. "Can I feel free to leave the other important costume decisions in your hands, KJ?"

"Feel free, Mr. Katz. Feel free," Andy said before I could respond. "She's really good. I mean, I assume she'll be really good. Although you know what they say about assuming. They say it makes an—"

"I know what they say, Andy," Mr. Katz said, raising a hand. "KJ?"

"I'm on it."

"Cool." Mr. Katz smiled. "See you two tomorrow." He turned and strolled out of the building, already fishing in his jacket pocket for his Marlboros.

"Fine! Fine!" Tama shouted into her phone. Then she clapped it closed. She did a double take when she saw me and Andy standing there. "KJ! Thank God you're still here. I need a ride."

My face lighted up. "No problem." I tried not to sound too excited, but I have always wanted to see the palace Tama reportedly lives in. It's way up in the hills near the edge of town and even has a fountain out front. Or so I've heard.

"So, KJ, I'm going to Whole Foods now before I go home," Andy said, falling into step with us as we walked toward my car. "Do you want me to get you anything? For tomorrow, I mean. What are your five favorite fruits?"

He took out that little notebook of his. Tama shot him a confused look, like he was of some species she didn't recognize.

"Actually, Andy, I'm all set in the fruit department. But thanks," I said, pausing by my car.

"Oh." He looked disappointed and slipped the notebook away. "Okay. Well. See ya."

He pushed his glasses up, then turned and walked back to his Prius. I shot Tama an apologetic look.

"What happened to 'no, stop, go away'?" she asked.

"Well . . . I said no to the fruit," I replied.

She rolled her eyes and we got in the car.

"Hey, guys!"

"Omigod!" I blurted, hand to heart. I looked in the rearview mirror. Fred was sitting in my backseat, all bright-eyed and happy. "Fred! How did you get into my car?"

"It was unlocked," Fred told me, leaning forward. "That's

really not a good idea, KJ. Someone could come in here and steal all your CDs."

He already had half of them open all over the backseat, the liner notes pulled out everywhere. Tama sighed impatiently.

"Fred, I'm going to give Tama a ride, so it's going to take a little longer than usual," I attempted.

"That's cool," he said, reaching for his seat belt. "I'm up for a ride."

"Get out!" Tama snapped.

Fred froze. So did my heart.

"What?"

"Get out!" she repeated, turning around in her seat. "Go! We want to be alone."

Fred looked at me in the mirror. I shrugged, at a loss. "Oh. Okay. Okay. Girl talk. I got it." He scrambled out of the car, catching his huge bag on the door before finally yanking it free. "I'll talk to you later, KJ."

He slammed the door and took a step back.

"Guess that's what you meant by being mean," I said, my hands actually shaking as I reached for the ignition.

"God! How do you live like this?" Tama said. "They're all over you!"

I smirked. Finally, somebody got it. Stephanie tried to be supportive, sure, but she never really seemed to understand how annoying all the stalking could be.

"Fred's not *that* bad," I said. I felt the need to defend him since he was still standing right outside my car, looking like a puppy that had just been smacked by a rolled-up newspaper. He even waved as I pulled out of the spot.

"Not that bad?" Tama was incredulous. "You need to grow a backbone, like, yesterday."

I paused at the exit of the parking lot, feeling like a total loser. "Which way's your house?" I asked, happy to have an excuse to change the subject.

"I'm not going home," Tama said. She ran a fingertip over her eyebrow and slapped the visor up. "I'm going downtown."

"Oh." I swallowed my disappointment. "What's downtown?"

"I have a doctor's appointment," Tama said with an impatient sigh. "Leo was supposed to come take me, but no-o-o. He's too busy to help me out."

All the tiny hairs on my arms stood on end. The Fred confrontation was instantly forgotten. Was this, like, the kind of doctor's appointment that a boyfriend was *supposed* to bring a girlfriend to? Tama wasn't pregnant or something, was she? Oh, God. If so, Leo was a total jerk. How could you not take your girlfriend to . . . to . . . wherever she needed to go?

"Hey! Watch the mailbox," Tama said, slamming her hands against the door and center console just like my mother did pretty much every time she rode with me. I veered back toward the center line and took a deep breath.

"Where's your Thunderbird?" I asked. I worshipped Tama's car: a light blue throwback convertible T-bird. She looked like a movie star behind the wheel.

"My mother grounded me from it," Tama said with a scoff. "One time she finds me passed out in the front seat and it's like I'm an irresponsible driver all of a sudden." She sighed and stared out the side window. "Whatever, I guess Leo's right, though. He's busy. He has a job. I can't just expect him to drop everything and come chauffeur me around. Even if he does always say he'd do anything for me."

"He does?" I asked.

"Sure," she said with a shrug. Like it was the most normal

thing in the world to have people saying they'd do anything for you. "Plus he's dealing with all this crap right now. His dad wants him to go to college, but he wants to stay at the garage. . . . I would die if he left. Seriously. Just die. But it's not just about me. He doesn't *want* to go. It's just his dickhead father getting into his brain. Turn right here."

"Sounds like you really care about Leo," I said, trying to keep the surprise out of my voice. Considering the hot-and-cold nature of their relationship, I never thought of them as being so deep.

"He is one of the few good things in my life," she said, looking down at her hands.

Pardon? Everyone knew that Tama Gold's life was just chock-full of sugary goodness. The palace, the car, the stunning good looks, the popularity. Girl was even an honors student. It was so unfair. Plus I would bet money that her newscaster father didn't come home every other night trashed off his ass to throw fits over nothing. Tucker Gold probably drove home from his ten P.M. show each night, kissed her forehead and tucked her into her gold-plated bed. Not that I'd ever put much thought into it.

"It's right here," Tama said, pointing.

I pulled into the parking lot of one of those square brick buildings you never notice until someone tells you to go there, and stopped in front of the door.

"Thanks a lot," Tama said. She gathered her things, got out and slammed the door. I stared at the little placard on the side of the building, trying to figure out which doctor she might be going to. There were no GYNs listed, so that was a plus. Suddenly, the door opened again and I jumped, snagged.

"Oh, hey, I forgot to tell you—you're coming with me to the St. Luke's party this weekend," Tama told me.

"I . . . what?"

"Yeah. We're going to do a little experiment," she said with a mischievous smile. "You, KJ Miller, are my new project. Project KJ Gets Mean."

"Project? Uh, no. I don't think so."

"Well, I do and you are. Especially after that stalkeresque behavior I just witnessed."

"I can't go to a St. Luke's party," I told her, my heart already pounding with nerves. "They're totally insane." Or so I'd heard.

Tama looked at me like I was so third grade. "KJ. That's kind of the point."

Then she slammed the door and traipsed off.

ACT ONE, SCENE EIGHT

In which:

I'M APPARENTLY BRAINWASHED

I WAS AT THE SELF-SERVE SODA MACHINE AT WENDY'S THAT NIGHT, trying to decide between root beer and Sprite, when Stephanie nudged me with her tray. Her doctor parents had some charity thing at the hospital. Mine had teacher conferences at Christopher's school. (Well, Mom did anyway. Whether Dad would show was anybody's guess.) Therefore, the midweek fast food. Andy would be so appalled.

"Wanna go see the new Mark Wahlberg on Saturday?" Stephanie asked. She has a thing for Mark Wahlberg that I cannot wrap my brain around.

I bit my lip. "Actually, I might be going to a St. Luke's party with Tama." Stephanie cracked up laughing and I felt a chill all through my body. My toes curled inside my pink and brown Kangaroos. Finally, the laughter stopped.

"You're serious?"

"Um . . . yeah," I said.

Stephanie's entire face shut down. She grabbed her tray and her ice water and tromped over to a table near the window, her pink purse bumping against her hip. I sighed and quickly filled my cup with root beer.

"*You're* going to a St. Luke's party. You," Stephanie said.

"What? Is that so insane?" I asked, already knowing the answer as I slid into the chair across from her.

"Are you kidding me? It's all drinking and hooking up," Stephanie said. We'd both heard the same rumors, after all. "Neither of which you do."

The ball of dread that had formed in my stomach the second Tama brought it up started to expand. I had spent the first two and a half years of my high school career studiously avoiding any and all situations that might lead to drinking-related peer pressure. Anything to keep me from turning into my father. Was I really going to give up on that now just because Tama wanted to make me her project?

"You're right. I can't go," I said, feeling relieved even as I said it. "What was I thinking?"

"You weren't. Tama does that to you," she said.

"Pardon?" I asked, reaching for a fry.

"It's like whenever she's around, you're brainwashed," she said matter-of-factly. "Like this whole idea she has about you being mean to everyone. You're not actually going to do that, are you?"

Maybe. "No," I said, squirming.

"Good. Because it's just not you, KJ. You're nice. It's good to be nice," she told me, taking a sip of her water.

Easy for you to say, I thought. All being nice had ever gotten me was a steady stream of unwanted attention from guys with visible nose hair and major B.O. Why did she not understand this?

"So. The new Mark Wahlberg?" she asked again, her eyebrows raised.

"Yeah. Sure," I replied.

I took a deep breath and dug into my food, trying to ignore the sinking sensation her brainwashing comment had given me. Was that what my best friend really thought of me? Well, I'd prove her wrong. I was not going to go to that insane party. Tama and I would just have to work on Project KJ Gets Mean some other time.

ACT ONE, SCENE NINE

In which:

I RECEIVE AN UNEXPECTED GIFT

FRIDAY AFTERNOON, WHEN THE BELL RANG TO END ENGLISH class, I gathered my books slowly, stalling for time. Ever since that one brief encounter with Cameron, I had been salivating for another. Today, I was going to make it happen. From the corner of my eye I saw him coming down the aisle toward me. I was a genius! There was no way he could get past me without at least asking me to move. But he didn't. He stopped. Stopped and smiled.

Breathe. Breathe. Breathe.

"Hey, KJ."

Tingles everywhere. I loved not being invisible anymore. He slung his backpack over his shoulder. The leather arms of his varsity jacket creaked.

"Hey."

"I heard you're going to the St. Luke's party with Tama on Saturday," he said. "That's cool."

I froze. How had he heard about that?

"Yeah. Um . . . I guess."

Actually, after dinner last night I had spent the rest of the night trying to figure out some unobvious way to beg out and not look like a total dork. I was going to be at the movies with Stephanie on Saturday night. But he didn't need to know that.

"Cool," Cameron said. "I just broke up with a girl who goes there; otherwise I'd probably be going, too."

"Really?" I practically squealed.

Way to be cool, KJ.

"Yeah. Don't usually miss 'em. But I guess I'll have to find something else to do," he said.

Thank God. He didn't notice my piglet imitation. But he was single! Single and talking to me!

"Do you guys hang out a lot? You and Tama?" he asked as we walked to the door.

"Uh . . . not . . . sort of—"

" 'Cause that's cool. You and Tama hanging out. She's cool and you're cool, so it's . . . cool."

I'm cool? I am? What? We stepped into the hallway, my mind buzzing with excitement. Cameron thought I was cool. My life simply could not get any better.

Until Glenn Marlowe was all up in my face.

"Hey, KJ," he said to my right breast. He sucked his teeth, then moved his gaze to the left. "Wow. Someone got up on the sexy side of the bed this morning."

Cameron snorted a laugh, but covered it with a cough. This. Was not. Happening. Did the geeks have some kind of secret pact to embarrass me in front of Cameron? Were they trying to ruin my life?

"Got you something!" Glenn sang. He held up a big package wrapped in the Sunday comics and tied with a red bow.

"What is it?" I said warily. I glanced at Cameron. He was blatantly amused.

"Open it!" Glenn said, shoving the box at me.

A few passersby glanced over and whispered to each other. This was so not good. Probably the best thing to do was to just get it over with. I tore open the paper and peeled the top off the box. Please just don't let it be a French maid's outfit. . . .

But it wasn't. My eyes widened as I pulled out the exact same light blue sweater that Glenn had ruined with his Yoo-hoo projectile the first day of rehearsal.

"Glenn! You didn't have to do this!" I said, unfolding it and holding it out. I was amazed by the gesture. Glenn had done something right. Not just right, but sweet.

"Yeah, I did. I had to sell my Aragorn sword on eBay to pay for it, but it was worth it," Glenn said with a nod.

"Thank you," I told him, overwhelmed. "This is unbe—"

"I hope it's big enough," he interrupted, staring down at my chest. "Because you are very, you know, *endowed*."

The hallway and all the people in it blurred. My face seared and my eyes stung and I actually felt faint. This was it. I was going to be the first person in the history of the world to actually die of embarrassment. He hadn't just said that. Not in front of Cameron.

"You like it?" he asked.

"I have to go," I heard myself say.

Hugging the sweater to my chest, I turned around, vaguely recalling that there was a bathroom somewhere near here. As always, however, Glenn stepped in front of me.

"Wait. KJ. Do you like it?" he asked, totally clueless. "C'mon, do you?"

I stared at the ground. One tear escaped and I quickly wiped it away. Leave me alone. Please, please, please, leave me alone!

"Dude. Back off," Cameron said, lowering his voice.

Glenn flinched and I ran. By the time I shoved my way into the bathroom, tears were streaming down my face. A couple of senior girls eyed me warily as I careened by them. Safely inside a stall, I sat on the toilet and pulled my feet up, willing myself to stop crying.

This was so pathetic. Me, balled up on top of a toilet bowl, sobbing into Glenn's sweater. What did Cameron think of me right now? Was he ever going to speak to me again after that display? That comment? And why couldn't I stand up for myself? Why was I such a huge-mongous loser? Tama was right. I had to stop this. I had to show these people that they couldn't walk all over me. Forget Stephanie and Mark Wahlberg. Saturday night I was going to that party with Tama. I was going to stop this once and for all.

ACT ONE, SCENE TEN

In which:

DIVORCE SOUNDS LIKE A PLAN

"I'M NOT EATING THIS, JILL! THIS IS SLOP!"

There was a crash. The sound of ceramic plate hitting steel sink. Christopher and I both flinched.

"Well, maybe if it hadn't sat around for two hours before getting reheated, it wouldn't *be* slop!" my mother shouted back. It was Friday night. Bad Dad Night. And this one was turning especially bad.

I hugged Christopher a little bit closer to my side on my twin bed. On the TV, a family sitcom was all but drowned out. Two sisters were pulling on the sleeves of one sweater between them as the laugh track applauded their efforts.

"What's that supposed to mean?!" my father shouted. A cabinet slammed. The bottles in the door of the refrigerator jangled.

"It means that if you weren't three hours late . . . if you were here when the rest of the family was eating, your food would have been fine!" my mother shouted.

"Who the hell do you think you are, talking to me like that?"

my father yelled. Another slam. "This is my house! I paid for this food! I have a right to expect a real dinner whenever the hell I choose to come home!"

God, I hated him. What did he want my mother to do, make two dinners? One for us and another for him? And when should she prepare this meal exactly? Was she supposed to psychically intuit the exact time at which he was going to deign to roll through the door and time his meal accordingly?

"Oh, so I should just sit here all night cooking meals until you come home so that one of them will happen to be fresh?"

"Yeah! Maybe you should!" my dad screamed.

Christopher moaned and curled into a ball with his head on my upper thigh. My heart felt sick.

Throw the food in his face, I willed my mother. My fingertips curled in toward my palms. Tell him you've had it. You're leaving. Tell him to get the hell out of our house.

I'm, like, the only kid in the world who wishes on a daily basis that her parents would get divorced. But life would be so much more peaceful if he would just go away. I couldn't imagine what it would feel like to come home and know that there was no possible way the night would end in a fight. That my father wouldn't be around to blow up for no reason. To not have to always wonder what might set him off, who he might choose to focus his venom on that night. To not be scared all the time.

Come on, Mom. You don't have to take it.

"Fine! Don't eat! I don't care! Do whatever you want!" my mother shouted.

Her pounding footsteps crossed the kitchen and moved down the hall.

"Screw you!" my father roared.

Their bedroom door slammed and I flinched.

A hollow pit of disappointment opened in my gut. Once again, she'd decided to just take it. To walk away and let him get away with it. I felt my heart rate start to quicken as my father continued to pound around the kitchen. I should just go down there and scream at him myself. Tell him he couldn't talk to my mother that way. Tell him what a freaking hypocrite he was, expecting everyone to treat him like the god of the household when he treated everyone else like dirt. I grew warm just thinking about it and my breath started to shorten. I wished I could do it. I wished so badly I could. But I knew that I never would. It was just like being cornered by the geeks, but ten times more intense. I was trapped there inside myself, dying to say what I really wanted to say, and frustrated to know that I would never have the guts.

"KJ. You're squeezing me," Christopher whined.

I realized how tightly my arm muscles had coiled, and released him.

"Sorry."

Down below, the basement door banged closed and my father's heavy footsteps barreled down the creaky stairs. That was "game over" in our household. Now he would throw darts for a while and drink from one of the bottles he had "hidden" down there among his books—because clearly he hadn't had enough tonight. Then he would pass out in my grandfather's old recliner until sometime in the early morning when he would crawl up the stairs and into bed with my mom. How she tolerated that so often, I have no idea.

Christopher's little body relaxed and my blood stopped

rushing through my ears. I breathed in and lifted the remote to turn up the volume. The dad on the TV had the two sisters gathered into his arms on the couch as they all laughed over the now torn and ruined sweater. Christopher giggled at a lame joke. I closed my eyes against the burning.

ACT ONE, SCENE ELEVEN

In which:

WE ALL PLAY OUR ROLES

I AWOKE THE NEXT MORNING TO THE STOMACH-GRUMBLING SCENTS of pancakes and bacon. At first, I smiled, but then I woke up and realized what this meant. Dad at the stove. Mom sipping coffee. Christopher emptying half a bottle of syrup onto his plate. The Millers play *7th Heaven* for a day. So very fake.

I whipped my covers off and got right in the shower, scrubbing my skin so hard I scraped a big line up my arm with a fingernail. I put on my softest cargo pants and a black sweater, wrapped my wet hair back in a ponytail, shoved my marked-up script in my bag and trudged downstairs.

"There she is!" my father sang. He wore a sweatshirt and jeans and his "Quiche the Cook" apron—an ill-advised Father's Day gift from a few years back. When I still liked the pancake-flipping, cheerful guy he was on Saturday mornings. "Two pancakes or three?"

"I'm not hungry," I said.

There was a bottled smoothie in the fridge somewhere. I dove in to look for it and to cool down my angry, overheated face. How could he be so chipper? After his performance last night shouldn't he at least be punished by a massively painful hangover? But no. He was a "functioning drunk." At least that was what my mother called him. She got the rhetoric from her Al Anon meetings. They were for family members and loved ones of alcoholics. Every once in a while she'd get on this big "I'm so healthy" kick and go to meetings once or twice a week, then come home acting like she was all wise and had my father all figured out. And when I had my normal emotional reactions to his insanity, she'd look at me in this condescending, piteous way like I was just *so* unenlightened. "Oh, KJ. When you're older, you'll understand," was her catchphrase. I hated that version of my mom almost as much as I hated the sloshed version of my dad.

"KJ. You should eat something. You have a long day," my mother said.

I turned and let the fridge door slam. Both my mother and my brother stared at me with pleading eyes. This was one of the few hours of total peace we were granted each week. They didn't want me to ruin it for them. I heaved a sigh.

"Fine. I'll have two."

"A*ha*! No one can resist my perfect pancakes," my father said.

Yeah. You're, like, the coolest dad ever. Just keep telling yourself that.

I yanked out a chair and dropped into it so hard I bruised my butt. My father deposited two pancakes on my plate and kissed the top of my head. Such the doting dad. As if twelve hours ago Christopher and I hadn't been huddled up in my room hating him with everything we had in us. I watched my brother as he lapped up his syrup, happily swinging his legs under the table. Traitor.

"So you have a long day?" Dad said. "What's on the agenda?"

"I have an all-day rehearsal and tonight I'm going to a party with Tama." I ate the pancakes dry. It wasn't like I wanted to enjoy them. Take that, Superdad.

He turned to me, his eyebrows coming together. "Tama? Do I know Tama?"

He had to be kidding me. He loved Tama. "She was Kim in *Bye Bye Birdie* last year? You drove us to Friendly's that one night after rehearsal and you let her crank up the stereo?"

Nothing.

"You said she looked just like Whitney Houston back when she was normal?"

There was an edge in my voice now that earned me an admonishing look from my mother, which was so unfair. She wanted me to spare his feelings? Please. How ridiculous was that? And besides, my father should know who Tama was. He'd even met her a few times when he was stone sober.

"Oh, right! The girl with the nose ring," he said finally. "I like her."

"She doesn't have one anymore, but whatever," I replied.

"Well, I suppose you can go to this party as long as you promise us you'll be responsible," my father said.

I laughed. I couldn't help it. Like he could really tell me whether or not I could go to a party. He had no idea about my life, let alone what was okay to do and what wasn't. That was my mother's department, and she had already told me I could go.

"Something funny?" my father said.

My bones burned, heating me from the inside out. Yeah, something's funny. How about the very idea that you have any clue what the word *responsible* means? Next you should tell me not to drink. Please, please, *please* hit me with that one.

He hovered over me with another pan of sizzling bacon. My mother's brainwaves were pounding against mine so hard my temples hurt. Christopher's legs had stopped swinging. I swallowed a lump of dry pancake and sucked down some orange juice.

"No. Just got something stuck in my throat," I lied.

I played my part like a good little actress. I hated it, but it was easier that way.

ACT ONE, SCENE TWELVE

In which:

I SING IN PUBLIC . . . SORT OF

THERE'S ALWAYS A LOT OF MAYHEM AT AN ALL-DAY SATURDAY rehearsal. There's something about having the run of the school that makes an already-prone-to-mischief set of people just a little bit wackier. There's a lot of whooping in the lobby, skateboarding in the main hall and raiding the vending machines, as if they're not there every other day of our lives. But today, I just couldn't get into it. I watched all the revelry going on around me with a detached impatience.

Yeah. Look at you people having tickle fights backstage. You're so very carefree. I get it. Now shut up.

Finally Mr. Katz set us free for lunch. I grabbed my stuff and went right outside to wait for Stephanie, who was upstairs in the home ec room getting measured for costumes. I took a big gulp of fresh air and glanced at my watch as everyone poured out the doors behind me. Including Robbie and Tama. Who walked out together. Interesting. Had Robbie already made his move?

"Hey, KJ, we're gonna hit Wendy's for a little Biggie this and some Biggie that," Robbie said. "Wanna come?"

I kind of didn't. I had been looking forward to venting all over Stephanie at lunch. But behind Robbie, Tama waved her hands and pressed her teeth together, begging me to be her wingman. I felt a flutter of pride. Needed by Tama Gold.

"Sure. I could use a Biggie this," I told him.

"Don't forget the Biggie that," he replied. "The Biggie that is very important."

Stephanie pushed through the door. Andy was with her, that damn little pad of his at the ready.

"So, where are we going?" Steph asked, shrugging her coat on.

I bit my lip. Steph was already irritated at me because I'd busted our plans for the movies so that I could hang with Tama. She was not going to like the idea of having lunch with the girl as well. "We just decided on Wendy's," I said.

Stephanie looked at Tama and Robbie like they were alien beings potentially interested in sucking her brain matter out through her ears. "We just went there."

"So what?" Tama said.

"So I didn't want anything too heavy," Stephanie replied.

"They have salads, you know," Tama shot back, semi-condescendingly.

What was with these two? Why did they always have to be at each other's throats?

"Sure. Salads with processed fried chicken on them. Only forty grams of trans fat," Andy scoffed.

"Not *all* of them have fried chicken on them," Tama sneered.

"Well, I'm out." Andy put the pad away and I found myself breathing again. "I brought tofu tacos."

Gross. "Okay. So let's go!" I said happily.

Stephanie hesitated, shifting her weight from foot to foot. I couldn't believe it. Didn't she see how rude she was being? I knew we usually ate together alone, but what was the big deal if a couple of people came along?

"Okay. Fine. Whatever," she said finally. Thank God.

We were almost home free when Fred came barreling in out of nowhere, yanking down on his T-shirt. "Where are we going? BK? Mickey D's? Panera?"

I looked at Tama desperately. Tama shot me a pointed look. Like this time it was my job to get rid of him. I opened my mouth, not entirely sure what we were going to say, but Stephanie beat me to it.

"We're going to Wendy's, actually," she said, looping her arm through his. She shot me a tight smile. Her way of getting me back for forcing Tama on her and ditching her tonight. She could be vindictive sometimes, that Steph. "Let's go!"

"Ooh! I love Wendy's!" Fred said, wide-eyed. "I call—"

"Shotgun!" he and Robbie both said at the same time.

I looked at Robbie gratefully. "Sorry, Fred. I think Robbie beat you out on that one."

"Darn," he said, hanging his head.

"Better luck next time, Freddy." Robbie patted him on the back.

And we were off.

Tama refused to sit in the middle of the backseat, so Fred offered and wedged himself in between my two friends, both of whom looked stonily out their respective windows. On the way out of the parking lot, Robbie cranked up my stereo and started to sing along at full voice. I glanced nervously in the rearview mirror. Tama eyed Robbie with mild distaste.

"Robbie," I said under my breath. He could not dork out in front of Tama. Not if he wanted to date her.

"What?" he said loudly. "I love this song."

"Oh. Yeah? So do I," I told him. Clearly he wasn't getting my hidden meaning, so I tried to be supportive instead.

"So sing it, baby!" he cheered, turning it up even louder.

He was insane. "No."

"Come on! Sing! You know you want to!" he teased, opening his mouth to belt out the chorus. Fred leaned forward and joined right in with him. Robbie laughed. "See? Fred knows! It's fun!"

"Come on, KJ! You can do it!" Fred chided me.

I rolled my eyes at them and started to sing. Thanks to the volume, I couldn't even hear me, so I sang even louder. I glanced in the rearview mirror and saw that Tama and Stephanie were singing along now, too. Robbie was that infectious. Suddenly I couldn't stop laughing. Between the sun and the cold breeze and the singing . . . I just felt free. For the first time all day, I felt like nothing at all could be wrong. Maybe I wouldn't have to vent about last night after all. I looked at Robbie and smiled. He had no idea the favor he'd just done for me.

The song came to an end just as I stopped at a red light. Robbie turned the radio down.

"You know, KJ, you should really talk to Ms. Lin about her choice of costumes," Tama said. "She's giving Ashley all the good poodle skirts and sweaters."

"So?" Stephanie said.

"So isn't Rizzo supposed to be, like, badass?" Tama replied. "She should be in hot pants and tight tops. Instead they've got her looking all Sandy-like. I should stand out from the rest of the Pink Ladies, shouldn't I?"

"I don't think you need a costume to do that," Robbie said.

"Robbie!" Tama said gleefully, shoving his shoulder.

"Just stating an undisputed fact," he said with a casual shrug.

Tama blushed. I'd never seen her do that before. This kid was good.

"You're right. Sandy should look more pure than the other girls, especially in the beginning. It just makes sense, artistically," I said.

"This is what I'm saying!" Tama announced.

"I'll see what I can do."

"Thanks, KJ," Tama said, patting me on the shoulder. "I knew you'd make a good stage manager."

I beamed at the compliment.

"Brainwashed!" Stephanie sang under her breath.

I shot her a look of death in the rearview mirror.

"What was that?" Tama asked.

"Oh, nothing," Stephanie said sweetly.

The light turned green. I ignored Stephanie and hit the gas.

ACT ONE, SCENE THIRTEEN

In which:

I HAVE A BREAKTHROUGH

"WASHINGTON HIGH, HUH? YOU KNOW THAT'S THE ONLY SCHOOL in the L.W.A.L. that I haven't hooked up in?" The St. Luke's boy snorted, sucking phlegm into the back of his throat, and swallowed. I tried not to grimace. He had bulging eyes and ears like Dumbo. His name was Otto. I had a hard time believing he'd ever hooked up with anyone anywhere, let alone in every school in the L.W.A.L. Whatever that was.

All around us, unfamiliar people laughed and flirted and kissed and drank while I . . . I was being systematically tortured, praying every second that Cameron wouldn't walk in and see this guy inching closer to me with every rancid breath. He had told me that he wasn't going, but he'd also said he never missed these things, so my radar was up and running just in case.

Anyway, this was Tama's plan. Throw me to the geek wolves so she could study and analyze my behavior. She stood back by the bookshelf near the wall, watching my every move. I was starting to hate her a little bit.

"You mean, like, *in* the school, or with girls from the school?" I asked, because I had no idea what else to say.

He guffawed. "No! Not *in* the schools! What kind of a male slut do you think I am?"

The annoying kind.

"So, what do you think? You wanna go find someplace private and help me run the table?" he asked, looking me up and down.

Not even a little bit.

My face warmed up as he moved in closer. I looked past him at Tama, pleading silently for mercy. As soon as Otto's fingertip touched my arm, she crossed the five feet between us in two long strides, tapping him on the back.

"You need to go now," she told him.

"Excuse me, but we're having a conversation."

"Not anymore!" she announced. Then she took him by the shoulders, steered him around and gave him a push in the center of his back. Otto tripped away, cast one forlorn look over his shoulder and disappeared into the next room.

"Thank you! Omigod. He was about to stick his tongue down my throat!" I said.

"Why didn't you stop him?" Tama blurted.

"I don't know! He was all over me! I was all trapped and stuff," I said, feeling like a weakling.

"It's not like you two were alone in some dark alley somewhere. There are fifty people in this room," Tama said. "God, KJ. If you can't tell off a guy you don't even know, how are you going to ever tell off the geek posse?"

I sighed morosely. "I don't know."

"Let me ask you this. What were you actually *thinking* when he was about to rub himself up against you?" Tama asked.

"Uh . . . well? He asked me if I wanted to hook up and I thought, 'Not even a little bit.'"

Tama's eyes widened. "There! That's *perfect!* See? You do know what to say, you just have to say it."

"Wait, so that would have worked?" I asked.

"Yuh-huh!" She threw up a hand.

"But it would have crushed him," I said.

"So what? Why does he get to make you uncomfortable, but you can't make him uncomfortable? If that were me, he would have felt my discomfort right in his itty-bitty boy parts," she said, leaning back against the wall next to me. "Oh! Here comes that horror show who was talking to you before."

I looked up to see Peter, a tall guy with broad shoulders and a somewhat pockmarked face, approaching with two drinks. The last time he'd been over here, he'd spent the entire time channeling Glenn—talking to my breasts and calling me J.J. At least Glenn got my name right.

"Do it to him! Tell him what you really think!" Tama hissed as she moved away.

"No! Tama! Don't leave me!" I pleaded.

But it was too late. Pockman Peter was there.

"Hey, J.J. Got you that root beer," he told my breasts.

He held the cup out. I automatically took it. From the corner Tama groaned and rolled her eyes.

"Saw you talking to Otto," Pockman said to my chest. "I know you don't go to St. Luke's, so let me clue you in—you don't want to be talking to Otto. He's kind of a loser."

Gee, thanks. And what does that make you?

Tama stared me down. I was so hot I could feel sweat prickling under my arms. I had to say it. I had to.

"Gee, thanks," I said. But my throat closed and I couldn't get out the second part. Why, why, why would my body not cooperate with my brain?

He smiled. At my boobs. "You're welcome. So. You want something harder than that?" he asked. "Maybe have some real fun?" Then he turned slightly, crooked his elbow out and rubbed it against my chest. He blatantly felt me up with his arm joint, right there in the middle of the party. That was it. My internal thermometer shattered.

"What the hell was that?" I blurted, shrinking toward the wall.

His arm flattened at his side and he turned white. "What?" he asked. For the first time all night he looked at my face.

"That!" I glanced at his elbow. "Do you really think it's okay to feel someone up in the middle of a crowded basement without even knowing her name? What's wrong with you?"

His jaw dropped slightly and he reminded me so much of Glenn. Glenn, who I really *should* have been yelling at for six years of invading my personal space. But Glenn wasn't here. Peter was.

"I wasn't—"

"Yes, you were," I shouted. I slapped the root beer cup down on the shelf next to me and it splattered everywhere, but I didn't even care. "You know what? Otto's not the only loser at St. Luke's. Maybe you should go find him and compare notes."

A few people around us chuckled. Peter once again glanced at my breasts. "I . . . I . . . ," he stammered.

Un. Be. Lievable. His complete gall gave me the one last push I needed to finish him off. I snapped my fingers in front of his face. "Up here, Peter." He looked me in the eye, snagged. "You need to go now," I said, mimicking Tama's words.

He ducked his head and finally went.

"Nice one!" some stranger shouted as a couple of girls near the basement's wide bar applauded. I grinned from ear to ear.

I'd done it. I had told someone off. And I had never felt lighter in my entire life.

"KJ, that was amazing!" Tama cried, grabbing my arms. "Man, I'm good at this! I should go into the empowerment business or something."

"Yeah," I said vaguely.

I didn't have the heart to tell her that it was thinking of Glenn and the many indignities he'd put me through that had actually inspired that rant. She was still partially responsible. For bringing me here. For cheering me on. For giving me the "you need to go now" line. I would never have done that without her help.

Tama's cell phone rang and she rolled her eyes at the caller ID before picking up. "Where are you?" she said without greeting. Then she rolled her eyes at me. "No. No . . . *fine*! We'll meet you there." She clicked the phone closed and tilted her head. "Come on. We're out. Leo's not coming. I said I'd meet him at the diner, and we have to stop and buy him cigarettes on the way."

"But how—"

"I have ID." Tama rolled her eyes at me this time. "God! Grow up already."

I narrowed my eyes as I followed her out. She had been in a perfectly fine mood before Leo had called and now look at her! All tense and snapping at me and being bossy. Robbie was right. Tama deserved much better than Leo. And tonight, when I hadn't been getting accosted by geeks, I had been taking notes. Details I could pass along to Robbie. Seeds, as he so liked to call them. As I followed Tama out the door, I couldn't help hoping that very soon, Tama and I would *both* have brand-new boyfriends.

ACT ONE, SCENE FOURTEEN

In which:

I PUT MY NEW SKILLS TO GOOD USE

THE STAGE COACH DINER WAS JAM-PACKED WITH KIDS FROM school, playing table hockey with sugar packets, dumping over sodas and acting like general morons. I caught a few of them eyeing Tama and me with interest and tried to look aloof, like the two of us hanging out was a totally normal occurrence.

"There he is," Tama said, beelining it for a booth in the back of the room.

Leo sat with his arms splayed out atop the maroon vinyl bench, his blond hair back in a ponytail. He had a healthy blond stubble all over his chin and his blue eyes were droopy, making him look about twice his age and not at all attractive, in my opinion. Tama slid in next to him and they shared an extremely short, but still wet and tongue-heavy kiss.

"Got my cigarettes?" he asked by way of greeting.

Tama dropped them on the table and he slid them into the pocket of his black leather jacket. "KJ, Leo, Leo, KJ," she said.

"We've met," I said, sitting across from them.

"We have?" he asked.

I blushed. "A few times." Jerk.

"Okay, KJ. Time to work on your image," Tama said.

My eyebrows shot up. "My image?"

Tama nodded. "I was watching you at the party and your body language is all wrong. You've got the hunched shoulders, the darting eyes, the apologetic smile. It all just screams 'victim.'"

Wow. Tell me how you really feel.

"But the fix is very simple," Tama continued. "First. You want to keep your shoulders back and your chin slightly raised. Like this."

She sat forward, resting her elbows on the table and bringing her hands under her chin. Instant model. I tried to do the same, and my boobs hit the edge of the table. I immediately shrank back. She gave me a withering look. Leo, luckily, was oblivious.

"Sorry," I said, and tried again. This time I angled myself slightly so that my boobs faced the room instead of the table.

"Good," Tama said. "Now, don't make eye contact with anyone, but don't let your eyes dart around. Either stare at a fixed spot near the ceiling like you're thinking about something truly fascinating, or let your eyes slowly wander the room with disinterest. Like this."

Tama demonstrated. Her face was pure boredom as she scanned the restaurant full of hotties and dorks, jocks and wannabe jocks, princesses and emo chicks. Like it was all just *so* lame. I took a deep breath and tried to do the same. My eyes instantly fell on Jonathan Marsters, the oversexed burnout who was playing Kenickie in the musical. He stuck out his tongue and waggled it at me like a lizard. I quickly averted my gaze.

"KJ! Come on! This is not that complicated. Watch," Tama said.

As she scanned the room again, Leo started to chuckle quietly.

"What?" she snapped.

"You!" he cried mirthfully. "This!" He threw his hand out at me. "This is hysterical. Are you really trying to teach her to be more like you? And you're really trying to learn?"

"I'm just trying to help her," Tama said.

"Well, I think you both need help, because after that display, I'm not sure which one of you's more pathetic." Leo laughed.

"Screw you!" Tama shouted.

A few people around us shut up and stared. I sank a bit lower in my seat.

"What's your problem? We said we were gonna be more honest, right?" Leo said, turning toward her in his seat. "Well, that's my honest opinion, babe, so deal."

"Okay. Why don't you deal with this? I would *honestly* appreciate it if you'd get the hell outta my face," Tama replied, all business.

"Oh, really. That's what you want?" he demanded.

"That's what I want," she shot back.

Tama slid out of the booth and Leo got up, shaking his head. "Bitch," he said under his breath.

"Jackass," she replied loudly.

Leo stormed out, leaving me completely and totally shell-shocked. I couldn't believe Tama had just told him off like that in front of everyone. I was half awed, half mortified.

"God, it's like he's PMSing," Tama said, loud enough for the people around us to hear. A few of them laughed and everyone went about their business.

"Are you okay?" I asked Tama quietly.

"I'm fine. He'll have a smoke and come back all smoochy. It's what he does."

Great. Sounds like a real prince.

"Uh-oh. Incoming," Tama said.

I glanced over my shoulder. Glenn Marlowe had just walked in with two of his friends from the chess club. He hadn't spotted us yet, but I knew it was only a matter of time. His KJ radar was as reliable as my Cameron radar.

"This is your chance," Tama said under her breath. "Remember what you did at the party and just do it."

Glenn spotted me. Gave me a particularly lecherous smile. My palms were moist.

"Oh, God."

"You can do this, KJ. It's time. It's *beyond* time. Look at the guy. He's undressing you with his eyes right now," she said with disgust.

She was right. I felt violated just looking at him.

"Here he comes," Tama whispered. "You have to be mean, KJ, or these people are never going to leave you alone." Tama gave me a serious, bolstering, dead-on glare. "Remember the party. Do it again."

I nodded, but inside I felt sick. This wasn't some random guy at some random party. This was Glenn. And okay, he sucked, but I had to face him every day at school and at rehearsal. How was I going to do this?

"Katie Jean Miller." Glenn dropped into the seat next to me. Before I even knew what was happening, his leg was pressed into mine and his arm was draped over my shoulder. "I knew you were going to be here tonight. I just knew it."

His breath smelled like guacamole. My skin burned. My

vision blurred. I looked at Tama. She clenched her teeth as she stared back.

"Glenn, go away," I said, stomach turning.

He laughed and squeezed my shoulder. "Why don't you come over and sit with me and my friends? I've told them all about you."

Like what? How much I hate you?

I wanted to say it, but I couldn't. The lump in my throat was too huge.

"I mean *all* about you," Glenn said, running his beady eyes over me like a slithering reptile.

And that was it. Something inside of me just snapped.

"Really? Have you told them how much I hate you?" I blurted, pushing him away from me.

All the tables around us fell silent once again. Glenn went ashen. I felt that annoying thump of guilt.

"What?" Glenn said.

"Go away, Glenn," I said again, lowering my voice. My heart was pounding so hard it was tough to breathe, but somehow, I forged ahead. "Leave. Me. Alone."

I stared at him, my face growing redder with each passing moment. I was doing it. I was being mean. I was finally saying how I felt. So why wasn't he going away?

"Do you not understand English, Marlowe?" Tama said finally. "She said go away."

Stunned, Glenn pushed himself up from the table. He paused in the aisle, and I was sure he was going to say something crude, but instead he turned and walked stiffly out of the diner.

"Wow. You guys are really setting 'em up and knocking 'em down tonight, huh?" Jonathan shouted, earning a round of laughter.

I stared at Tama, stunned. Stunned and suddenly twenty pounds lighter. For the first time in as long as I could remember, I felt good. Proud. Confident. I'd actually gotten rid of Glenn. Glenn "Human-Flytrap" Marlowe. I had taken charge of my own personal space. From this moment on, everything was going to be different. Tama was a freaking genius.

I sat up straight in my seat and smiled. Tama lifted her water glass in a toast.

"Now, *that*, KJ Miller, is how it's done."

END ACT ONE

ACT TWO, SCENE ONE

In which:

GLENN FIGHTS BACK

I WALKED INTO SCHOOL ON MONDAY MORNING FEELING LIKE A new person. The sun was shining, there were no clouds in sight and my hair had even done exactly what I'd wanted it to do. I'd told off Glenn Marlowe. I was a Glenn-free zone. It didn't get much better than this.

"Hey. Have you seen Glenn yet?" Stephanie asked, pushing herself away from the wall in the lobby to fall into step with me.

My stomach clenched. I'd told Steph all about what had happened on Saturday night and she hadn't been quite as proud as I'd hoped. In fact, she'd sounded disappointed.

"No. Why?" I asked.

"Because. He's looking for you," she said, all ominous-like. "Apparently he wants to 'talk,'" she added with air quotes.

My hair actually drooped. Come on. I couldn't even get one school day out of this Mean KJ thing? What the heck had I gone to all that trouble for?

We came around the corner and my Cameron radar went off. He stood in the center of a group of jocks and jock worshippers in the general vicinity of my locker, going over a play-by-play of some game or other, but when he saw me, he slapped hands with one of his buddies and jogged over. I went catatonic. I merited a jog-over? How had this happened?

"Hey, KJ," he said, resting his basketball between his hip and his wrist. He used his free hand to adjust his hair, pulling his bangs forward, then pushing them back. "How was your weekend?"

"Good," I replied.

Please don't let Glenn find me now. Please, please, please.

"I heard you and Tama had a good time at the St. Luke's thing," he said, his blue eyes sparkling.

Stephanie shifted next to me, irritated at the very mention of my Saturday night out with Tama. Couldn't she keep the judgmental thing under wraps for five seconds? I was talking to Cameron Richardson here!

"Yeah. It was fun," I lied. At least the last two minutes when I'd finally told off Pockman Peter had been fun.

"Well, maybe I'll see you at the next one," he said, knocking my arm with his elbow. "You can help me make the ex jealous."

I made a noise that was half laugh, half snort, then almost threw up from embarrassment. But Cameron just laughed. "Well. See you later."

"Yeah. Later," I managed to say.

He jogged off and I turned to Steph. "Oh. My. God! Did you hear that! He wants me to help him make his ex jealous!"

Stephanie's face was white and expressionless. Why was she not celebrating with me? Why was she not doing cartwheels right now in the center of the hallway?

"Uh, KJ?" she said.

And then, I felt a chill down my back. The Cameron radar's freak-out must have caused a temporary malfunction in my

Glenn Marlowe Early Warning System. Because he was poking me on the shoulder. Hard.

I turned around, head held high, and looked Glenn right in the eye.

"KJ. I need to speak with you," he said, all formal.

"What is it, Glenn?" I asked, trying to keep my voice calm.

He folded his hands in front of him. "I just wanted to inform you that the manner in which you spoke to me on Saturday night was inappropriate and unacceptable."

I laughed. I couldn't help it. He had to be kidding. The way I'd treated him was inappropriate and unacceptable? How about the way he treated me every single day of my life?

"I don't appreciate you laughing," he continued. "This is very serious."

"Oh, well, of course it is. I'm dying to know where it's going next," I said sarcastically.

"KJ," Stephanie said under her breath.

I looked over at her. Oh no. She was not taking his side. She was not scolding me in front of him.

"Well, I wanted to let you know that I don't think I can be friends with you anymore," Glenn said in a clipped manner. "I don't wish to surround myself with people who have so little respect for me."

A choked laugh strangled its way out of my throat. I had to be hallucinating. There was just no way that Glenn "The Groper" Marlowe was dumping me as a friend because I didn't respect him.

I opened my mouth to say something, anything, but Glenn was already turning around.

"Good-bye, KJ," he said stiffly.

"Ugh! I . . . Bye!" I shouted after him at the top of my lungs. This was insane. This was totally and completely otherworldly insane. "Did that really just happen?"

"Wow. You must have really hurt his feelings," Steph said, staring after him.

"I hurt his feelings? *I* hurt *his* feelings?" I blurted. "How can you stand there and say that after all the times he's grabbed me and all the awful things he's said?"

"I'm sorry! It's just . . . he doesn't know any better," Stephanie said with a shrug. "You did what you did on purpose."

"Yeah, well, I thought that maybe saying what I said would wake him up, but clearly it didn't," I told her, shaking. "He is beyond all hope."

"KJ, calm down," Stephanie said.

"I have to go," I told her. "I'll see you in class."

I stormed off, not knowing which was worse—Glenn's self-righteousness or Stephanie's scolding.

ACT TWO, SCENE TWO

In which:

WE'RE GOING TO CHANGE THE WORLD

I OPENED ONE OF THE CABINETS IN THE LARGEST OF THE THREE dressing rooms that afternoon and started to shove aside hanger after hanger. I hadn't been able to get that conversation with Glenn out of my head all day. Where did he get off telling me we couldn't be friends anymore? I had basically already told him that, hadn't I? He was the one in the wrong, not me. Couldn't he just leave me alone? Let it be? No, he had to make a statement right in the middle of the crowded hallway. Had to have the upper hand.

He was just like my father. Thinking he was some perfect dad and expecting us all to treat him that way, even though all he did was screw up and make us all miserable. Glenn thought he was above reproach, too. He thought he could tell me that *I* was wrong? What was the matter with these people?

"Men suck," I said through my teeth, yanking a silk dress out of the closet and tossing it on the "possibly useful" pile. "Every single one of them sucks."

I slammed the cabinet door, turned around and gasped. Robbie was standing in the doorway of the dressing room, wearing a T-Bird T-shirt.

"Are you gonna punch me?" he asked, hands up.

I sat down on the only empty chair in the room and put my head between my legs. I had riled myself up to the point of nausea, and the shock of seeing him there didn't help.

"No," I said, my voice muffled.

"You okay?" he asked.

I took a deep breath and flipped my hair back as I came up again. "Fine. Why?"

Robbie shot me a look that told me he'd heard exactly what I'd been ranting about. "No reason."

He leaned back against the makeup table and crossed his legs at the ankle. The drumsticks in his back pocket were forced into an odd angle, but he didn't adjust them. He was wearing yellow Chuck T's that were so dirty they looked more mustard. Was it possible that Robbie owned as many pairs of sneakers as I did? For a moment, he contemplated me. I stared back.

"I don't suck, though, do I?"

"What do you mean?"

"Well, I'm a man and you said that all men suck, so—"

"You're not a man. You're a boy," I improvised. Even though that logic would exonerate Glenn as well.

"*I* . . . am not a boy," Robbie said, an incredulous laugh in his voice.

"Okay then, you're a guy," I amended. "Happy now?"

He nodded. "I'll take it." He stood up straight and pulled his T-shirt off over his head.

"What're you doing?" I blurted.

And how the hell did you get that absolutely perfect body? We're talking lean torso, visible pecs, arms with actual definition.

Robbie paused, his hair sticking straight up. "Giving you this T-shirt. Ms. Lin asked me to ask you to put it with the other T-Bird stuff." He tossed it to me, then yanked his long-sleeved Red Hot Chili Peppers tour shirt out of his backpack and put it on.

"Oh." I cleared my throat and hung up the T-shirt. My hand was shaking. I wasn't used to seeing half-naked boys in school. Or anywhere, for that matter.

"So anyway, I just wanted to see if you've gotten anywhere with Tama yet."

"Actually, yeah. I do have a few seeds for you," I said, grabbing my bag and jacket. I think I'd suddenly had too much stimulation for one day.

"Really? Oh, this is great." He rubbed his hands together. So excited it was almost annoying. "Okay, hit me."

I sighed, feeling tired. "Actually, I was just on my way out, so . . ."

"Okay. Cool. We'll go to your place."

My brain automatically assessed the situation. It was Monday. Mondays were generally okay. Except for last week. But usually, Dad didn't get to the heavy drinking until Thursday. Wednesday if it was a bad week. I could take the risk. I hated having to say no to stuff like this, because of him. Coming up with excuses was always very awkward.

"Okay," I said. "Sounds good."

Robbie hooked his arm over my shoulder and we walked toward the door together. "I knew teaming up with you was a solid idea, Farmer Miller," he said, giving me a little squeeze. "Together you and me are gonna change the world."

ACT TWO, SCENE THREE

In which:

ROBBIE AUDITIONS FOR THE FOOD NETWORK

WHEN WE GOT HOME, MY MOTHER WAS STANDING AT THE counter, her blouse untucked from her wool skirt, her hair falling out of its ponytail, chopping vegetables like she was seeking revenge. What the vegetables had done to her I had no idea, but I instantly tensed up. I hoped she'd just had a bad day at school (did I mention my mom teaches first grade?) and that there wasn't something bigger going on.

"Hi, Mom."

She blew out a sigh. I could tell she was about to order me to do something (unpack the grocery bags still standing all over the counters, perhaps?) when she saw Robbie standing there.

"Oh. Hello," she said.

"Mom, this is Robbie. Robbie, my mom."

"Hi, Mrs. Miller." Robbie swung his bag onto a chair and walked over to wash his hands in the sink. He scrubbed them, dried them on a dish towel, then shoved up the sleeves on his shirt. My mother and I watched all of this in mute fascination. He then pulled a knife out of the block on the counter and held it up. "What're we making?"

My mom gave me this look like *What kind of psycho did you bring into my house?*

"Uh . . . stir-fry?" she said.

His eyes lighted up. "Great! Can I do the carrots?" He reached for the bag. My mother watched them go like they had walked off on their own. "Oh, unless you wanted to do them. I didn't mean to swoop in. I just love to chop."

He said this matter-of-factly. Like he was saying he loved chocolate.

"No. I don't mind at all."

My mother pushed one side of the cutting board toward him and he peeled the carrot in about half a second, then started chopping. Slowly I unpacked the first bag of groceries, keeping my eye on him the entire time. It was fascinating, really. On so many levels. A boy in my house was strange enough. But a guy who was that comfortable in someone else's house, around a parent? A boy who knew how to chop vegetables? A boy who voluntarily helped with anything? Was he one of those adults masquerading as a teenager? Was he a narc or something? Maybe there was a big drug problem at my school and twenty-five-year-old Robbie had been sent in to fix it.

Except that he'd been around since kindergarten, so unless the cops planned way ahead, that was out of the question.

"Are you sure you want to chop them so small?" my mother asked as she worked on an onion.

"Yeah, well, carrots are a dense vegetable, so you either need to cook them longer or chop them smaller so they keep up with the rest of the food," Robbie said. He smacked his hands together and walked to the stove, where the wok was already set up. "May I?" He put his hand on the knob next to the burner.

I'm pretty sure my mom thought she'd died and gone to heaven. "Sure."

"The wok should heat up for a while so it's nice and scalding," Robbie said, flipping the flame to life.

I slammed the door to the refrigerator. "Okay, what are you? The Iron Chef?"

Robbie laughed. "No, I just do a lot of the cooking in my house. My brother and my dad can't cut butter, so . . . I just learned."

"What about your mom?" my mother asked. She had backed to the opposite counter now and was leaning back against it. Robbie had taken over.

"My mom left when I was five," Robbie said as he went to work on a head of broccoli. "Someone had to step up. I cooked my first Thanksgiving turkey when I was ten."

"I'm so sorry to hear that," my mother said.

"Eh, I figure we're better off," Robbie said with a shrug. "It'd be worse living with someone who didn't actually want to be there, right?"

My mother and I looked at each other, stunned. So offhandedly, he'd shared this information. Like it was nothing big. Like he wasn't even embarrassed by his situation. I wondered if I would be able to just say it like that if it ever happened.

Yeah, my dad moved out. We're better off without him.

It had a certain ring.

Robbie threw a little oil in the wok and then added the already chopped chicken. Sizzles and pops filled the room and he shook the wok up like a pro. It was so surreal watching Robbie Delano cooking in my kitchen, I couldn't tear my eyes away.

Then I heard my dad's car pull up. Once again, Mom and I exchanged a look. It was early. Way early. What was he doing here already? My mother went for the kitchen door and opened it. I heard his engine die, the pop of his car door closing. My heart pounded with nervous fear. This was completely out of the ordinary, even for a good night. Had something happened at work? Something bad?

Please, God, just don't let him be drunk. Please, please, please don't let him embarrass me.

"What's the matter?" Robbie asked me as he stirred.

"Greg! You're home early!" my mother said brightly.

"Well. To what do I owe this greeting?" my father replied.

Normal. He sounded normal. His footsteps on the side porch weren't heavy or dragging. Normal. My shoulders started to relax. My father stepped into the kitchen, his suit jacket folded over his arm, his briefcase in hand, his tie slightly undone. His face was white, not red. His hair combed, not mussed. His eyes not swimming. His nose of normal size. I was so happy I sprang forward and hugged him.

"Hi, Dad!"

"KJ." He gave me a little squeeze. "What's this?" he asked Robbie.

"Just a little stir-fry, sir," Robbie said.

My dad grinned. Sir. He had to love that.

"Dad, this is Robbie Delano," I said.

"Robbie." My dad reached out his hand and Robbie wiped his on his jeans before they shook. "Any man who comes in here and gives my wife the night off is okay by me."

He kissed my mother and she beamed, and then he headed off for his bedroom to change. My mother and I couldn't stop grinning. Robbie must have thought we were on something, but I didn't care. It was a rare moment when I actually liked my father.

ACT TWO, SCENE FOUR

In which:

ROBBIE EXPLORES MY BEDROOM

I TRIED TO SEE MY ROOM AS ROBBIE SAW IT. WHAT DID IT LOOK like upon seeing it for the first time? The dark purple walls. The sketches and paintings tacked up over my bed. The four long, built-in shelves with their alphabetized books and CDs. The easel in the corner with the red-and-black piece I'd done last week still sitting there, awaiting completion or destruction. The teetering piles of magazines—*National Geographic*, *Vogue*, *Entertainment Weekly*, *Paper*, *W*, *Interview*, from my artistic collage phase. The desk chair piled with ten days of discarded clothes.

Maybe I should have thought this through better.

"So this is where you live."

Robbie went to close the door and I grabbed it. "No!"

"What?"

"House rules. I'm not allowed to close the door if there's a guy over," I said. Then wanted to shoot myself.

Robbie's eyebrows arched. "And do you have a lot of guys over?"

"No. You're the first." I blushed. "Well, not in that way, because you're not here in a *guy* capacity—"

"I am *always* in a guy capacity," Robbie joked.

"Ha ha. But no. You're here . . . we're here to talk about Tama. And the seeds," I said. I shoved all my clothes off my desk chair and onto the floor and sat down.

"Right. The seeds." Robbie inspected my anger painting, his back to me. I was glad I couldn't see his face. He was probably wondering where I was hiding the chicken heads and hacksaws.

"So, here's what I learned about Tama Saturday night," I said, soldiering forward. "She likes salty snacks, not sweet."

"Okay. Got it. Good to know."

He moved on to my books and CD collection. Pulled something out, inspected it, put it back. He strolled along the shelves slowly, as if he were reading each and every title.

"She absolutely hates it when guys check themselves out and fix their hair and stuff," I continued. "Which is weird because Leo's pretty vain, I think."

"Right, but he probably doesn't admire himself in public. Too 'cool' for that," Robbie said, adding air quotes.

He scoffed at something on my shelves. Shook his head. Moved on to the paintings over my bed. I watched him closely. What had he scoffed at? Could you really come into someone else's room and mock their stuff? I hoped he didn't mock my work. That I could not handle.

"Anything else?" he asked, walking around my bed so he could see the paintings on the other side. He passed right by my knee, but didn't look at me. What was he thinking right now?

"Oh! Yeah. She likes guys in turtlenecks," I said.

"Turtlenecks?" His eyes finally met mine.

"Yeah. Turtlenecks."

He frowned and touched his neck. "I hate turtlenecks. They chafe."

"No they don't," I said. I was wearing one at that very moment.

"I don't even own a turtleneck."

I shrugged. "Sorry. Just reporting what I know."

He nodded and returned his attention to the paintings. "You did all these?"

"Yeah." I held my breath.

"They're cool."

I blushed. "Thanks."

"But your music collection needs serious help."

My heart dropped. "What?"

"This is pathetic," Robbie said, striding back to my media wall. "What are you going for here? Unoriginality?" He gestured at my magazines. "Do you just buy whatever *Entertainment Weekly* tells you to?"

Yes.

"No," I said defensively. "And I like my music."

"You don't like this stuff. Trust me. You just don't know any better."

"Thanks a lot." My face flushed with embarrassment.

Robbie's face fell. "Sorry. I just . . . sorry. I guess I'm kind of a music snob."

"You guess?"

He came around my bed and sat on the edge to face me. "I'll burn you some stuff, if you want me to," he offered. "You like metal, obviously. Classic rock. No emo, thank God. At least you've got that going for you."

"You don't have to burn me anything," I said, humiliated. "I have a Best Buy gift certificate from Christmas. I can use that."

"You still have a gift card from Christmas? I would have scorched that sucker the next day. We are so going shopping."

The embarrassed heat that had overtaken me ebbed a bit. "We are?"

"We are. Soon," he replied.

The phone rang and I grabbed it off my desk without checking the caller ID. Steph pretty much always called after dinner.

"Hello?"

"Hi . . . Can I speak to KJ?"

My heart stopped beating, then gave an overly huge thump. This could not be what I thought it was. It was a telemarketer or something. Robbie got up again to take a look at my Happy Meal toy collection from my youth, which I had yet to bring myself to toss. I spun the chair toward my desk, away from him.

"This . . . this is KJ."

"Hey. It's Cameron."

Holy. Holy. Crap.

I gripped the edge of my desk. Cameron Richardson was on the phone! He had called me! He had my number! Wait a minute, how did he get my number? Had he looked it up or . . . Who cared!? He was on the phone at this very second and . . . I wasn't saying a thing.

"Hello? You there?"

"Yeah, I'm here."

I stood up. I couldn't help it. I could not sit still.

"Okay, so, you know that project Mrs. Driscoll assigned today?" he asked.

"Yeah?"

"I was wondering if you wanted to maybe work on that together," Cameron said.

No way. No. Freaking. Way.

"Really?" I said. "Uh . . . sure."

"Cool," Cameron said. "Do you want to set up a time? To, you know, work on it?"

"Yeah! Sure. Definitely," I said.

Robbie was staring at me quizzically now. I couldn't believe I had to do this with an audience. Breathe, KJ. Breathe.

"How about tomorrow? After school? We don't have practice since there's a game tomorrow night."

Tomorrow. Tomorrow. What was I doing tomorrow? I couldn't even remember what day it was. Like it mattered.

"Tomorrow is perfect," I said.

Robbie crossed his arms over his chest, staring blatantly at me now.

"Good. Okay. So we'll meet in the library after eighth. Cool?" Cameron said.

"Cool," I replied.

"I guess I'll . . . see you in class."

"Yeah. See you in class," I said.

We hung up. I felt a scream bubbling up in my throat so I grabbed a pillow and let 'er rip. I didn't even care that Robbie was watching me. Let him think I was weird. Who cared? I had a study date with Cameron Richardson!

"Okay, I give. Was that Ryan Seacrest or something?" Robbie asked. "There was another sex scandal on *American Idol* and they need you to take over a vacancy in the top ten, am I right?"

"Nope," I said happily, dropping down on my bed. I still had the phone in my hand and my scream pillow across my lap. "That was Cameron Richardson."

Robbie blinked. "Cameron Richardson," he said flatly.

"Yeah. What?"

"Cameron Richardson made you scream into a pillow."

"Yeaaaahhhh?"

"Huh."

The smile started to fade. Something about his tone was not right. Robbie turned around and picked up a plastic Bugs Bunny from my collection. He rearranged the arms so that it was strangling the Bob the Builder next to it, and set him down again.

"Huh what?" I said.

"Nothing. I just would have thought a girl like you would be able to see right through a guy like that."

"A guy like what?" I asked. My skin prickled.

"Like him," Robbie said with a shrug. "He's shallow as a puddle, which does make him pretty see-through."

"He's not shallow," I protested. I was getting all hot again.

Robbie laughed. "Uh, yeah. He is."

Wow. Could he be any more condescending? I stood up, dropping the pillow to the floor. "How would you even know? It's not like you guys hang out."

"Okay. Fine. So, what do you guys talk about?" Ronnie asked, crossing his arms over his chest.

Nothing.

"Lots of things," I lied. "We talk about our classes, for one. He's a really good student, you know."

"That doesn't automatically make someone unshallow," Robbie said.

I rolled my eyes. "Oh, and what makes you unshallow? The fact that you're a music snob who uses sixties slang and tries to impress their parents with his cooking skills? Big whoop."

Did I just say "big whoop"? Robbie stared at me for a long moment. I couldn't believe I'd just blurted all that to him. I never said what I really thought. And the kicker was, I didn't really think all those things were bad things. I just couldn't deal with him insulting the love of my life.

"Sorry," Robbie said, raising his hands. "I'm just trying to be honest."

My jaw clenched as we stared at each other. That was so weird. He'd just sounded exactly like Leo. What had Tama said to him again?

"Well, *honestly* . . . ," I began. Then I paused. I couldn't tell him to get the hell out of my face. That was not in me. But I could get the same effect. "I kind of have a lot of homework to do," I finished, deflating.

I sat down at my computer and opened a random Word document. He hovered behind me. What had just happened? We'd been having fun, making plans. And now I couldn't even look at him.

"All right, then," Robbie said. "I guess I'll see you tomorrow."

"Yeah! See you tomorrow!" I said with false brightness.

My blood was rushing so loudly in my ears, I didn't even hear him leave.

ACT TWO, SCENE FIVE

In which:

TAMA AND I GO TO WORK

"HEY, KJ! WANNA HANG OUT AT LUNCH TODAY?" FRED ASKED, walking sideways down the hall next to me, practically tripping himself with every other step. "I need someone to test me on act one. I think I can go off book!"

"I can't today, Fred. I already have lunch plans," I told him. Or I would, I hoped. I was on my way to ask Tama to hang out right then so I could get her advice on Cameron. There was just no way I could go into this study date cold turkey. I needed help. Normally, I would have asked Steph, but she was even more boy-clueless than I was. Plus I was still a little annoyed at her about the whole Glenn thing. The last thing I wanted was for the day of my first Cameron date to be tainted by one of Stephanie's Be Nice to the Geeks speeches.

"Oh. Well, that's okay. Maybe after school. You think?" Fred asked, hiking his pants up.

My impatience mounted and my fingers clenched. Maybe I should just tell him off the same way I had Glenn. Be done with this once and for all. But one look in his puppy-dog eyes and I couldn't do it. This wasn't creepy Glenn. It was sweet little Fred. I couldn't crush him. Not yet. Baby steps, KJ.

"I have plans then, too," I told him, trying to keep my voice even. "But I'll call you tonight and we'll figure it out, okay?"

"Promise?" he asked, all excited.

I laughed. I was Cameron-inspired giddy. "Promise."

"Thank you, KJ! Thank you so much!"

"No problem. Bye, Fred!" I hightailed it up the hall, dodging a big group of freshmen who ideally would confuse him enough to give me a head start. By the time I got to the drama room, I was Fred free and, luckily, the door was still closed. Katz had kept the class late. My hero.

Inside, the lights were out and a movie played on the TV screen at the front of the room. A couple of people were packing up their stuff, but most of them, including Tama, were riveted. I angled myself to better see the television through the skinny window. On the screen, two old-fashioned people with old-fashioned hairdos and old-fashioned clothes waltzed together in black and white. As the music swelled, the man dipped the woman and leaned in to kiss her. Then the words *The End* appeared over their faces and the lights came up.

"All right! You can all go now!" Mr. Katz announced, stepping away from the wall. He opened the door and I sprang back. "We'll discuss the movie tomorrow."

Ashley Brown sniffled as she walked out, clearly moved by the film. Tama followed after her, shaking her head. "That girl must have missed her meds this morning. She just bawled through that whole thing."

"You didn't like it?" I asked.

"No. It was cool," Tama said as we turned down the hall together. "Especially the dancing. There was this waltz at the end . . ." She sighed dreamily. "I can't even get Leo to step from side to side with me."

Ooh. Another seed for Robbie. Nice. That was, if Robbie ever wanted to talk to me again. And vice versa. I still hadn't decided. Partially because I had other, more important things to focus on.

"So, you're never going to believe this," I said under my breath. "Cameron called me last night."

Tama gasped. "No way! I knew it! I *knew* my plan was working! What'd he say?"

"He wanted to set up a study date. For this afternoon," I told her.

"This afternoon? This is so killer," Tama said. "I told you I would help you snag him!"

I wasn't entirely sure what Tama had done to help in this particular matter, but I decided to just let that go. Maybe she had been talking me up to him, as she'd said. I had no idea. But I wasn't about to question her when I was here to ask for a favor.

"I know. I can't believe it," I said. "So what do I do?"

"What do you mean, what do you do? You go!" she said.

"But what do I say? How do I act? What if I dork out in front of him?" I asked desperately.

"You are not going to dork out in front of him," Tama said. She took a deep breath and paused. "Okay. Here's the plan. You, me, lunch in the library. I'm going to give you some pointers."

"Really? Thank you so much," I said, already relieved.

Tama smiled. "No problem. But first, we must go over the

lighting rundown. Yesterday Glenn had me in a yellow wash during my solo. I don't do yellow. I mean, does he want Sandy to look like she has jaundice during a romantic song?"

"I'm on it," I promised her. "I'll talk to him."

Even though I hated him. After all, what were friends for?

ACT TWO, SCENE SIX

In which:

FOOTSIE IS PLAYED

"SO, DID YOU TALK TO GLENN AT ALL TODAY?" STEPHANIE ASKED me as we stood outside the library that afternoon.

I had to practically eat my tongue to keep from saying something I'd regret. I mean, was she really bringing up Glenn two seconds before I was supposed to be meeting Cameron? Had she ever heard of bad karma?

"No. And even if I did want to talk to him, he made it pretty clear he doesn't want to talk to me, remember?"

"Yeah. I just . . . I hate it when people are fighting," Stephanie lamented, looking at her toes.

"Steph, don't take this the wrong way, but can we talk about something else?" I asked, glancing nervously around the hall. "I don't really feel like thinking about Glenn right now, you know?"

Stephanie blinked and suddenly seemed to remember what we were doing there. "Right. Sorry. So, are you ready for this?" she asked.

"I hope so," I said. I was, in fact, hardly breathing.

"Well, don't worry. It's going to be great," Stephanie assured me. Her eyes shone the exact same way my mom's had before my confirmation. Like she was so proud of her little girl. "Call me later and tell me *everything*."

"I will," I promised, bouncing up and down on the balls of my feet as I looked past her down the hall. It sounds awful, but I just wanted her to go. I couldn't be Cool KJ with an audience. Especially not one who would know how much I was faking.

"Okay. Bye! Call me," she said again before hugging me one last time and going.

"Bye!"

Of course the second she was gone, I wanted her back. I couldn't do this. Who was I kidding? Maybe I should just go down to the auditorium and stay there. Mr. Katz had given me the day off to work on my biology project, but still. At least there I knew what I was doing. At least there I was in charge. Standing here I could barely even control my bladder.

Okay. Forget this. I started to turn. To flee. But Cameron chose that exact moment to show up, freshly showered after gym class, the curls along his collar still darkly wet.

"Hey." He smiled. "You ready?" He touched my arm as he slid by me, and my nostrils filled with the scent of his spicy soap. Every joint in my body weakened.

"Okay," I squeaked.

As I followed him, Tama's mantra repeated itself over and over. *Confident, Cool, No Giggling. Confident, Cool, No Giggling. Confident, Cool, No Giggling.* She was really into the three-pronged plans of action.

Cameron looked up from the table where he'd already settled in. "So, you sure you don't mind working with a B student?"

And I giggled.

Dammit! Foiled already. Frustrated, I pulled out the chair across from his and sat down, remembering to sit up straight.

"No. I'm good," I said.

"I know you are. That's why I'm here," Cameron replied with that ridiculously sexy smile.

And I giggled again. His grin widened. If my face got any hotter, he was going to get a sunburn off me.

"Okay, so, should we pick a topic?" I said, pulling out my notebook. "I was bored in French, so I made a list of possibilities."

"Cool."

Cameron reached for my notebook and his pinky grazed mine. There was such a burst of excitement inside every inch of my body I thought I might faint. While he scanned the list, Cameron's brow wrinkled in this totally adorable way. If only I could take a picture with my cell without him noticing . . .

"I like this one," he said. "Chemical tests for nutrients in food. That could be kinda cool."

"That's my favorite, too!" I announced.

"Shhhh!" someone behind me said.

Cameron smiled.

"I mean, yeah," I said, looking away and uncapping my pen. "Sure. Let's do that."

This was cool KJ. Super-cool, unaffected, confident KJ. I pulled the notebook to me and turned calmly to a clean page.

"So, are you coming to the game tonight?" Cameron asked.

"Me?" I asked, surprised.

"No. The kid behind you," Cameron joked.

I glanced over my shoulder. There was no one behind me. Cameron laughed. Nice one, KJ. Tama never would have fallen for that. Never would have looked. But KJ Miller? Of course! I just fell off the turnip truck yesterday.

"Um . . . I don't really go to games," I said.

"Why not?"

Because none of my friends go to games. Because only the cool kids go to games. Because if I went there, I'd have no one to sit with and it would be completely obvious to the world what a total dork loser I am, including you?

"I'm just not that into basketball," I improvised.

"Well, you should be," Cameron said. "We're good this year. You should come."

Did he want me to come? Was it possible that Cameron Richardson was telling me, KJ Miller, that he wanted me there to cheer him on?

"I don't know," I said.

"Come on." His foot nudged mine under the table. I blushed scarlet. "Come on. You know you want to, KJ. Come on . . . come to the basketball game. . . ."

"Cameron!" I hissed as the librarian looked at us over her desk.

"Come on, KJ. All the *cool* kids are doing it," he teased, nosing his foot beneath mine now. "Come to the game. Come on!"

Everyone in the library was staring at us. "Cameron! We're supposed to be studying!" I hissed, grinning like mad.

"Oh, right. Studying. Sorry." He suddenly sat up very

straight and poised his pen over his notebook. "I'm very serious now. Teach me, oh wise one."

I snorted a laugh and pushed myself up straight in my seat as well. My mind was still reeling, though. Was Cameron flirting with me? That had certainly felt like flirting. Maybe I could go to a basketball game. Maybe if I offered to drive Tama, she'd let me sit with her. But then I'd have to sit with all those popular people I never spoke to. Wouldn't they be wondering what I was even doing there? What if they made me leave? Did people do stuff like that, or was it only in the movies? But still, if Cameron wanted me to go, how could I *not* go? That would be like dissing him. Omigod. Did I really have the power to diss Cameron Richardson?

"KJ? You in there?"

Right. Focus. Task at hand. Confident, Cool, No Giggling.

"Um . . . okay," I said. "I guess we should start by figuring out which foods we want to test. Then we can write the hypothesis. And tomorrow we're going to have to talk to Mrs. Driscoll about lab time."

"Okay. Good plan. I knew you were going to be a good person to partner with."

And there it was. The truth. The real reason we were here. I knew it was too good to be true. I was good in bio and Cameron wanted an A. He'd asked me to be his study partner. He hadn't asked me on a *real* date. Maybe he was just trying to get me to come to his game because they needed more fans there or something. Or he was just trying to be nice.

I couldn't believe I'd almost risked the total public humiliation of sitting alone at a basketball game for a pipe dream. Or worse, trying to sit with the popular kids. Okay, KJ. Work time. No more reading "date" into every little thing he said.

"But I still think you should come to the game," Cameron said, nudging my foot one more time.

And after that, I couldn't stop smiling.

ACT TWO, SCENE SEVEN

In which:

THERE'S A BETRAYAL

I SHOWED UP AT STEPHANIE'S HOUSE THAT NIGHT WEARING MY ONE and only Washington High T-shirt under my coat—the one we had all been issued the first day of freshman year. I knew there was no way she would have agreed to a basketball game ahead of time, so my plan was to drag her out to it. I bounced up and down on my toes as I waited.

"Surprise!" I squealed when the door swung open. "Get your coat! We're going to—"

She held up a finger. She was on the phone.

"Okay. Yeah. No. She's here now." Her eyes flicked to me. "No. She looks fine."

Wait. She was talking to someone on the phone about me? Who was it?

"Yes, I'll ask her. I'll talk to you later," she said into the receiver. "It's okay. Don't worry about it. Bye."

"Who was that?" I asked, stepping inside.

"That was Fred," she told me flatly.

Okay. Major downer. "You talk to Fred on the phone? Since when?"

"Since he called me freaking out because you promised to call him tonight and didn't," she said, crossing her arms over her chest.

Oh. I had promised that, hadn't I?

"Why didn't he just call me?" I asked, walking down the hall toward her room.

"He said he tried, but he kept getting your voice mail," Stephanie said. "He thought you were, like, dead or kidnapped or something."

I snorted a laugh. "He's even more dramatic than the Drama Twins." I pulled out my phone and sure enough, it was turned off. I guess I'd never turned it back on after my afternoon in the library.

"KJ, this isn't funny," Stephanie said, tossing her phone on her canopied bed. "Fred's really hurt. Why didn't you call him?"

I saw red. This was so not the way this surprise drop-in was supposed to go. It was one phone call, not the end of the world. Why did she have to make a federal case out of it?

"Oh, I don't know, because I was out with Cameron all afternoon and I've been kind of distracted ever since?" I said pointedly.

The guilt was evident on Stephanie's face. "Oh my God. I totally forgot. Your date with Cameron!"

"Yeah. Only the biggest moment of my life," I told her. "I came over here to tell you about it, but if you'd rather jump all over me about one forgotten phone call to Fred—"

"No! No. I'm so sorry. We can talk about that later," Stephanie said, bouncing down onto her bed. "Tell me all about Cameron. How was it?"

This was more like it. But when I tried to muster the

excitement, it was gone. I picked up one of her ceramic horses from a shelf and toyed with it listlessly. "Fine. It was fine."

"Come on, KJ! Tell me!" She hugged a throw pillow to her stomach. "What did he say? Did you guys just study or was there actual flirting?"

"There was flirting . . . I think," I said, warming to the subject a bit. "Why? Did you think there wouldn't be flirting?"

"I don't know. It *was* a study date," she said with a shrug. "He didn't ask you to hang out, he asked you to study."

"What's that supposed to mean?" I demanded. All the annoying negative thoughts that had been circulating in the back of my brain all afternoon came zooming to the forefront. "You think he's just using me?"

"No. Not exactly." Stephanie pushed herself up off her bed and shoved her hands into the pockets of her sweatshirt. "It's just that, it could have gone either way. Either he wanted to hang out with you for you or he just wanted to study. So I wasn't entirely sure if it was a *date* date."

"Oh. You don't think he likes me, do you?" I said. I couldn't believe she was saying this. It was one thing for me to think it. I was allowed to be insecure about myself, but Stephanie was supposed to be my best friend. She was supposed to tell me my insecurities were silly and that of course Cameron was totally in love with me and we were going to live happily ever after!

"No! I think he likes you! Why wouldn't he like you? I just think maybe he asked you to study instead of something else because then he could play it off to his friends like it was just a study thing. You know, so he could still look cool."

"Well, if he was so afraid of being seen with me, then why did he ask me to come to his game tonight?" I demanded.

"He did?" she asked.

"Yeah! Nice to be shocked," I told her.

"I'm not shocked. I'm just—"

"I was going to ask you to come with me, but you know what? I think I'll go by myself," I told her. "Wouldn't want you sitting there the whole time telling me what a bad person I am and that Cameron doesn't actually like me."

Stephanie's face fell. "KJ! That's not fair. I—"

"Forget it. I don't know why I came over here." I hadn't even gotten my coat off yet, which was a plus for making a speedy exit. "You know, sometimes this whole glass-is-half-empty thing of yours really sucks!"

"Thanks a lot!" Stephanie said, her cheeks coloring. "I didn't . . . I was just theorizing."

"Well, now you can theorize to yourself," I said.

I stormed out of her house without looking back. Stephanie and I had never fought before. Had never actually yelled at each other in the ten years we'd been best friends. But now I was so angry I actually peeled out of her driveway. Until that moment, I hadn't even known I could do that. Guess you really do learn something new every day. Including who your real friends are.

ACT TWO, SCENE EIGHT

In which:

TAMA TRUMPS STEPHANIE

THE NEXT MORNING, STEPHANIE WAS WAITING FOR ME BY MY locker. I took one look at her and everything inside of me clenched. Thanks to her, I had missed the basketball game, unable to bring myself to show up alone. Thanks to her, my giddiness over Cameron was all mired in doubt. Thanks to her, I had barely even been able to sleep all night, tossing and turning over the fact that she was gabbing with the geeks about me behind my back. And now she was waiting for me at my locker? Why? So she could pants me or something? Seal the deal?

I paused in the middle of the hallway. The last thing I wanted to do was endure another lecture about how awful I was. But there she stood. Hovering. I was trapped. She noticed me. Our eyes locked. All I wanted to do was turn the other way. And then—

"Cage! There you are!" Tama came swooping in, all cashmere sweater and dangling earrings and perfume, and hooked her arm through mine. "I've been looking all over for you. How was your date with Cameron?"

I looked at Stephanie and smiled triumphantly. My date

with Cameron. See? Some people thought it was an actual date. People who actually knew Cameron. People who hung out with him all the time. And finally I was going to get to tell someone all about it. Someone who actually wanted to hear the story.

"Omigod, it was so amazing," I said to Tama. "He actually played footsie with me under the table!"

"He did?" Stephanie said.

"No he did not!" Tama protested with a grin.

"Yes he did! I mean, I think he did! I don't know. No one's ever played footsie with me before." I ignored Steph and focused on Tama.

"If you think he did, then he did. There's no mistaking a good game of footsie," Tama said. "Cage. I am *so* proud of you! My little protégé! What else? Tell me everything."

"KJ, wait," Stephanie said. "We have to talk."

But I didn't want to talk to her now. Didn't want to hear more about how I was wrong about everything. So instead, I decided to bypass my locker.

"Later, Stephanie. I have to go."

Then I walked off down the hall with Tama, relating every little detail I could remember. And unlike a certain other supposed best friend, Tama had the perfect, psyched reactions to every last thing I said.

ACT TWO, SCENE NINE

In which:

THERE'S FORGIVENESS . . . FROM SOME

CAMERON TALKED TO ME THREE WHOLE TIMES IN BETWEEN classes, whereas not one geek talked to me all day long. Not Glenn, not Fred, and not Andy, who spent lunch in the courtyard taking notes and clutching at his hair all mad-scientist like, while I helped Tama memorize lines at our own private table. I only hoped that it wasn't notes about me he was going over, but then, who cared? As long as he wasn't in my face it was fine by me. Never in my life had I been blessed with such a stalker-free day. It was bliss.

But my good mood hit a road bump when I saw Robbie waiting for me at the end of the hall after the final bell. He was wearing a black We Are the Fury T-shirt and a gray skullcap and listening to his iPod, but he pulled out the ear buds when he saw me. Today's sneakers were gray Chucks with little black stars all over them. Cool. They almost distracted me from the fact that I hadn't spoken to him since Monday evening.

"Hey," he said.

"Hey," I replied nervously.

Robbie pushed himself away from the wall to walk with me. "So, this guy walks into a bar and says 'Ow. That hurt.'"

I stared at him. "What're you doing?"

"Trying to make you laugh," he replied. "People hate you less when you make them laugh."

"I don't hate you," I replied with a smirk. I was feeling very benevolent thanks to my geek-free day.

"You don't?" He drew his hand across his head dramatically. "Good. 'Cause that was my best material."

We were both grinning as we crossed the hallway toward the auditorium. "Somehow I doubt that."

"So listen, I was thinking we could hit Best Buy tonight after dinner."

"Tonight?"

It was Wednesday. A could-go-either-way night. Might be good to avoid home.

"I've been thinking about your CD collection pretty much nonstop," he told me. "Seriously. It's kept me up at night. I'm concerned for your well-being."

I rolled my eyes and yanked open the door. "All right, fine. We'll go tonight."

"Yes! Thank you!" He clapped his hands. "You will not regret this."

Then he ran down the aisle and up the steps and disappeared into the wings. Very excitable, that one. Up ahead, Glenn sat on the edge of the stage, staring me down. He'd been staring at me like that every single time I'd been in his presence since Monday morning. It gave me the willies, but at least he wasn't grabbing me anymore. That was something.

I cleared my throat and was about to go talk to him about Tama's yellow wash, but Stephanie caught up with me from behind.

"KJ," she said, taking my arm.

Her tone was all serious. I knew she was going to be irritated after lunch, but I'd seen her sitting with Ashley and the Drama Twins, so she hadn't been entirely alone.

"Okay, are you going to hate me forever?" she asked.

I flung my bag on the first seat of the first row. All the tightness I'd had in my chest about her that morning was long since gone. Cameron had loosened it bit by bit each time he'd spoken to me, because each time, he was proving Stephanie wrong. It was much easier to forgive her, knowing she was wrong.

"Why does everyone think I hate them?" I asked.

"Well, you were sure giving off that vibe this morning," she said.

"I don't hate you," I said. I put my hands on her shoulders and looked her in the eye. "It's fine."

"Really?"

"Yeah." I pulled my script and notebook out of my backpack, smiling pretty uncontrollably. This had been a good day after all. A really good day.

"Why is it fine?" Stephanie asked, ever suspicious. "What's with the doofball grin?"

I glanced around for spies and waved her closer. Stephanie stepped in, clearly intrigued. "Because I really think he might like me," I whispered.

"Really?" she gasped.

"Yes! Really. He talked to me so many times in the hall

today, and you should have seen him yesterday, Steph. He was dropping all these signals . . . Well, at least Tama thinks they were signals."

"Yeah, I heard about the footsie," she said pointedly.

"There were other things, too."

Her eyes were wide. "Like what?"

"Well—"

"Hey, KJ," Andy popped in out of nowhere, his notebook out and a pen at the ready. "I have some more questions for you."

Stephanie stood up straight and cleared her throat.

"Maybe we can do this later?" she said. "Wanna come over tonight?"

"Oh, I can't. I have plans with Robbie," I said, biting my lip.

"You have plans with Robbie?" Andy blurted. I could tell he totally had the wrong idea, but I wasn't about to correct him. Let him think I had something going on with Robbie. Wasn't exactly a Mean KJ diss, but it couldn't hurt my cause.

"Yeah, we're going shopping," I told them.

Stephanie stared at me as if I'd just told the whole school about her secret unicorn obsession. "Okay. Do you think maybe you'll have time this weekend?" she asked, her voice tight.

"Yeah. Definitely," I replied, wondering what was wrong. "Everything okay?"

Mr. Katz chose that moment to walk in and smack his hands together. "Magic time, people!" he shouted at the top of his lungs. "I want all my actors backstage! Now, now, now!"

Wow. He was in rare form today. Must have had an extra Red Bull at lunch.

"Guess you'd better get back there," I told Stephanie.

Her face was sour. "Yeah. Guess I'd better."

She turned to go, and I was about to follow her and ask what was wrong when Fred tried to slip past me, bumped into the arm of one of the seats, tripped and sprawled facedown in the aisle.

"Oh my God! Fred! Are you okay?" I asked automatically.

He jumped up, the change in his pockets jangling, and straightened his Spider-man T-shirt. His face was even redder than usual.

"I'm okay. I'm okay," he said, trying to make a quick getaway.

Acidic guilt surrounded my heart. I knew what Tama would tell me to do. To let him go. Or finish him off with some scathing remark about how his plumber's crack was not for public viewing. But did I really have to be mean to all of them all at once? I mean, poor Fred. Clearly he was really upset about yesterday, however much I thought he was overreacting. Besides, I wasn't feeling quite so belligerent today, thanks to Cameron. I didn't feel caged or trapped or angry, which made it a lot harder to be mean. I glanced around quickly, making sure Tama was nowhere in sight. The coast was clear.

"Fred, I'm really sorry about yesterday," I blurted.

He looked at me hopefully. "That's okay."

"No, it's not. I promised I'd call you and I didn't," I told him. "I shouldn't have done that."

"Thanks, KJ. It really means a lot to me that you said that," Fred said, tilting his head to the side. "Really a lot."

"No problem," I told him. "You'd better get backstage. Katz means business today."

"You got it!" Fred said loudly. He practically skipped backstage. I shook my head, laughing as he went, then turned around and walked right into Andy. I had totally forgotten he was there.

"So, top three dream vacation destinations?" he asked me, his pen hovering.

I sighed, my shoulders slumping. So much for my geek-free day.

ACT TWO, SCENE TEN

In which:

COMPROMISES ARE MADE

SOMEWHERE BETWEEN MAKING PLANS WITH ME AND APPEARING on stage, Robbie changed into a black turtleneck and lost the skullcap. He looked like a soulful poet dude straight out of some 1960s movie. Tama couldn't take her eyes off of him as they rehearsed the drive-in scene. The seeds were being sown.

"All right! Let's take five!" Mr. Katz shouted.

Everyone scrambled for the bathrooms and the vending machines. Robbie walked over to his backpack, pulled out a jumbo-sized bag of Chex Mix and tore it open.

"A little salty goodness?" he asked, holding it out to Tama with one eyebrow raised.

"Thanks," Tama said. She reached into the bag for a handful.

"I'll go get us some drinks," Robbie said. He jumped down off the stage and winked at me as he passed me by. Then grimaced and pulled at the turtleneck. I had to stare straight into my lap to keep from laughing out loud.

The boy was good. I'd give him that. Give him some seeds and he got right to planting them.

"KJ! I need to talk to you!" Ashley shouted from across the room.

"*We* need to talk to you," Cory corrected.

"All of us!" Carrie added.

I stood up as the three of them stormed over. All three were red in the face. Ashley towered over the Drama Twins and her blond hair was up in two buns, which, with her roundish face, gave her a serious giant Mickey Mouse look. The Drama Twins flanked her on either side, their dark hair worked into identical braids down their backs.

"What's the matter?" I asked.

"Tama took over the big dressing room," Cory and Carrie said as one.

"She just took everyone else's stuff out of there and shoved it all in the small dressing room," Ashley added. "She didn't even bother to hang it up."

They all glared over at Tama, who was obviously pretending she couldn't hear anything over the crunching of her Chex Mix.

"This would never happen in summer stock," Ashley said, rubbing her temples. "I am just not used to working with this lack of professionalism. You know, if we were in Actors Equity, this could not go on."

"We know, Ashley," Carrie said, laying a comforting hand on Ashley's shoulder.

"Don't worry. I'm sure KJ will work it out," Cory added, taking the opposite shoulder.

"Well?" they all said in unison, looking at me.

"Well, what?" I stalled.

"Well, what are you going to do about this?" Ashley demanded.

I took a deep breath and looked at Tama. This was not going to be fun.

"Tama? Could you come here for a second?" I called. My gut was all twisted into knots as she jumped down and made her way over. I hated confrontation. What was I thinking, taking this job when I hated confrontation?

"What's up, Ms. Stage Manager?" she asked.

"Did you move everyone else's stuff out of the big dressing room?" I asked her.

She shrugged. "It was in my way."

"In *your* way?" Ashley blurted.

"Ashley, calm down," I said. "Tama, you can't just claim the big dressing room for yourself. There are a dozen other girls in this production, and they can't all fit in the small room."

"I have, like, a million more costume changes than anyone. My stuff has to be organized if I'm going to get back on stage in time."

"Oh, and ours doesn't?" Cory and Carrie asked.

"You have fewer costumes," Tama snapped. "Ergo, you need less space. Freaks," she added under her breath.

"Ugh! How dare you talk to us that way?" Carrie and Cory blurted.

"Why doesn't one of you try having an original thought and then you can get back to me?" Tama shot back.

"Ugh!" they cried, offended.

"Everyone just chill for a sec!" I said. I grabbed my costume-change flowchart and flipped through it. Tama's name *was* all over it, and she did have a lot more quick changes than everyone else.

"See?" Tama said, coming around to look over my shoulder. "It totally makes sense for me to have my own dressing room.

I'm never going to be able to do any of this if I have all these people up in my face the whole time."

"She does have a point," I said.

"Oh no," Ashley protested. "No way. I have just as big a part as she does! I am so sick of everyone acting like *Grease* is Sandy's show. Rizzo is just as big a lead! There would be no conflict without Rizzo! No drama! No—"

"God, Ashley, maybe you should just change backstage. I don't think your ego's gonna fit in either one of the dressing rooms," Tama said with a laugh.

Ashley turned red and she emitted a high squeal. I had to stop this before it got out of hand.

"All right, all right. Here's a compromise," I said. "Tama can have the *small* dressing room. The rest of you will have the large dressing room to share. How's that?"

Tama sighed hugely, clearly put out.

"What?" I said. "I think that's fair."

"Well, I already moved all that stuff, but whatever," Tama said, making a face.

My skin heated up. "So I'll help you guys move it back."

"Oh, would you? Would you please, please, please help us clean out Diva Gold's dressing room for her?" Cory said.

"You really suck at this, KJ," Carrie added before she and her sister linked arms and walked away.

Ashley took a deep breath and looked at me. "I'll respect your decision, KJ." Then she slid a scathing look at Tama. "That's what professionals do. Even if they don't agree."

Then she followed after the Drama Twins. I glanced at Tama. She had to say something. I mean, she *had* to agree that I'd been fair. There was no way the rest of the Pink Ladies *plus*

Stephanie *plus* every other girl in the cast could get changed in the small room. No one would be on time for their curtains.

"I'm gonna go do some scales," she said grumpily.

And that was it. No sorry. No thanks. No nothing. She just moved over to the piano and started singing. What, exactly, had I done wrong?

"A good stage manager's work is never appreciated," Andy said, appearing at my elbow out of nowhere.

I blew out a sigh. "Tell me about it."

He held out a bag of squishy-looking black stuff. "Prune?"

I wrinkled my nose and walked away.

"Don't like prunes! Got it! I'll make a note!" he called after me.

I shook my head, walking right past Glenn, who glared me down as I headed backstage to the dressing rooms. My fingers curled into fists as I went and I took a deep breath, resolving not to let the geeks get to me. Not today. Today I was going to focus on the good if it killed me.

ACT TWO, SCENE ELEVEN

In which:

I'M A ONE-GIRL SHOW

"WELL. THAT TOOK FIVE SECONDS," I SAID, HOLDING THE FOUR CDs I was told I must purchase. Oasis. Run-DMC. The Beloved. R.E.M. I'd never heard one song by any of these bands. At least, I didn't think I had. Of course, I hadn't told Robbie that.

"I told you. I haven't stopped thinking about it for the last forty-eight hours. There was a whole elimination process, but if I let you in on how that worked, you might have me committed."

"I'd never do that," I said.

"Why? 'Cause you'd miss me too much?" Robbie asked, walking backward.

"No. Because if you can barely handle a turtleneck, you'd never make it in a straitjacket," I said.

Robbie laughed. "I'm touched you care so much."

He had, in fact, changed back into a T-shirt before picking me up for our shopping spree. I have to admit, I missed the turtleneck. It did have a certain something. He picked up a mini digital camcorder and flipped open the viewfinder, training it on me. I blushed and put my hand up to shield my face.

"Stop it!" he said, slapping my arm down. "It's time for your close-up."

"I don't do close-ups," I replied, blushing.

He gazed through the screen like a pro. "Sure you do. KJ Miller, you've just stage-managed an award-winning production of *Grease*. What are you going to do next?"

"Murder the star?" I said, grabbing for the camera.

He dodged me easily, moving as far away as the chain connecting the camera to the counter would allow. "Which one? Ashley? Jonathan Marsters? Not Tama. Don't murder the love of my life."

I paused, my face flushed. "I was talking about you, actually."

"Moi? Please! I am a pleasure," he said, hand to chest. He held the camera up again. "Seriously, though. Ashley would have to be the first to go."

"Omigod, seriously," I said. I struck a haughty pose and put on Ashley's slightly nasal voice. "When I was in the Wee Ones Summer Camp production of *Jesus Christ Superstar*, I never had to deal with this level of unprofessionalism!"

Robbie cracked up laughing. "That is dead-on. Do Katz!"

I rubbed my hand up and down my face a few times, then made my eyes all heavy. "KJ, do the blocking for this scene, would you? I've got—" I paused to add a burp. "—heartburn."

Robbie laughed and closed the camera. "You're really funny, you know that?" he said.

"No I'm not." I blushed. "I can't even believe I just did that."

"You're kidding. I think you should do it more often," Robbie said as we made our way to the register. "How come you never try out for the musicals?"

I laughed out loud. So loudly the woman in front of me in line jumped.

"Yeah right."

"Why not? You've never thought about it?"

"No," I lied. "I'm a behind-the-scenes kind of girl."

"Whatever you say," he replied dubiously.

I had thought about it. Wondered what it might be like to surprise everyone and get out there and act. Whether I'd be any good. I'd imagined the whole auditorium applauding for me, giving me a standing ovation. But that was just for fun.

The truth was, it could never happen. Because the very idea of being out there under the spotlight in front of all those people made me break out in the sweats. I had nightmares about it every musical season and always woke up relieved to recall that I was only working on the sets. This was one girl who was never going to be ready for her close-up. Not by a long shot.

ACT TWO, SCENE TWELVE

In which:

AN INVITATION IS EXTENDED

"ALL RIGHT, PEOPLE, GOOD REHEARSAL, BUT I SEE WAY TOO MANY scripts out there. I want to be off book by the end of the week," Mr. Katz said, standing in the center of the stage. It was Monday and he was looking good. Refreshed. And like maybe he'd gone tanning over the weekend. "I know you know your lines, so stop using your scripts as a crutch."

Ashley raised her hand.

"Yes, Ashley."

"I've been off book since early last week," she announced with pride.

"Yip-de-freakin-do for you," Tama said, earning a round of laughs.

"That's fantastic, Ashley. I wish I had twenty more like you," Mr. Katz said pointedly, which brought the temporarily lost grin back to Ashley's face. "Now, before I dismiss you for the day, I believe Fred has an announcement to make."

Fred jumped up, yanking on the waist of his jeans, and grabbed a plastic grocery bag from the floor. A murmur of mirth ran through the crowd.

"Here we go," Tama said under her breath, leaning back on her elbows.

"Party, party, party!" the Drama Twins trilled.

"Uh, well, in case you don't know this, every year there's a midway-through-the-musical party, and I've been hosting it for the past couple of years," Fred said. He pulled a stack of big white envelopes out of the bag and started to hand them out, sidestepping around the inside of the circle. "These are your official invitations, but everyone's allowed to bring one guest. But just one. My mom's pretty strict about that."

"Aw! Mommy doesn't like crowds?" one of the drama dudes teased.

"Maybe I'll distract her for ya, Freddy. Is she hot?" the other one cackled.

"I bet she's a MILF!"

Fred turned royal purple.

"Dude. Not cool," Robbie admonished, whacking the kid on the back of the head with his invite.

Stephanie opened her invite and Tama grabbed it right out of her hand. I leaned over to check it out. There were the two drama masks in the center, made out of silver and gold foil. At the top of the card were the words "All the World's a . . . Party!"

"Omigod. So lame," Tama whispered.

"So there's gonna be chips and dip and pizza and cake," Fred said, clasping his hands together when he was finished. "I just got the movie *Grease* on DVD, so maybe we'll watch that . . . and we'll listen to some music and stuff, you know. It's always a good time, so . . . ."

Fred ran out of things to say. Robbie put him out of his misery by shoving himself up from the floor. "Thanks, Fred. Sounds like a serious shindig. We'll be there."

The circle started to break up. I stood and brushed the dust from my butt, then took Tama's outstretched hands to pull her up.

"So, we're going, right?" I said. Everyone always went to Fred's party, and I knew him well enough to know that if we didn't all show up, he'd take it personally. "It's, like, Fred's favorite day of the year."

"Chips, dip *and* pizza? Like I'd ever miss out on that," Tama joked.

"Well, I know *I'm* gonna be there," Stephanie said, glancing at Andy as he stood and made a note in his planner.

"Me, too," he said, snapping the book closed. "I promised Fred I'd help him set up, so that's what I'll be doing."

"That was nice of you," Stephanie said.

"I like to help people," Andy said, shooting me a smile.

"Speaking of which, I wanted to go over that last problem from calc today," Stephanie said. "If you have a minute."

That was weird. Since when did Stephanie need help with math? She was usually the one who did the helping.

Andy's face lighted up. "Absolutely. I always have time for math. I mean, unless KJ needs me to do anything, because then I'd have to, you know, stay, since I'm the assistant stage manager and all. . . ."

"No. I'm good. Thanks, Andy," I said.

"Call you later, KJ," Stephanie said. Then she snatched her invitation out of Tama's hand as she and Andy walked by.

"God. You could warn a girl first," Tama said, checking her fingers for paper cuts.

"But you are going to come, right? To Fred's party?" I asked. She followed me off the stage, where we slipped into our coats.

Mine plain, black wool. Hers creamy suede with a fur collar. Me, sailor. Her, supermodel.

"What's the obsession with Fred's party all of a sudden?" Tama asked. "You, of all people, should probably avoid it. Aren't you supposed to be, like, freezing him out?"

"It's just one party. And everyone's going to be there," I told her. "It's not like I'm agreeing to date him or something by going."

"Whatever." Tama rolled her eyes. "Of course I'll go. It's tradition." She touched up her lip gloss with her fingertip and shrugged. "You know, as long as nothing better comes up."

ACT TWO, SCENE THIRTEEN

In which:

WE PHILOSOPHIZE ON POPULARITY

LATER THAT WEEK I SAT ON THE FLOOR BACKSTAGE, PAINTING A Rydell High banner. On the other side of the curtain, Ashley rehearsed "There Are Worse Things I Could Do" for the fourteenth time. I was going to be singing that tune in my sleep.

"I have a theory about set crew," Robbie announced, appearing around the side of the curtain.

"What's that?" I asked.

"We should get the cheerleaders to do it," he said, sitting cross-legged next to me. "Think about it. Half their time is spent making banners and signs for the football team and the basketball team, and they have to do all new ones every week. They'd probably have this whole thing done by now."

"You're forgetting one small detail," I told him, bending over the white *R* with my paintbrush.

"What's that?"

"They wouldn't be caught dead on set crew," I replied.

"Ah. Right. Social hierarchy rears its ugly head again," he said. "I, however, have no such qualms. May I? Katz gave me fifteen." He reached for a paintbrush.

"Knock yourself out," I said.

We worked in silence for a few minutes. At one point, Robbie scooted in my direction to get a better angle on the page and his knee sort of came down on my lower thigh. I was about to flinch away, but I thought I might look like a prude, so I stayed there. And so did he.

His knee was touching my thigh. Pressing into it, even. Did he not realize this? Was he as completely freaked by it as I was, or was it no big deal to him? Maybe his knee touched other people's bodies every day of the week.

This was ridiculous. I had to say something. Just to break the tension. Something.

"So . . . you're going to Fred's party, right?" I asked.

"Definitely," Robbie replied.

He left his knee there. I watched his profile. His concentration was unbroken. How on earth did he do it? How was he so entirely comfortable with himself that he not only went around touching his body parts to other people's body parts with the complete confidence that it was okay, but also wore whatever he wanted, did whatever he wanted, acted however he wanted, and didn't seem to care at all what anyone else thought?

"Can I ask you something?" I said finally.

"Just did," he said.

"Ha ha. Seriously."

"Shoot." He leaned back to check his work and his knee pressed even farther into my leg. My entire body stung with heat.

"Why did you stop hanging out with Cameron and those guys back in middle school? You used to be, like, best friends."

"I decided I didn't want to be a part of that scene in high school," Robbie said, still working.

"What scene?" I asked.

"That whole . . . fake scene," he said. "All these supposed athletes walking around like they're perfect specimens of teenagerdom, being all worshipped by the parentals and the teachers when they're just a bunch of lying hypocrites."

"They are?" I asked.

He put his paintbrush down and looked at me. "They drink. They do drugs. They trash their bodies every chance they get, and they want everyone to believe they're these perfect, pristine athletes. All-American, boys next door. It's such a sham."

"They're not *all* into drugs and drinking," I said, even though I had no proof for my argument. How did I know? I never hung out with any of those people.

"No, not all. But most," he said. He blew out a sigh and pressed his hands into the floor so that he could turn and face me fully. His knee moved and I was clear. I missed it the second it was gone. "I watched my brother go through it. He was on the football team and the basketball team and he was always partying—half the time at our house. I can't tell you how many times I walked in on one of his friends—one of these guys I looked up to—booting it in our bathroom after a bender. And then this one time his girlfriend, Kristy Sandless, almost drowned in our hot tub because she was so stoned she couldn't keep her head up and all the kids around her were so stoned they didn't realize she was in trouble."

"Oh my God," I said.

"I know. The 'popular kids'? It's like they feel like they have to do all this shit just to keep up the ruse of being popular. Like they have to push the envelope or something," he said. "Well, that's not me. And I knew Cameron and those guys were headed that way, so I just sort of separated myself from them."

"Was it hard?" I asked. I was still trying to wrap my brain around the idea of Cameron doing drugs. I wasn't totally naïve. I knew this stuff went on. But I always sort of thought he was above that kind of thing.

He shrugged. "Not really. All you gotta do to drop-kick guys like that is start talking about anything original. Like acting or singing or poetry. They lose your number pretty fast."

"So you decided not to be popular," I said, incredulous. "That took guts."

"Nah. Just common sense," he said, returning to his painting. "But you pretty much did the same thing, didn't you?"

I felt like I'd just tripped, even though I was sitting still. "What do you mean?"

"You've never bothered with the pretty posse. Why not?" he asked.

More like they never bothered with me, but whatever.

"We don't have a whole lot in common," I said.

"Exactly. You're not shallow like them. You'd rather do something cool with your time like painting or studying instead of being obsessed with clothes and makeup."

I looked down at my paint-stained T-shirt and baggy, fraying jeans. "What? You don't consider this the cutting edge of fashion?"

Robbie laughed. "Well, I like it, but then, what do I know? I'm not exactly Versace," he said, glancing at his own faded Arctic Monkeys T.

I grinned and picked up a new paintbrush. Suddenly I felt all warm inside. Part of me had always felt ashamed by the fact that the popular kids had never accepted me. That was why hanging out with Tama meant so much to me—she was at the center of that crowd, and she still chose to hang out with me. It was kind of like flicking off all the girls who had always ignored my existence before Tama moved here.

But now, Robbie had put a whole different spin on things. He saw my less-than-popular status as a conscious decision. As something to be proud of. And maybe, in a way, he was right. If I'd wanted to, I could have gone to parties every weekend, but I didn't want to be around drinking any more than Robbie did. Though for different reasons. And I could have worked really hard and kept up with fashion and makeup and all that, but clearly that hadn't been a priority for me. I was my own person. I had *decided* to be less than popular.

I liked that theory. I liked it a lot.

ACT TWO, SCENE FOURTEEN

In which:

ANGER ISSUES ARE DISCUSSED

"If I hear the phrase *When I did summer stock* one more time, they're gonna need the Jaws of Life to remove my foot from Ashley's face," Tama grumbled. She flipped down the visor in my car so hard it popped out.

"Okay. Let's not take it out on the auto," I joked, trying to lighten the mood.

Tama gave me an irritated sidelong look and shoved the mirror back into place. It was Thursday afternoon, and after a long week of tense rehearsals, I was looking forward to the weekend. After I dropped Tama off at the doctor—again—I was going straight to Stephanie's house for her family's weekly Chinese food and movie fest. Thereby avoiding my family's wait-for-Dad-and-see-how-drunk-he-is fest. I was looking forward to chilling and to chatting with Stephanie. Things had been a little off with us all week, and I was hoping that we could fix all that tonight.

"Whatever. I just want this night to be over with already," Tama said, pressing her hands into her thighs.

At a stoplight, I glanced over at her. She was chewing on

the inside of her cheek and her fingers were all curled up. Totally nervous. What were all these doctor appointments about, anyway? Was something really wrong with her?

"What?" she snapped, glaring at me.

"Nothing. Sorry. It's just . . ."

"The light's green," she said.

I took a deep breath and drove through. "Tama, is everything okay?"

"What do you mean?"

"I mean . . . all these doctor appointments," I said tentatively. I pulled into the parking lot I now knew well, having driven her a few times over the past couple of weeks. "Are you . . . sick?"

Tama blew out a laugh through her lips. "Depends on who you ask."

My fingers tightened on the wheel. "What do you mean?"

It was dark in the car, the only light coming from my headlights, which were bouncing back at us off the wall of the office building. Tama looked at me for a long moment.

"No one knows this. I mean, no one other than Leo," she said. "But he thinks I stopped going last summer."

I was intrigued. I'm only human. "Okay."

"I'm not going to a doctor doctor," she said finally. "I'm seeing a therapist."

"Really?" I blurted.

"My mom's making me go." She shook her head and toyed with the lock on the glove compartment. "She thinks I have anger issues and that I'm self-destructive."

I was blown away. I couldn't help it. Tama Gold was in therapy? But her life was perfect. If anyone should have been in therapy, it should have been me. I spent half my life ready to punch someone and the other half feeling guilty about it, thanks to my screwed-up family. But Tama . . . Tama lived in a palace, and her parents were totally normal and sober. What did she have to be angry about?

Although she had just made reference to kicking a fellow student in the face so hard it stuck there.

"What?" she demanded. "What's with the face? You think I'm a freak now, don't you?"

"What? No!" I protested. "Honestly, I just . . . I think it's cool that you're talking to someone. It's good."

"Uh-huh," she said wryly.

"No, it is," I said. "And thanks for telling me."

I was touched. I mean, if she was sharing private info like this with me and Leo and no one else, then clearly she thought of me as a good friend.

"Yeah, well, who're you gonna tell?" she said with a shrug. "Thanks again, KJ. And if you talk to Cameron, tell him you *love* him for me," she teased.

I laughed as she slammed the door behind her. I sat there for a long moment, listening to the hum of my car's engine, marveling at how quickly everything had changed. I was friends with Tama now. Real friends. And it was actually in the realm of possibility that I might talk to Cameron Richardson later. Maybe not a probability, but it was possible. Plus I was down one geek. It was amazing how much having the threat of Glenn gone had changed my outlook on things.

I felt a lightness in my chest I had never felt before. Life really could get better. I sat there for a little while longer, clinging to the novelty of it all, not wanting to go home.

ACT TWO, SCENE FIFTEEN

In which:

THERE IS DANCING

THE NEXT DAY, I BORROWED THE MOVIE FROM MR. KATZ. THE one Tama had watched in his class with the dance scene at the end. I told Robbie we had some more seeds to sow and he agreed to stay late after rehearsal. When Mr. Katz headed upstairs to go over a few things with Ms. Lin, Robbie and I slipped backstage.

"So, what's this all about?" Robbie asked.

"You'll see," I teased.

It felt very quiet and still in the backstage area, after all the bustle of rehearsal. I pulled the television cart out of the prop room, and the wheels squeaked and squealed in protest. Robbie found an outlet behind a fake palm tree and plugged everything in. The VCR groaned and clicked and whirred to life. I put the tape in and hit the fast-forward button.

"This isn't gonna be some dirty video, is it? Because I'm not allowed to watch that kind of thing," Robbie said with mock piety.

"Yeah, I wanted to show you all the positions Tama likes to do it in."

"Whoa! X-rated KJ!" Robbie exclaimed. "I like it!"

I couldn't believe I'd just said that. I blushed and Robbie pulled over a couple of prop chairs from the back wall. The tape finally neared its end and I hit play. The black-and-white image popped up on the screen.

"Okay, in a minute, these two people are going to start dancing," I said, stepping back.

"Ooooookay," Robbie said, perched on the edge of his chair.

"The other day Tama told me that she would give anything to dance like that," I said. "Well, she said she'd give anything for Leo to dance with her like that, but you get the idea."

"Interesting," Robbie said.

"So how do you feel about dancing?" I asked, knowing most guys hated the very idea with every macho fiber of their being. Although I had a chance with Robbie, considering he was dancing in the musical and all.

"I'm not morally opposed to it," he answered pragmatically.

He rested his elbows on his knees and leaned forward as the dance sequence began, the picture of perfect concentration. On the screen, the actress's dress billowed and fluttered as the actor twirled her out, then brought her back to him. It really was kind of romantic. In an old-fashioned, stiff kind of way. The dance ended with that kiss—that closed-mouthed kiss that they tried to make look all passionate by moving their heads around. The music swelled, and then it was over.

"Okay, let's do it," Robbie said, slapping his hands together as he stood. He stepped toward me with his arms outstretched and I tripped back.

"What? No."

"What? Yes," he said. He hit the rewind button and the tape

zipped backward. He paused it right as the dance began. "You don't really expect me to ask Tama to dance with me without any practice. Even I'm not that stupid."

I was suddenly very aware of my heartbeat. "There's no way I'm dancing with you."

"You really know how to stroke a guy's ego," Robbie joked. "Come on. I'm not that repulsive."

"You're not repulsive at all, it's just—"

"Well, that's good to hear," Robbie said with a teasing smile. He was enjoying this.

"It's just that I don't dance," I admitted. Never had. Not once. Not with a guy. I was a dance-free zone.

"Well, neither do I—I mean, except on stage. But I've never danced like this, so we're even," he said.

He hit "play." The music started and Robbie pulled me toward him by my wrist. He grabbed my hand, which was sweating, and held it, then put his other hand on my waist. My boobs pressed into his chest and I flinched, but Robbie didn't even seem to notice. He was too busy consulting the TV screen.

"Here goes nothing," he said. "Okay, it's a waltz, so one, two, three . . . one, two, three. Looks like a big step on one and two little steps on two and three. Got it?"

"Sure." I so didn't have it.

"Okay, go."

He started to step in a circle, pulling me with him. I staggered along, mortified. "One, two, three. One, two, three," he counted under his breath.

My foot caught on his ankle. "Oops! Sorry." I was sweating like mad now, wishing I'd taken off my sweater, at least.

"I got ya," he said, his grip tightening on my hand. "Keep going."

"One, two, three," I counted, staring down at our feet. He slammed his hip into one of the set chairs.

"Ow! Dammit!"

"Are you okay?" I asked.

"Yeah. Keep going," he said through his teeth.

"One, two, three," I counted. I glanced up at the TV screen, and the second I took my eyes off our feet, they got hopelessly tangled. I felt that instant swoop of gravity and shouted as we went down. The floor was not soft.

"Oof!"

"Ow. Okay, ow," Robbie said, grabbing his elbow. "That was not a good bone to fall on."

He shook his arm out and I brought my knees up under my chin. "Maybe this wasn't the best idea."

"No! No. We cannot quit that easily," Robbie said, standing. He took my hands and hoisted me up. "Maybe we just need to simplify it a little."

"Actually, I think it's the twirl and the dip at the end that are really important," I theorized. It seemed like the most romantic part to me.

"Okay, good." Robbie was psyched by this development. "So maybe instead of going in circles, we just step side to side and do the twirl thing a couple of times."

"Sounds like a plan," I said.

"Let's do it."

Robbie rewound the tape and we started from the beginning of the music. He took my hand again and held it up, then placed his other hand on my waist. This time we simply swayed back and forth. I was just getting used to the motion, when I realized that Robbie was staring at me. Big time.

"What?" I said, my skin prickling.

"Trying to make eye contact," he said. "I hear eye contact while dancing is key."

"Where would you hear something like that?" I said.

"My grandmother. She's a wise woman," he said.

His grandmother. How cute was that?

His eyes were completely focused on my face. I tried to stare back into them, but I kept cracking up laughing. And he thought I'd make a good actress.

"Wow. You suck at eye contact," he said. "Come on. Give me something to work with here."

I took a deep breath and steeled myself. It's just Robbie Delano, KJ. You can do this. And so I did. I looked right back into his eyes. And we continued to sway to the music. His hand around mine. His hand on my hip. Our chests pressed together. I stared into his eyes, and soon I found that laughing was the last thing on my mind.

"How's this working for you?" Robbie asked me quietly.

"Good!" I blurted, my heart slamming against my rib cage. "It's . . . it's good."

"Good," he replied.

My palms were totally slick by now. My pulse a rushing freight train. What was going on here? This was how I felt around Cameron, not Robbie. This was all totally wrong.

It's just the slow dance, KJ. It's just because it's your first slow dance. Don't get all carried away.

"Okay, here comes the twirl thing," Robbie announced. "Let's try it."

He pulled me closer to him and my breath caught, then he

spun me away and I almost lost my balance, but he pulled me back in, slung his arm around my back, and dipped me, never letting me fall. By the time I stood up again, the whole room was reeling and the people on the screen were kissing passionately and Robbie was holding me, his breath short and quick, his face ever-so-close to mine.

"How was that?" he asked.

"That was . . . that . . . was . . ."

Just the dance, KJ. Just the slow dance.

Cameron was the guy I liked. Cameron, Cameron, Cameron.

"Perfect."

ACT TWO, SCENE SIXTEEN

In Which:

THERE'S A SURPRISE VISITOR

"SO, WHO'S COMING TONIGHT?" STEPHANIE ASKED AS SHE WRAPPED my big-barreled curling iron around her hair.

"Almost everyone, I think. Ashley, Jonathan, Cory, Carrie, Robbie . . ."

Which will be great, as long as there's no dancing.

I glanced at Stephanie, wondering if I should tell her about that weird moment I thought I'd shared with Robbie, but decided to keep my mouth shut. It was nothing, after all. And how was I supposed to explain it after freaking on her for not taking my thing with Cameron seriously? Things were tentatively normal between us. I didn't want her lecturing me for being a total flake.

"Anyone from the crew?" Stephanie asked.

"Well, I'd bet money Glenn is coming, though luckily he doesn't apprise me of his every move anymore," I said with a shudder. "And Janice and Andy . . ."

Stephanie turned back toward the mirror. "That's good. Sounds like it'll be a good turnout."

I dug through the pile of clothing on my desk chair, looking for my black cardigan sweater. It was times like these that I secretly wished I listened to my mother when she told me to clean up my room. If I hung all my clothes in the closet after I took them off, she would say, then they would be there when I went to look for them and I wouldn't have to go through this. But at the end of the day, throwing them on the chair was just *so* much easier.

"Aha!" I yanked the sweater out from the bottom of the pile and pulled it on over my burgundy T-shirt. This was about as close as I got to dressing up. Instead of a baggy sweater or T-shirt, a less baggy T-shirt *and* baggy sweater. Plus dangly earrings instead of studs. Plus my favorite plaid sneakers, of course. Which, unfortunately, were tangled up in a mess of dozens of other pairs of sneakers on the floor of my closet. They took about ten minutes to extricate. But at least all my sneakers were *in* my closet, right? That had to count for something.

"I wonder if anyone's bringing anyone," Stephanie said. She let her hair go and a perfect spiral curl fell down around her face, joining all the other perfect spiral curls.

"No one ever does," I said. "It's not exactly the social event of the year."

"I guess not."

I did a double take as she leaned toward my mirror to apply some extra lip gloss.

"Steph, you look . . . hot," I said. The girl was wearing eyeliner. Last I checked she didn't even know how to apply eyeliner.

She smiled. "I do?"

"Uh, yeah. What's with the primp?" I asked.

She blushed under her powder blush. "I just thought it might be nice to, you know . . . look nice."

"Okay."

This was so not Stephanie. It was so not Stephanie, I was a little confused by it. Why would she get all dressed up and made up for Fred's party, of all things? And then, out of nowhere, a thought hit me. Was Stephanie crushing on someone I didn't know about? Was that why she was wondering if people were bringing dates? Maybe I wasn't the only one holding back. Which was so wrong. If Stephanie had a new crush and hadn't trusted me enough to share it, I'd be heartbroken. Our friendship couldn't have changed that much, could it?

"Steph?" I asked tentatively.

She stopped fluffing her hair. "What's the matter?"

And then, the doorbell rang.

"Who's that?" I asked.

"Your house," she said with a shrug.

I ran downstairs and over to the door, shoving aside the window curtain. Tama was standing on my front step chatting with Leo, and Cameron Richardson.

No. Freaking. Way.

The curtain fell back into place. I pressed my back against the door. Cameron Richardson was at my house. He was standing on my doorstep at this very moment looking all beautiful in his brown leather jacket and jeans. Cameron Richardson was here!

The doorbell rang again. "God, if she left already—" Tama said.

I held my breath and flung the door open. "Hi!"

"There you are!" Tama said.

"Hey, KJ," Cameron said with a smile.

"S'up," Leo added.

"What are you guys doing here?" I asked.

"We're taking you out," she said, glancing into my house. "Get your coat."

"What do you mean? What about Fred's?" I asked.

Cameron scoffed a laugh and I instantly wanted to bitch-slap my tongue.

"I'm ditching that cheese-fest. We have something *so* much cooler planned," Tama said. "Come on."

A car turned onto my street and my heart leapt into my throat. But it wasn't my dad's car. Too quiet. Still, I had to get these people out of here before he came home. It was Friday night—Bad Dad Night—and God only knew how he'd react to me standing here with the door open (losing heat) talking to three people he didn't know (he wouldn't remember Tama), one of whom was smoking (Leo).

"You guys, I can't ditch Fred. He'll die," I said, wishing I didn't have to say it. But I did. Because it was true.

"So what? It's Fred Frontz," Cameron said. He ran his finger through his curls and glanced in the window at his reflection.

"Exactly. And this is me. And Cameron," Tama added through her teeth, widening her eyes.

Okay. She had a point. Was I really going to choose a night of *Grease*-watching and fruit-punch-sipping in Fred's moldy basement over going out and doing something cool with Tama and Cameron Richardson? Answer: hell no.

"KJ?"

I glanced at Stephanie, who was standing in the kitchen. "Could you guys hold on just a sec?" I asked.

Tama groaned. "Fine, but hurry up. It's freezing out here."

I closed the door after one last glance at Cameron, just to make sure he was actually there, then grabbed my coat off the hook and ran over to Stephanie. "It's Tama and Leo and they have Cameron with them."

"No way," Stephanie said, her eyes wide.

"I swear! He's out there right now! And they want me to go out with them." I shoved my arms into my coat and grabbed my purse.

"But what about Fred's party?" Stephanie asked.

"I know. I know. I don't want to ditch it, but Steph, this is Cameron!" I wailed quietly. "This is practically a double date! I have to go!"

Please let her understand. Please, please, please don't let her make me feel guilty about this, too. Stephanie took a deep breath. "You're right. It's Cameron."

Thank you!

"So will you cover for me? With Fred?" I asked.

"Sure. I'll just . . . tell him you're sick or something," she said grudgingly.

"Are you mad?" I asked.

"No! No, of course not. This is Cameron Richardson. You've been waiting for this your entire life."

"I know!" I hugged her hard and she hugged me back. "I can't believe this is happening!"

"Me neither," she replied. She picked up her own coat and put it on, lifting her freshly curled hair over her shoulders. I realized that I had never gotten a chance to ask her about her potential crush, but there wasn't time now. I'd have to grill her later.

The doorbell rang again and my heart jumped. "Okay, I gotta go. Have fun!"

"You, too!" Stephanie replied.

We walked out together. Tama was irritated at the sight of Stephanie. "Oh. You're here."

"Don't worry," Steph said flatly. "I'm just going to walk up to Fred's party."

"Oh! Cool!" Tama said, suddenly bright as a floodlight. She wrapped her arm around mine as we all turned back down the path. "Say hi to everyone for us!"

Stephanie rolled her eyes and waved at me. Five seconds later I found myself in the backseat of Leo's pickup truck with Cameron Richardson sliding in next to me.

"So. This should be cool," he said. His leather jacket squeaked as he sat back.

"Yeah. Definitely," I replied.

I glanced out the window to hide my giddy smile. Leo revved his engine and zoomed backward out of my driveway. He roared past Steph, walking up the street with her hands in her pockets, alone. I felt a lump of guilt in the pit of my stomach until we got to the top of the hill and she dipped out of sight. Then it was just me and Cameron and the whole night ahead of us.

ACT TWO, SCENE SEVENTEEN

In which:

I WANT TO DIE

O'REILLY'S. O'REILLY'S POOL HALL. THE VERY NAME MADE ME nauseous. Made my heart sick in a way that was almost unbearable. I had always wondered what it looked like on the inside behind those blacked-out windows. What, exactly, the appeal of the place was. And now that I was seeing it for the first time, I was disgusted. The dark, low-ceilinged room was filled with stale gray smoke. Every guy in sight was sucking on a beer bottle. Every woman, too, though there were far fewer of them. I stood near the wall, clinging to my own elbows, trying to make myself as small as possible. Every time the heavy wooden door squealed open, I flinched and my heart stopped.

I could not be here. Could not. But how could I possibly tell Tama and Cameron and Leo that? What, exactly, was I supposed to say?

Uh, guys? My dad comes here practically every Friday for the nightcap to cap his many nightcaps. I know this because my mother has had to pick him up here semi-unconscious on more than one occasion. So if we could just hoof it on down to Friendly's now so that I can avoid the most horrifying experience of my life, that would be super cool. I'll even buy the Fribbles.

Yeah. That was not going to happen.

"This is a cool place, huh?" Cameron said. He took a slug of his beer—Leo had bought bottles for all four of us without being carded—and placed it down next to mine on the tall table. Mine was still full. His, half drained.

This was wrong. This was all wrong. This was where the smell came from. That awful Bad Dad Night smell. And Cameron was drinking. Perfect, boy-of-my-dreams Cameron. The last person I wanted to think of when I was with him was my father.

The door opened again. A large man in a leather vest walked in. I gulped smoky air. Tried not to cough.

"Yeah. Cool." I rearranged my cardigan over my chest and held it there with folded arms. Two old men with beards had been ogling me all night and they both laughed when I made my adjustment.

"You okay?" Cameron asked me.

No. This is my worst nightmare.

"I'm fine," I said brightly. I tried to make my face match my voice, but it came out kind of tight and manic. Cameron looked disturbed. God, I hated my father. I just hated him. He had made me this way. The thought of him was making it impossible for me to relax. Impossible for me to be a normal freaking teenager. Thanks to him, this whole night was ruined. Thanks to him, watching other people ingesting alcohol made me want to gag. And cry. And hit something.

"You haven't even touched your beer," Leo pointed out, sucking down his own. "I paid for that, you know."

I'd been hoping against hope that no one would notice that.

My life was over. I was failing miserably at this. I was uncool and I was never going to convince Cameron otherwise. I had to just accept it.

"That's mine," Cameron said.

He reached for my bottle and took a big swallow. When he put it down again, he smiled at me with his back to Leo. My insides went all warm and gooey. For a moment, I even forgot where I was. I wished Robbie could have seen that. Shallow my ass. Cameron was as chivalrous as Robbie Delano any day.

"Whatever. You're up," Leo said to me.

I slid down from my stool awkwardly. Glanced at the door. The coast was still clear. Maybe my father had already gone home. Maybe he'd skipped O'Reilly's that night. Maybe, just maybe, luck was on my side today. Cameron picked out a pool cue and handed it to me.

"You know what you're doing?" he asked.

"Not really," I replied. "Or, at all."

"Here. Let me help you," Cameron said. "Hold it like this."

He moved his fingers over mine. His hands were soft and warm, and suddenly my mind was swimming. "Now, you want to try to hit the cue ball into that red ball over there and get it into the corner pocket," he instructed. "So bend over the table and line it up, like this."

He put his arm around me and got behind me, nudging me into a bend. He was so very, very warm and close, and he was breathing in my ear. The stale beer smell of the bar faded away, replaced by the clean leather and spicy-soap scent of him.

I really thought I might faint.

"Get really close and try to line up the angle," he instructed.

My whole side tingled at the proximity of his voice to my ear. I squinted one eye closed and tried to concentrate on the ball. It was extremely difficult with Cameron Richardson's hip pressed against my backside.

"Okay, now pull the cue back."

He guided my arm with his hand.

"Now you want to pop it forward and follow through," he said. "Try to hit the ball right in the center."

"Okay." I wondered if he could tell my voice was trembling in two syllables.

"Okay, ready?" he said. I somehow managed to nod. "Go for it."

I did. And the tip of the cue hit the table and the white ball bounced half an inch forward and stopped. Leo cracked up laughing.

"Well. That sucked," I said, embarrassed.

"Uh, no shit," Leo said mirthfully. Jackass.

Cameron stood up and moved away. It was all I could do to keep from pulling him back. "Nah. It was just your first time. You'll get the hang of it. You just gotta practice, like anything else."

"Thanks," I said, grinning. He wasn't mocking me. He was being sweet. See? I knew this boy was different. The door opened again and I held my breath. It was just a couple of people leaving.

"So, how're we doing over here?" Tama asked, sauntering up to Leo and slinging her arm over his shoulders. She'd been in the bathroom for the last ten minutes. "Are we winning?"

"We got this one in the bag, baby," Leo said, leaning into her for a kiss.

A kiss that was way too long and gross to be just a kiss next to a pool table. Cameron looked at me and widened his eyes, and I smirked. It was like we were sharing a personal joke.

"So, Leo," Cameron said when their lips finally unlocked. "What's up with you, man? You still working at your dad's shop?"

"For now," Leo said with a shrug.

Tama, who had leaned in to take her shot at the table, paused. "What do you mean, for now?"

Leo glanced at me and Cameron, then shifted his feet. Nervously. Uh-oh. Something not good was about to happen here. "Actually, I've been filling out some applications," he announced. "For next year."

"Excuse me?"

Tama stood up and tossed her pool cue on the table. Balls raced everywhere. Game over. Cameron and I both moved instinctively toward the wall. My heart started pounding sickly, not unlike the feeling I got when my father started up a fight with my mom. I looked at the door again. It was closed.

"I'm, uh, thinking about maybe going to school next year," he said. "I've been putting away some money and—"

"You've been putting away some money?" Tama blurted. "For how long? How long have you been planning this behind my back?"

"This is not good," Cameron said to me under his breath.

"Why did he decide to tell her this now?" I whispered back.

"Uh, because he's a moron?" Cameron joked.

"I'm not doing it behind your back," Leo replied. "I just told you about it."

"Yeah, when all your applications are already done. What were you going to do, just leave town and not even tell me?" she blurted. "Since when do you make decisions like this without me? God, Leo, you can be such a little—"

"Tama! Chill!" Leo shouted. So loud it startled me. "I haven't made a decision yet. I'm just keeping my options open. And maybe I didn't tell you because I knew you'd be a total bitch about it."

"Oooooh," a couple of guys at the next table sang.

Tama looked at them, then at me and Cameron, as if just realizing she was in a public place. A public place where we were two of the only five women. A public place where the bartender was eyeing us menacingly and reaching for something behind the counter. The phone? A bat? Didn't matter. I suddenly wanted to be far away from here all over again.

I looked up at Cameron, wondering how far that chivalry of his would extend. "Cameron? Maybe we should—"

"Go? Yeah. I can find us a way home."

Thank God. Cameron grabbed our stuff and we started for the door. In two seconds I was going to be out of this nightmare—out of danger of bumping into my dad—and alone with Cameron on a Friday night. I could practically taste the freedom. The possibility.

"You want bitch? I'll give you bitch," Tama said as we slipped by. Quickly, shakily, she gathered up her things. "We're out of here! You can go home by yourself tonight!"

"Fine!" Leo shouted.

"Fine!" she replied. She grabbed my wrist. "Come on, KJ. We've got a party to go to."

I looked at Cameron, desperate.

"But Tama, I—"

"Come *on,* KJ!" she said through her teeth.

She begged me silently with her eyes. It was a female

solidarity thing. Leave no woman behind. I shot Cameron an apologetic look.

"I guess I'm going," I said morosely.

"Yes. You are." Tama yanked me away toward the door and I tripped forward.

"But what about—"

"Cameron's a big boy. He can get home on his own," Tama snapped.

I paused, stalling for time as I pulled my coat on. "I guess I'll . . . see you on Monday?" I said.

"Yeah. I guess," he replied.

We looked at each other for a long moment. Something in his eyes made me feel warm all over. I wanted to say something cool, but was at a total loss. What if this was it? What if I never got a chance to hang out with him outside of school again? There had to be some way to end this night well.

"KJ! Let's go!" Tama shouted.

Then she grabbed my arm and tore me away from Cameron and out into the cold, where we found ourselves face-to-face with my father.

ACT TWO, SCENE EIGHTEEN

In which:

TAMA FINDS OUT

HIS EYES SWAM IN HIS SOCKETS. HE LOOKED AT ME. LOOKED AT the glowing green sign over O'Reilly's front door. Looked at me again. My heart slammed around in my chest. For a split second I thought about just running. He was already so drunk, maybe he wouldn't even realize it was me. Maybe we could make a quick getaway and I could deny it all in the morning. He'd think he just dreamt it. Or imagined it. Yes. That was it. Just go. But then, Tama spoke.

"Mr. Miller?"

He blinked. Fire lighted his eyes. Suddenly he knew exactly who I was, and exactly what was going on.

"Katie Jean? What the hell—?"

He went to grab the handrail on the side of the wheelchair ramp and missed it, falling sideways into it before straightening himself out. My heart turned with embarrassment. I looked at Tama. Tama, who quite obviously understood exactly the state he was in.

"We were just leaving," I said to him. I took Tama's hand

and tried to get around him—to get out of here before this got any worse—but he reached out and grabbed my arm.

"You're seventeen! You're not supposed to be here!" he said, his eyes wild.

I looked up at him. Was he more pissed that I was underage drinking (which I was not), or that I had just caught him red-handed?

"I know. That's why we're leaving," I said flatly.

"Don't take that tone with me, Katie Jean! You are in a world of trouble right now!" he roared, fumbling in his pocket for his keys. "We are going home right now and we're going to discuss this."

His keys dropped on the ground with a clatter. He crouched down to grope for them blindly. I couldn't believe this was happening. Not in front of Tama. Not now when Cameron could walk out the door at any second. Hot tears burned my eyes. I felt as if my head was about to explode from the throbbing. Something was squeezing my throat. Squeezing all the air out of me.

The hatred bubbling up inside of me was so fierce, so hot, it frightened even me. I wanted to hit him. Wanted to kill him. Wanted him dead, dead, dead so I wouldn't have to feel this way ever again.

"KJ. KJ! Ow!" Tama whined. She tore her hand from mine and I realized I was squeezing her fingers to pulp.

"Let's go," my father said, standing finally. Unsteadily. He took my arm again. Started to lead me across the parking lot. My heart pounding, I looked back at Tama. She looked scared. Uncertain. I had never seen her look that way. Ever. I had to stop this.

"Dad, no!" I cried, ripping my arm away from him. It took

him a second to stop walking, and by that point I'd backed up, all the way to Tama. Tears of fear and anger spilled down my cheeks as I glared at him. Tama clung to the sleeve of my jacket. "No. I'm not going with you!" I yelled at him.

"Oh yes you are," my father shouted, red with rage.

He took a step toward us and I backed up more, taking Tama with me.

"No! I'm not! You're drunk!" I screeched, doubled over slightly, my stomach knots so tight they were dragging me down. "You'll kill both of us! I don't care if you kill yourself, but I am not getting into the car with you!"

"What did you just say to me?" my father roared. "Get back here! Get back here right now, Katie Jean!"

"No!" I shouted. "No!" And then I turned around and, half blinded by tears, started to run.

ACT TWO, SCENE NINETEEN

In which:

I LOSE IT

I SQUEEZED MY EYES SHUT IN THE BACK OF THE CAB, TRYING TO squeeze out the image of my father. His red face. His staggering. His fury. It kept coming back to me in waves. The humiliation. The anger. The embarrassment. Every time a new detail shoved itself into my brain—his swimming eyes, his imbalance, his groping for his keys—I had to close my eyes, clutch my fists, will it away.

I hated him. I hated him so much. Why couldn't he just go away? He obviously didn't care about us at all. Why couldn't he just leave us? Just get the hell out of our lives. Why did I have to live like this? Why?

"God. And I thought my family was whacked," Tama said lightly.

"I don't want to talk about it," I snapped.

She raised her hands in surrender. Like I was so out of line. And I instantly felt guilty. Horrible. Stupid. She was never going to speak to me again after this, was she? Now that she knew what a freak show my family was. And she'd probably tell

Cameron, too. Unless he already knew. Unless he'd witnessed the whole thing out the window.

My eyes squeezed shut again as my heart seized with pain. No. No, please, no.

"We're here," Tama said.

The cab brakes squeaked. I looked out the window at Fred's one-story house. The sad helium balloons on the mailbox. This night had started out full of possibility and now, here we were, back at Geek Central with no Cameron. And just down the street, my house, where if my father didn't pass out the second he got home, he'd be waiting for me.

Tama paid the cabdriver. "Let's go."

As we approached the door, my heart was still pounding around all shallow and fast. I could hardly breathe. I was trembling from the exertion. From the embarrassment. From the fear of what might happen when I got home.

Calm down, KJ. Maybe seeing Steph and Robbie will help. Just relax. Your friends are right inside.

Fred's mother let us in. I tromped down the steps to the basement behind Tama. I could hear "You're the One That I Want" playing at a low volume, but something was off. When I hit the basement floor, I realized what it was. The music was the only noise. No voices, no laughter, no singing along to anything. Why? Because there was no one there. No one except Robbie, Steph, Andy, Glenn and Fred. They were all sitting on the corduroy couch, looking bored, watching *Grease.*

"KJ! You're here!" Fred exclaimed, jumping out of his seat and rushing to my side. "Are you okay? Do you want something to drink?"

"I'm fine," I snapped, pulling away from him.

"No you're not. You look pale," he said. "You're still sick. You should sit."

He took my wrist and tried to pull me toward his vacated seat on the couch.

"I'm not sick, all right? I was out with Tama and Cameron," I said, snatching my arm back.

Fred looked crestfallen. "What?"

"KJ—" Stephanie said in that admonishing tone of hers.

"What? What's the big deal?" I asked, my blood boiling.

"On the night of my party?" Fred asked, pouting. "But you said you were coming! You promised you were going to be here!"

More expectations. More accusations. I felt as if the walls of the basement were closing in on me.

"Fred, I'm sorry, all right?" I said, trying to get control of my heart. "At least I'm here now."

"Yeah, like two hours late!" Fred cried, raising his voice. Raising his voice to me for the first time ever. I felt as if I'd just been slapped. My eyes burned as I looked at the others. At Stephanie and Robbie and Glenn and Andy and their accusing faces.

"What's the big freaking deal?" I shouted back. "Obviously I'm not the only person who didn't come. Why don't you call all of them up and yell at them!?" I said, throwing my hand out at the empty room.

"KJ!" Stephanie stood up, her expression appalled. "What's the matter with you?"

"Yeah, KJ. Calm down," Robbie added.

"Why are you all ganging up on me?" I cried, backing toward the wall. "It's not my fault nobody's here. It's not my fault your party is so totally lame!" I shouted at Fred. "Why do you have to put everything on me? I wanted to go out with Cameron Richardson tonight, all right? For *once* I did what I wanted instead of feeling bad for you and putting your crap ahead of me. I'm sorry if that upsets you, Fred, but I'm sick and tired of always protecting your feelings!"

"Protecting my feelings?" Fred repeated dumbly.

"Yes! All those times you followed me around, hid out in my car, jumped all over me in the cafeteria or the hall or the theater! All those times I bit my tongue, but I can't do it anymore. I can't take having to deal with your little gifts and your poor, pathetic puppy-dog eyes anymore. I quit! As of this moment, I'm done!" I rambled, hardly even aware of what I was saying. "And you!" I cried, reeling on Andy. "Enough with the survey questions, all right? I'm on to your experiment and I don't like you that way. I don't like any of you that way!" I added, looking at Glenn and Fred. "So you can stop staring at me and stop following me around and just . . . just . . . *stop*!"

For a long moment, no one said a word. On the TV screen behind me, the cast of *Grease* ramalamalam-ed away. Robbie and Stephanie stared at me like they'd just seen my eyeballs implode. Tama had her hand over her mouth, but I couldn't tell if she was laughing or appalled. And suddenly, the weight of what I had said started to sink in on me.

"I have to go," I heard myself say.

And just like that, I was gone.

ACT TWO, SCENE TWENTY

In which:

A CHOICE IS MADE

TAMA FOLLOWED ME OUT, SLAMMING THE DOOR BEHIND US.

"That was *so* classic!" she cheered, following me across the front yard to the street.

Tears spilled over onto my cheeks. I felt anything but triumphant. "What is the matter with them? Why were they all over me?"

"I have no idea. But at least you just put your dad-related anger to good use," Tama said.

"What?" I snapped.

"Well, that's what my therapist would say!" Tama said, raising her hands.

The door closed and I saw Steph coming toward us out of the corner of my eye. "KJ! What was that?" Stephanie demanded.

"Don't even get all high-and-mighty on me right now, Steph," I replied, storming down the street toward my house. Tama fell into step with me, and Steph took my other side.

"I'm not!" she replied. "I've just never seen you like that. Are you all right?"

"Yeah, she is," Tama said. "For the first time in her life, probably."

"Excuse me, but you don't even know her," Stephanie shot back.

"Don't talk to her like that," I shouted.

Stephanie stopped walking. "What is the matter with you?"

"I freaked out, all right? I can't take it anymore!" I replied. "You know I've been wanting to say that to Fred and those guys forever. Well, now I did."

"I know, but . . . did you have to be so mean about it?" Stephanie said. "You're acting like—" She glanced over at Tama and bit her tongue.

"What? Me? Is that what you were going to say?" Tama asked. "That she's acting like me?"

"Yeah," Stephanie said, lifting her chin. "That's exactly what I was going to say."

Tama laughed. "Well, good for her!"

"Could you have a bigger ego?" Stephanie said. "No one besides you thinks it's a good thing."

Wait a minute. What did that mean? Did that mean that people had been discussing me? "Oh my God! You *are* talking about me behind my back!" I blurted. "I thought you were my best friend!"

"KJ, I am your best friend," Stephanie said.

"No, you're not. All you do is judge me and tell me how everything I do is wrong!" I cried. "You think me and Cameron are a joke. All you want to do is keep me down! Stay friends with Fred and Andy and be nice to Glenn. You just want me to be a loser all my life!"

I was rambling. I knew I was rambling. But even so, it all felt very true.

"No. I just want my friend back," Stephanie said calmly. "I don't even know who you are anymore."

"Well, here's news. I'm still me," I told her, my heart breaking down the middle. "I'm just realizing all my friends suck."

Stephanie looked at me, utterly and completely betrayed. "What?"

"Come on, Tama," I said coolly. "Let's go."

Tama smiled triumphantly. "Yeah. Let's."

I turned my back on Stephanie and walked down the street with Tama. I felt myself starting to come down from my ire high and my legs were shaky beneath me, but I kept right on walking. I was done with Stephanie. Done with Fred and Glenn. Done with all those people. I knew who had my back. I knew who I wanted to be with. And it was not them.

END ACT TWO

ACT THREE, SCENE ONE

In which:

THE WALLS CRUMBLE

I PULLED INTO MY DRIVEWAY AFTER DRIVING TAMA HOME, AND THE lights were still on. As I got out of the car, I could already hear the yelling. My heart moved up my throat and I had to swallow it back, but it wouldn't go. As I walked toward the door, my stomach started to twist and my hands trembled. I didn't want to go inside, but I had nowhere else to go. I shoved the key into the lock and walked in.

"What the hell is the matter with you!" my father screamed, his face as red as a hot poker as he glared down at my bawling brother. "Things cost money! Glasses cost money! You have no respect for anything!"

"Greg, it's just a glass," my mother said.

"You stay out of this, Jill! This has nothing to do with you!" my father screamed.

He slammed his own glass down on the counter so hard I was amazed it didn't shatter. Christopher jumped. The look of sheer terror on his face broke something inside of me. I slammed the front door and everyone whirled around.

"Leave him alone!" I shouted at my father.

Every single inch of my body shook as I moved forward and hugged Christopher out of the way. He turned his face into my side and cried.

"Where the hell have you been?" His eyes were so watery, his breath so rank, I was shocked he had been able to drive himself home.

"It's just a glass, Dad!" I shouted, ignoring the question. "Look at him. He's scared out of his mind and bawling his eyes out because he broke one little glass! He's just a kid! What's the matter with you!"

"KJ," my mother begged.

"How dare you talk to me like that!?" my father roared. "It's about time you and your brother learn a little respect!"

"For what? For *you*?" I spat, every ounce of my disgust toward him seeping into that one word.

"Yes, for me! I work my ass off every single day so that I can buy all the things you need and want, and all you do is take!" he shouted. "I work late every night for you kids and no one appreciates it!"

"Please! You do not work late!" I cried, tears springing to my eyes. "You work till five every day and then drink till eight and then come home and scream at everybody!"

I was so strangled by the end of the sentence, it came out like a wail. My father stared at me for a moment, shocked. Guess he was still getting used to the idea of me standing up to him. Actually, so was I.

"You have no idea what you're talking about, young lady," he said finally.

"Oh, so that wasn't you I bumped into outside of O'Reilly's Pool Hall tonight?" I asked, somewhat more in control.

"What? KJ, what were you doing at O'Reilly's?" my mother asked.

"Nothing," I told her. "And I know I'm probably grounded anyway, but I wasn't drinking. *I* know better," I said, turning judging eyes on my father.

"Katie Jean, go to your room," my father said through his teeth.

He was trying to avoid me saying more. Trying to avoid a discussion of where he'd been tonight.

"Do you really think we don't know, Dad?" I said. "Do you even realize how bad you smell at night? How it's so awful no one wants to go near you? You're always mad and you're always mean and we're all scared of you! We're scared to be in our own house half the time! I mean, break one glass and you react like we've just driven your car through the front of the house! You're the one who has no respect for us!"

I was just rambling now, spitting out all the things I'd thought all those nights while I'd listened to him and my mother fight. When I was finished, my father was silent. I couldn't even believe it. My mother sank into a chair in the corner and I grabbed my brother's hand and got the hell out of there. Christopher and I ran up to my room and closed the door behind us. My heart was pumping so fast I had to gasp for breath to calm it down. Christopher dried his eyes and heaved in a breath, watching me pace back and forth in front of him until I finally, finally quieted myself. I ran my hands through my hair and looked at him.

"Are you okay?" I asked.

He gazed back at me in awe. "I can't believe you just did that."

I felt an odd burst of joy in my chest. "Neither can I."

ACT THREE, SCENE TWO

In which:

ROBBIE SAVES ME, AGAIN

SATURDAY AFTERNOON I WAS WORKING ON MY THIRD PAINTING OF the day—each one darker than the last—while my father banged around his home office. As if slamming things at random would get all his anger out of his system. When he was in this kind of mood, there was no telling what might set him off again. So when the doorbell rang, I dropped my paintbrush and ran for it, knowing my mom and brother were out. I was shocked to see Robbie standing on my front step.

"Hey," he said, hands in the pockets of his blue puffer vest.

It was actually semi-warm out. One of those random early-March days that popped up to remind you spring was coming.

"What's up?" I asked.

"Nothing. Just thought I'd stop by to see how you were doing," Robbie said.

"How I'm doing?" I asked. "You mean you don't hate me?"

His brow creased. "Why would I hate you?"

"Everyone else does," I replied.

Well, Stephanie did, at least. She hadn't called me once. On a Saturday. That was unheard of. Not that I wanted to talk to her either, but the silence felt like a lead apron on my chest.

"So you freaked out," Robbie said with a shrug. "From what I could tell you were already upset about something the second you walked through the door, so I figured I'd come over and see if you wanted to, like, talk or whatever."

"So this is a house call," I said.

"Just call me Doctor Phil," he said.

"The doctor and the farmer," I joked.

Behind me, a door slammed, there were a few heavy footsteps and another door slammed. I glanced warily over my shoulder. When I looked back at Robbie again, his face was all concern.

"KJ, is something wrong?" he asked.

"Uh, can I plead the Fifth?" I asked.

"You're not gonna let me in, are you?"

I looked down at my feet. He knew. He knew that my family was dysfunctional and my father was scary and I was totally pathetic.

"Then do you want to come out?" he asked. "We could go for a walk. It's really nice out."

I took a deep breath and realized there was absolutely nothing in the world I wanted more than to get the heck out of my house.

"Definitely," I said. "Wait here."

I scribbled a quick note to my mom to let her know where I was going, then grabbed my coat and walked out. Within ten seconds of the sun on my face, I was smiling. I know I could have gone out for a walk by myself, but I never would have. Robbie was my knight in shining armor. Again.

"So, stopping by. Good decision?" Robbie asked.

I grinned at him and skipped a step to illustrate my glee. "Great decision."

ACT THREE, SCENE THREE

In which:

I BLAB

INSTEAD OF WALKING DOWN MY DRIVEWAY TO THE STREET, ROBBIE hooked a left, around the side of my house and into the backyard. He cut right by my brother's swing set and into the woods at the back. No one knew who owned the woods between my house and the houses on the next street, but they were thick and wide and ran all the way from Gerber Hill to the high school, like, a mile away. It was basically the only stretch of trees in town that hadn't yet been cut down to build McMansions.

"Where are we going?" I asked Robbie as he held a branch aside for me. The ground was muddy and covered with slick leaves left over from last fall. I was glad I was wearing my crappiest sneakers.

"To the bridge," he said. Like I obviously knew what bridge he was talking about.

Which made me feel stupid when I said, "What bridge?"

Robbie glanced over his shoulder at me. "What, you've never been back here before?"

"Not this far," I grumbled. My tentative good mood was

close to evaporating. I hated feeling stupid. Almost as much as I hated feeling trapped. Or embarrassed.

"I cut through here to get to your house. If you go this way, we don't live that far from each other."

I wondered when he had figured this out. Why he cared how close we lived to each other. Why he felt he needed a shortcut to get to me. But I didn't ask.

"Here. See? The bridge."

We'd come upon a tiny stream with a steep embankment. A sturdy wooden bridge with no handrails connected one side to the other over the widest stretch.

"What's this stream?" I asked as Robbie sat down and dangled his legs toward the water. The bottoms of his sneakers almost touched the rocks. He took the drumsticks out of his back pocket and laid them aside.

"It turns into Meadow Brook farther down. By the park."

He was looking at me like I was clueless. Like everyone knew this but me.

"Guess I'm not much of an explorer," I said, sitting down next to him. My feet came nowhere near the water. I picked up a pebble from the bridge and tossed it in.

"So, is everything okay?" he asked me.

I took a deep breath. Already my body heat was skyrocketing. "Yeah. Everything's fine." I tossed another pebble into the water.

"But not really."

I glanced at him from the corner of my eye. He was looking at me with those eyes of his. Those completely unteasing, interested, kind eyes. I felt the words bubbling up in my throat. Tried to hold them back. No one needed to know how much my life sucked, least of all Robbie Delano, whom I hardly even knew. But somehow, I knew I was going to say it anyway. Being out here in the middle of the woods with nothing but the sound of the babbling water and the birds flitting from tree to tree overhead made me feel safe.

"I had a fight with my dad last night," I said finally.

"About what?" he asked.

God, this was going to sound stupid. "Well, first he caught me and Tama at O'Reilly's Pool Hall."

Robbie winced. "Ouch."

"And then, when I got home last night, he was freaking out on my brother for breaking a glass. So I yelled at him."

"Really?" Robbie said.

"Yeah."

He crossed his arms over his chest, stuffing his hands under his elbows. "How bad was he freaking out?"

"Bad. Like, really bad," I said, my insides twisting at the memory. Another pebble plopped into the water.

"Over a glass?" Robbie sounded incredulous.

"He was kind of . . ." I looked at Robbie.

"What?"

My cheeks prickled with heat. "Drunk."

There. I'd said it. It was out there.

"Oh."

"He's always drunk. Every night. And he's always in a bad mood. Like, really bad. Like if you leave the light on in the basement or something, he just loses it. He goes ballistic. Like you burned the house down or something. And that's what he was doing to my brother last night, so I kind of freaked. I was all upset already after the party and I just . . . snapped."

"Wow," Robbie said. "He seemed so normal when I met him."

"Yeah, well, that was a good night."

"Oh." Robbie pondered this for a second. "KJ, he doesn't, like, hit you or anything, does he?"

"No! Oh no. Nothing like that," I said, rushing to my father's defense. "He would never do that. He just yells. A lot. And he gets all red and he throws things sometimes."

"He throws things?"

I felt like I was drawing this picture that was a lot worse than it was. "Well, yeah, but not *at* people."

"But still—"

"I know. It's bad. But it's, whatever. It's fine," I said with a shrug. I wished I had never opened my mouth. Now Robbie was going to think I was a freak with a crazy family. He wasn't going to want to be friends anymore and he was never going to stop by like this ever again. Nice one, KJ.

"That must suck," he said finally.

"Yeah, well."

I didn't know what else to say. I threw another pebble into the water. Flung it, actually.

"I can't imagine being afraid of my dad," Robbie said, which made my heart twinge painfully.

"I can't imagine not being afraid of my dad." I took a deep breath. "I'm scared all the time when I'm home. All the time."

I sounded pathetic. Why couldn't I make myself stop talking?

"Well, maybe it's good that you stood up to him. Maybe he'll realize how bad it is and he'll, I don't know, get help or something," Robbie said hopefully. "Maybe whatever you said will make a difference."

I sputtered a laugh. "Please. Nothing will ever make a difference with him."

"You don't know that."

"Yes. I do. A couple of years ago he was found passed out at his desk at work and my mom thought that would do it, but his boss helped cover it up because they're such old friends," I said. "Then last Christmas he went out to string lights during, like, fifty-mile-an-hour winds or something and he broke his arm and slipped a disk. We thought that would do it, but no. I think he'll end up dead before he changes. It's definitely not gonna be a lecture from me. He doesn't even care about me." I picked up another pebble and threw it so hard, my arm socket hurt. Robbie stared out at the water and I could practically hear him thinking. He was trying to figure out how to get away from me as quickly as possible. Get away from the freak. "You must think I'm such a loser," I said.

"What? No. Are you kidding?" he said. "Everyone has something screwed up in their lives. I just wish there was something I could do."

"Yeah, right. What's screwed up in your life?" I asked.

"Uh, my mother bailed on me and my brother when I was five?" he said.

Oh, right. Duh. I knew his mom wasn't around. What was wrong with me?

"Right. Sorry."

"Not only that, but we didn't hear one single word from her again until last summer, when she invited us both to her wedding in Maine," he said.

"No way," I blurted.

"Way," he said, widening his eyes.

I gaped at him. "So did you burn the invitation?"

"No. I went," he said.

"You did not."

"Did," he replied. "Tony, that's my brother, he couldn't handle it, but I was pretty much dying of curiosity. So I went. Good cake. Her husband's a tool, though. He's got a comb-over and he plays bingo. Like every Sunday."

"I can't believe you went," I said. "Wasn't it weird?"

"Kind of. But she was like a stranger to me. It was sort of like going to the wedding of a great-aunt you'd never met," he said. "We posed for a couple of pictures and she sent me a postcard from her honeymoon. Now she e-mails me all the time with these weird chain letters. And that is the extent of my relationship with my mother."

I shook my head. "See, I never would have gone. Once I go away to college, I never want to see my father again." I choked on the last couple of words. Suddenly I felt very tired. And pathetic. And sad. Why was this my life? It was so unfair. I just wanted to be able to come home and go to my room and not have to worry about whether or not my father was in one of his moods. I just wanted to be normal.

Robbie reached over and put his arm around my shoulder. The moment his fingers squeezed my arm, tears started rolling down my face. I tried to stop them, but the more I tried, the more they kept coming. Robbie scooted toward me until our legs touched, and held me a little closer without saying a single word. I couldn't believe I was doing this, weeping in the middle of the woods while Robbie Delano of all people hugged me, but at that moment, it was all I could do. I needed that hug. Between my dad and my mom and Stephanie and Fred and all the other crap going on, I needed it really badly.

ACT THREE, SCENE FOUR

In which:

CONFUSING EMOTIONS SURFACE

"ALL RIGHT! WE NEED ALL THE PINK LADIES AND T-BIRDS ON stage!" Mr. Katz called out. "We're doing a dry run of 'You're the One That I Want'!"

I cleared my throat and shifted in my seat, getting ready to make notes. Really, I was just trying to look busy for all the people who were glowering around me. Stephanie, Glenn, Andy, Fred. Not one of them had spoken to me all afternoon. Well, except for Andy, who kind of had to. But he only asked me questions about props and that was it. Guess he was too mature to let our personal issues get in the way of a great production. But it was so weird, sitting in the same room with Stephanie and feeling like I couldn't talk to her. So weird that she had no idea what had happened to me on Friday night and that she had no idea I'd spent lunch today with Cameron, hanging in the bio lab, trying to work but mostly just talking. But I couldn't bring myself to approach her first. I was still mad. She was supposed to be on my side no matter what, but lately, she'd aligned herself with the enemy one too many times.

"It's so gauche, taking the song from the movie," Ashley

said to Carrie as they strolled by. "When we did *Grease* at the Theater in the Round, we stuck to the *original* music."

Everyone gathered up on stage and Chelsea, the choreographer from a local dance school, snapped her fingers at Tama and Robbie, pointing to a place upstage. They looked at each other, confused, then moved to that spot. Chelsea turned to Mr. Katz and clapped her hands twice like a flamenco dancer.

"And now, we dance!"

Everyone laughed and she gave them all a sour look. Like Ashley, Chelsea didn't appreciate unprofessional behavior. Why she worked with kids was beyond me.

"All right, Jeffrey," Mr. Katz said, strolling over to the piano. "Whenever you're ready."

Jeffrey Porter played the intro, and up on stage, Tama and Robbie started to sing. They had these big grins on and moved through their dance sequences like they'd been doing it all their lives. A couple of times one of the T-Birds got in their way—usually Fred—but they moved deftly around him and kept right on singing. The background dancers were all over the place, but for the most part, it looked okay. Especially for the first time through with the whole cast. Watching it even made me forget, temporarily, that everyone hated me.

"Okay, everyone! Nice work!" Mr. Katz shouted as the final chord faded away. Everyone was posed on stage in their final move, hands in the air, fingers splayed, a crazy circus of wide eyes and huge grins. "Let's take five and then we'll go over that count by count."

The crowd broke up, but Jeffrey started playing another, slower tune. I recognized the music instantly and my pulse started to race. Up on stage, Robbie grabbed Tama's hand and pulled her to him. My heart caught in surprise. Was he doing what I thought he was doing?

"Uh, what's your malfunction?" Tama snapped.

Robbie ignored her. Slowly, he started to move back and forth, holding Tama against him. Right in front of everyone, he led her through the dance we had practiced backstage last week. Jeffrey continued to play expertly, the lilting music filling the auditorium, and every single person in the room was silent. Silent and watching in curious wonder.

I couldn't move. Couldn't look away. Robbie gazed into Tama's eyes like she was the only girl in the world. Tama blushed and looked away, then back again, like she couldn't help herself. I knew what that felt like. I knew *exactly* what that felt like. And suddenly, I couldn't breathe. I couldn't think. All I knew was I didn't want to see the twirl. The dip. The . . . the what came after that.

I was up the aisle and out the door before the song ever ended. The door slammed loudly behind me, which must have killed the mood inside, but I didn't care. I actually kind of hoped it would. Leaning back against the cool cinder-block wall in the lobby, I closed my eyes and breathed. This was wrong. This was very, very wrong. I was in love with Cameron. Always had been, always would be.

So why did I feel so utterly, indescribably . . . jealous?

ACT THREE, SCENE FIVE

In which:

I JUST WANT TAMA OUT OF MY CAR

"I MEAN, WHAT WAS HE THINKING? YOU HAVE TO ASK A GIRL TO dance first, don't you? Isn't that how it works?" Tama asked giddily. She was trying to act all offended by what Robbie had done, but she was actually beaming. "The boy can dance, though, can't he? Did you see the way he dipped me? It was right out of *Dancing With the Stars*."

I stared at the red light and willed it to turn green. Never in my life would I have imagined that Tama could make me feel this way, but right then I couldn't wait to get the girl out of my car. All she'd talked about the entire drive was Robbie. Robbie, Robbie, Robbie. Didn't she have a boyfriend?

"Cage? Hello?" Tama said, waving a hand.

The light turned green and I slammed on the gas. We lurched over the train tracks.

"What?" I said.

"I'm talking over here, in case you hadn't noticed," Tama said. "Or am I just boring you?"

"Sorry," I said. "Got a lot on my mind."

Tama laughed. "Like what?" she asked. Like there was no

possible way I could have anything important on the brain. I suddenly missed Steph. Badly. I turned in to the parking lot of her doctor's office and into the first space I saw.

"We're here!" I announced.

"What's with you today?" Tama asked, flipping down the visor to apply her lip gloss.

"What do you mean?" I asked.

"You're all bitched out," Tama said matter-of-factly.

"I don't have to drive you here, you know," I said. "I do have other things I could be doing."

Tama slapped the visor up and gaped at me. "Wow. One little unadulterated freak-out and it's like a whole new KJ," she said, referring to Friday night. "Fine. I thought friends did favors for friends, but if that's the way you feel about it—"

There was a roar of an engine loud enough to wake the dead and something zoomed past my window. I glanced up just in time to see Leo whipping his helmet off. He got up from his bike and walked around to Tama's side of my car.

"Get out," he ordered, jerking the door open.

"Leo! What the hell are you doing?"

"That's what I was going to ask you!" he shouted. "You're seeing the psycho shrink again?"

Tama got out of the car and slammed the door so hard the whole thing shook. My heart pounded with fear. Leo looked like he had blood on his mind. I killed the engine and stepped out as well. Maybe he'd double-think the violence if there were witnesses.

"Dr. Weiner? Yes, I'm seeing him again," Tama said. "Where did you come from, anyway? Are you following me? You won't answer my calls but you're following me?"

"I went to school to pick you up so we could talk and I saw

you getting in KJ's car, so I figured I'd just follow you home and talk to you there," Leo said. "But instead you come here. How long has this been going on?"

"I've been coming since Christmas," Tama admitted.

"Since Christmas? What happened to standing up to your parents? What happened to being in charge of your own life and not letting them control you?" he shouted.

"You're one to talk!" Tama said.

"What's that supposed to mean?"

"Oh, please, Leo. We all know who was behind you applying to college," Tama said with a disgusted look on her face. "You've never wanted to go away to school. Are you really going to tell me your dad didn't make you do it?"

"No, my dad didn't make me do it," Leo said. "We had some conversations about it, yeah, but I realized he was right."

"Ha!"

Leo's eyes narrowed. "Maybe he was right about some other stuff, too," he said. "Maybe you really are holding me back."

"What!?" Tama blurted.

"You know what, screw this," Leo said, turning around. "I'm outta here. I have some applications to send out."

He got on his bike and revved the engine.

"Well, fine! Go ahead and do that, then! I don't give a crap where you are next year!" Tama shouted, getting all up in his face. "There are a million guys in this town who would kill to date me!"

Leo backed up and turned the bike, Tama following awkwardly after him.

"You hear me? A million guys, Leo!"

He ignored her and peeled out. For a long moment, the both of us just stood there in the parking lot. A couple of faces stared down at us from the office windows. Finally, the sound of his engine faded to nothing and Tama turned around. Her chest heaved up and down. She had one tear on her face, which she quickly wiped away.

"Come on."

She walked by me and got back in the car. I slid in next to her.

"Don't you have an appointment?" I asked.

"I don't care." Her face was set like stone. "Let's just go."

I started the car. "Where are we going?"

She turned to look at me. "We're going to Robbie's."

ACT THREE, SCENE SIX

In which:

A DATE IS MADE

I PULLED INTO ROBBIE'S EMPTY DRIVEWAY, THE HEADLIGHTS OF MY car illuminating the basketball hoop hung over the garage door. There were only a few lights on in the house, and I found myself praying that no one was home.

This is a good thing, KJ. You've been trying to get these two together, and now, here you are, the farmer sowing the final seed.

So why did I feel like I was nailing the final nail in the coffin instead?

"Okay. I'm going in," Tama said, smoothing her hair. She got out of the car and straightened her skirt.

"Good luck," I said weakly.

She laughed and stuck her head back inside. "Like I need it."

Is it wrong that I wanted to pull her hair?

She sauntered around the car and up to the front door. I slid the car window down, needing to hear this. Tama rang the bell. I held my breath. The light on the front porch flicked on and Robbie opened the door. He didn't even look surprised to see her.

"Hey," Tama said.

"Hey," Robbie replied. He squinted past her at the car. My heart skipped a beat. I raised a hand. He raised a hand in return. Pathetic. I was totally pathetic.

"So, you want to go out this weekend?" Tama asked. Just like that. Like she was asking to borrow a pencil.

"Uh, yeah. With you? Sure. Absolutely." Robbie put his hand on the back of his neck. It was the first time I'd ever seen him flustered. Crap, he really liked her. Like really, really liked her.

My whole body sank. I wanted to drive away. I didn't need to see any more of this. My hand even reached for the gear shift, but I stopped. I was Tama's only ride home. And if I left her here, she'd have to stay here until Robbie's dad got back from work and drove her. And God only knew what they'd do together until then. The idea made my stomach very unhappy.

So I stayed. And I rolled up the window. I let them make their plans as I sat in the car and thought of Cameron. Cameron's laugh, Cameron's smile, Cameron's perfect hair. Cameron's scent, Cameron's clothes, Cameron's incredible shoulders.

Eventually a sort of calm resolve came over me. If Tama could do this, I could do it, too. It was time to take control of my life. I was in love with Cameron Richardson. No one else. And I'd waited long enough to do something about it.

ACT THREE, SCENE SEVEN

In which:

I TAKE THE PLUNGE

I DROVE TAMA HOME, THEN WENT BACK TO SCHOOL. I WAS SO pumped up with adrenaline and resolve, I felt like I was going to bust out of my skin. Our rehearsal had ended early, so even with all the driving around town, it was possible that the basketball team was still practicing. When I drove into the parking lot and saw Cameron's car sitting in its assigned space, I felt a rush of excitement and total dread.

This was it. This was my moment. Thank goodness my mother had believed that I wasn't drinking that night at O'Reilly's and had decided not to ground me as long as I promised never to go there again. Otherwise, I wouldn't even be free to do what I was about to do.

I threw the car into park before I hit the brake and lurched forward. Ow. Oops. Okay, I had to get control of myself. I killed the engine, checked my hair and got out of the car with only my keys. I tripped twice on my way up the steps. When I got inside, I heard the squeaks of sneakers on the hallway and the pounding of a basketball. My heart hit my mouth. Two seconds later, Cameron, Dustin, Tommy and three of their teammates walked into the lobby.

Perfect timing. It was like fate.

Please just don't let him walk by me like he doesn't know me. I'll never be able to do this if he does.

"KJ! What's up?" Cameron asked.

Yes. Yes. Yes. Another sign.

"I . . . uh . . . need to talk to you," I said.

The other guys exchanged looks behind his back.

"About the project!" I blurted.

"Oh. Okay," Cameron said. "Later, dudes," he said to his friends, slapping hands with all of them as they made their way out. "What's the matter? You hated what I wrote, for the procedure, right? I knew it sucked."

"No. It's not that! It didn't suck," I said. Even though it kind of had, but we could deal with that later. "Actually, I wanted to ask you something else."

Oh, God. Was I really going to do this? There was no way. No way I could possibly get the words out.

But Tama had asked out Robbie. Like it was nothing. Like no one else in the world mattered or cared or anything. I could do this. I was going to do this.

"Something else . . . ?" Cameron said.

"Would you want to go out with me? Maybe? This weekend?" I blurted.

Cameron looked like someone had just dropped something very heavy on his head. I swear he even got shorter. Or maybe he just bent his knees, I don't know. But he was going to say no. It was blatantly obvious by the look of abject terror on his face. What was I thinking? How could I have ever believed that Cameron Richardson would—

"Sure," he said.

"What?"

"I said sure," Cameron told me, passing his basketball from one hand to the other. "Unless you already changed your mind."

"What?"

He reached out and put his hand on my shoulder. "KJ. I said yes. You, me. This weekend. Sure."

Oh. My. God.

"Really?" I squeaked.

"Yes. Really." Cameron laughed. I was biffing this big time. Not cool. Not calm. Not even close. But I didn't care. He'd said yes! He couldn't take that back now. Or, wait, could he?

"Oh. Okay. Cool," I said, trying to regain some measure of composure.

"Good. Well. I have to go, sooo . . ."

"We'll talk about it on Friday," I suggested.

"Sounds like a plan," Cameron said. "Later, KJ."

He walked out of the lobby, tossing the ball in the air above his head. The glass door slammed behind him and I watched him walk all the way to his car. That boy was going out on a date with me. That piece of perfection that I had been daydreaming about ever since daydreams stopped being about horses and started being about boys. He was actually going out with me.

And it was all thanks to Tama. Now I was really glad I had not, in fact, pulled her hair back at Robbie's house.

I was just about to start jumping for joy when I heard singing. And piano playing. Had that been going on the entire time I'd been here? I walked over to the auditorium door and peeked in. Jeffrey was at the piano and Ashley, Cory, Carrie and Jane were all gathered around.

"Freddy my love, please keep in touch while you're away . . . ," Jane sang.

"Hey," I said loudly. The music stopped. I walked down the aisle, twirling my keys around my fingers. "What're you guys doing?"

"Working on our songs," Ashley said, lifting her chin. "Since we didn't *get* to them at rehearsal today."

Jeffrey looked at me sheepishly.

"We said we'd go over them tomorrow," I replied.

"Yeah, and then tomorrow we'll come in and Tama will just *have* to go over 'Raining on Prom Night' and once again, we won't have time to work on our harmonies," Carrie said.

"I am not going up there on opening night unprepared, KJ," Ashley told me, pointing at the stage. "That is not an option."

"You're not going to be unprepared. I—"

"Please, KJ! Tama has monopolized every single rehearsal we've had this year," Ashley said. "It's all about her. Her songs, her costumes, her blocking, her lighting. It's like the rest of us don't even exist."

"And you just give her whatever she wants," Jane grumbled, joining the mob.

"Is this about the dressing room again?" I asked.

"The dressing room is just one little part of it, KJ!" Ashley snapped. "Tama is a born diva, and you are only making it worse!"

"She's not a diva," I replied. "But she is the star. Certain things have to be done to accommodate her needs."

"Oh my God! She has you totally brainwashed!" Ashley said.

My jaw clenched. Was Stephanie comparing notes with Ashley Brown now, too?

"She's just using you, you know," she added.

"No, she's not," I said through my teeth.

"Oh, she *so* is," Ashley put in. "You're not a stage manager, KJ, you're Tama's glorified errand girl."

"Nice one," Carrie said, sliding her palm across Ashley's.

My face burned. "You guys have no idea what you're talking about," I said. "Tama and I are friends."

If we weren't friends, why would she have helped me lose the geeks and win Cameron? If we weren't friends, why did I know all about Dr. Weiner and why she was going there when no one else did? Ashley and the Drama Twins knew nothing.

"Whatever, KJ. All I know is, it's your job to get her ego under control," Ashley said, grabbing up her music. "Otherwise, this beloved production of yours is going down. Come on, girls."

All four of them strode by me, noses in the air. Jeffrey gathered his things and slunk away. I rolled my eyes and closed the piano cover. Ashley was such a drama queen, she just created it wherever she saw a void. Things had changed between me and Tama. We had been there for each other over the past few weeks. We'd helped each other. I was going out on a date with Cameron thanks to her, and thanks to me, she was going out with Robbie—a guy who would never yank her out of a car and bitch her out in a parking lot. Tama and I were friends now. Real friends. And nothing Ashley and her troupe of followers could say would change that.

ACT THREE, SCENE EIGHT

In which:

A PLOT IS REVEALED

TAMA HAD HER OWN BATHROOM. IT WAS ATTACHED TO HER bedroom and had a tub like a swimming pool, plus a separate shower with glass doors. It also had a separate vanity area, with a velvet-covered bench and a mirror the size of the wall, with hundreds of round lightbulbs surrounding it—the kind makeup artists always use in the movies. There were drawers and drawers full of makeup and brushes and hair products and perfume, and the music she was playing in her bedroom was pumped in over small silver speakers set in the ceiling. It was paradise.

The upstairs bathroom at my house had peeling flowered wallpaper and a tile stall shower with a fluorescent light that groaned whenever you turned it on. Not that I was jealous or anything.

I stood in front of the mirror, staring at my freshly made-up complexion, feeling unworthy. I couldn't even imagine living like this. If her dad was as psycho as mine, she'd probably never even know it. Her room was so far away from the front door, I'd be surprised if she ever heard anyone even come and go. God, that would be so incredible.

"Found it!" Tama cried, bounding in from her bedroom. She swung her leg over the bench and sat, leaning in toward the mirror to apply some kind of clear gloss to her lips.

"What is it?" I asked.

"Lip Venom. It swells your lips in, like, an hour. Makes them much more kissable."

My stomach twisted. She was going out with Robbie. She was plumping her lips for Robbie.

As you should be for Cameron. Cameron, I reminded myself, and felt a little thrill. I was actually going out with Cameron Richardson.

"Can I use some?" I asked.

Tama paused and flicked her gaze at my reflection. "Your lips are full already. Any bigger and you'd be Jolie-ing it."

Wait. Was that a bad thing? I looked at my lips in the mirror. Were they freakishly big? Tama quickly put the Lip Venom in her bag and snapped it shut.

"Almost time," she said.

"What are you guys doing tonight?" I asked, trying to distract myself from my balloonlike lips.

"He's taking me to dinner somewhere," Tama said with a shrug. "But after that I'm going to take him to the diner for coffee."

"The diner? Really?" I asked. That was, after all, not the most romantic locale.

"Totally. Leo's gonna be there," she said, running a finger over her eyebrow.

Hang on. Back up. "Leo?"

Tama heaved a sigh, like I was so irritatingly naïve. "KJ, if Leo doesn't see me and Robbie together, then what's the point of this whole charade?"

Charade? What the hell was she talking about? "I'm sorry, are you only going out with Robbie to get back at Leo?"

"Why else would I go out with him?" Tama asked. "You didn't really think I'd date a geek like Robbie Delano, did you?"

A geek like Robbie? A *geek?* Was she kidding me? Robbie was the least geeky guy I knew. And okay, maybe he didn't hang out with Cameron and those guys, but that was by choice. He didn't want to get sucked into their hypocritical popularity vortex of doom. Which made him, in my book, all the less geeky.

"What?" Tama said.

"What, what?" I replied.

"You're all red," she told me. "Do I offend?"

"Well, now that you mention it, yeah," I said. "You're using Robbie."

Tama laughed. "So?"

"Well—"

"Robbie is getting exactly what he wants tonight," Tama said, standing. "He's getting to go out with me. And who knows? Maybe I'll even let him kiss me for real. He does have the softest lips."

She grinned mischievously, then turned and strolled out. I felt like gagging myself. Robbie and Tama had closed-mouth kissed a couple of times in rehearsals, ergo her knowledge of his lip texture. But the idea of him kissing her for real, him not knowing that he was just being used, made me want to pick up her straightening iron and throw it at her.

I followed her into her bedroom, trying to think of something, anything to say, that would make her understand how absolutely awful she was being. Robbie really wanted to be with her, and she was toying with him.

"Speaking of stage kisses, you should really talk to Ashley.

When she kisses Jonathan, she looks like a blowfish," Tama said, tossing her cell phone and wallet into her purse. "It's going to get a laugh and it's *so* not supposed to."

"You know, Tama, people are getting a little sick of all your notes," I said angrily.

She stood up straight. "Excuse me?"

"It's just . . . you've been acting like a diva lately and people are starting to complain," I told her, trying to sound more diplomatic. "You might want to . . . I don't know . . . dial it down a notch."

Tama smirked. "Some people like who? Ashley? The Drama Twins?"

I said nothing. Thereby confirming her list.

"Unbelievable. They are just going to have to accept the fact that I'm the star," Tama said. "I'm sorry if that makes some people uncomfortable, but the sooner they realize it, the better off they'll be."

She turned around and grabbed her leather jacket, leaving me gaping behind her. They were right. Her ego was totally out of control. Even if she was the star, that didn't give her the right to run the production. That was, well, my job.

"What?" Tama said, noticing my pallor in one of her many mirrors. She sighed as I remained speechless. "Come on, Cage. You know all my notes have improved the show. You know that."

Unfortunately, she had a point. Other than the bizarre dressing room incident, she hadn't made any unreasonable or unintelligent demands.

"Right?" she prompted.

My shoulders slumped. "Right."

"Thank you," she said with a pleased smile.

The doorbell rang. The guys. Tama and her ego were instantly forgotten.

"Come on!" Tama said, shrugging into her jacket. "Let's go see which of our gentlemen callers is here."

Two minutes later (it took that long to get from her room to the front foyer), we swung the door open to find Robbie standing outside. He was wearing a black T-shirt with a gray shirt open over it, and he had a single white lily.

Damn, he was good.

"Hey, Tama," he said, his eyes shining annoyingly. Then he glanced at me. "KJ. I didn't know you were going to be here."

"We wanted to get ready for our big dates together," Tama said with a grin. She plucked the lily from his fingers. "Thanks. This is pretty. I'll go put it in water."

Her heels click-clacked as she walked away.

"You have a big date?" Robbie asked.

"Is that so hard to believe?" I replied.

He raised his hands. I had sort of bitten his head off there. Residual Tama anger. Dammit. Why couldn't I control my mouth? I wished Cameron had gotten here first so that I didn't have to witness this sham.

"Sorry," he said. "Who's the lucky guy?"

I blushed. Why did he have to say stuff like that? "I'm going out with Cameron."

Robbie blinked. "Really? That's—"

"You don't have to say anything. I know you don't like him."

Robbie put his hands in his pockets and looked at the ground. He was even wearing real shoes. Black, shiny things that looked really uncomfortable. He'd gone all out for this thing. My heart squeezed. Maybe I should tell him the truth—that she was using him, that she still wanted Leo. That all of our seed sowing had resulted in a sickly, wilting, mealworm-riddled crop.

"Hey, thanks for this," he said suddenly, quietly. "I wouldn't even be here if it weren't for you."

Or maybe not. Crap. He was right. This was all my fault. I'd gotten him into this mess with all my investigating and encouraging.

All you did was get him what he wanted, KJ, I thought, my inner voice sounding a lot like Tama. He wanted a date with her and now he's got it.

Maybe it would all be all right. Maybe Tama would spend the evening with Robbie and realize how totally incredible he was. I mean, he blew Leo out of the water. Tama would have to be blind not to see that.

"You're welcome," I said, feeling guilty, hopeful and pathetic all at once.

Tama returned and stepped out next to Robbie. "I'm ready," she said. "You can just hang out down here until Cameron shows. My mom knows you're here."

"Okay. Thanks," I said.

"Shall we?" Robbie said, lifting his hand toward the driveway.

"We shall," Tama said flirtatiously. I wanted to smack her upside the head. She walked toward his car and Robbie hung back for a second.

"You look really nice, by the way," he said, looking me directly in the eye. "I just hope . . . I just hope Cameron deserves you."

He gave me a sheepish sort of smile and walked off. Suddenly, I could hardly breathe.

But then he got in the car, and the heat passed. I was insane. Robbie Delano was just Robbie Delano. In about five minutes I was going to be out on a date with Cameron Richardson, the guy of my dreams. Cameron Richardson with his perfect hair and perfect lips and perfect eyes and perfect hands.

Get a grip.

ACT THREE, SCENE NINE

In which:

THERE'S PINKY CONTACT

THE MOVIE THEATER WAS DARK. CAMERON'S LEG WAS PRESSED into mine. During the quiet parts of the movie I could hear him breathing. He was chewing gum and eating popcorn and I could not figure out how he was doing both at the same time without being gross, but he was. He was Cameron Richardson. He could do pretty much anything.

I stared at his profile, unable to believe we were actually here. Together. Me and him. Him and me. KJ Miller. On a date with Cameron Richardson. I could reach over and pop his Hubba Bubba bubble with my fingernail. Even better, I could lean over and kiss him. That was how close he was. One lean in and my lips would be on his cheek. I wondered what he'd do if I had the guts. Would he flinch? Laugh? Turn his head and kiss me back?

I shivered. He turned and looked at me. Caught me staring.

"You cold?" he whispered.

Quite the contrary. But he was leaning forward and groping for his varsity jacket, which was mashed behind him. He was going to give me his jacket. Cameron Richardson's jacket on my shoulders.

He finally freed it, spilling some popcorn on the floor. I would have been embarrassed if I'd done that, but he didn't even seem to notice. He put his jacket on my lap, and it was all I could do to keep from lifting it to my face and inhaling forever.

"Thanks," I said.

"No problem. I just need it back after," he said.

"Okay."

I knew that if I tried to put the jacket on for real, I'd probably punch him in the face in the process, so I just laid it over myself like a blanket, cuddling back in the chair. Feeling giddy, I reached out for some popcorn and we knocked hands. My instinct was to pull my hand back, but Cameron caught my pinky with his and hooked it around mine. I glanced at him. He smiled at me.

My heart was never going to be the same again.

So we sat like that, for the rest of the movie, our pinkies entwined over popcorn. My arm went dead and my shoulder cramped, but I didn't even care. It was all my sappy dreams come true.

ACT THREE, SCENE TEN

In which:

THERE'S AN UNEXPECTED MELTDOWN

I WAS SHOCKED WHEN CAMERON DROVE TO THE DINER AFTER THE movie. Not that I thought he wouldn't want to be seen with me, but, well, part of me thought he wouldn't want to be seen with me. That sounds lamer than lame, but Cameron and I were just not on the same social level, and a lot of people at school would probably have something to say about the two of us being out together. But Cameron didn't seem to care about that. Not at all. And it only made me love him more.

"Richardson! Dude! Whaddup!" someone shouted the moment we were inside.

"Hey, Skeezo!" Cameron shouted. He glanced at me. "I'll be right back."

He left me standing there, in line for a table, by myself. I felt completely conspicuous, and caught a few sophomore girls staring at me, until I noticed Tama waving me down from across the room. Ha! Take that, sophomore haters.

I slid past the waiting crowd and over to her table. Lissa Burns and Jenny Fowler, a couple of Tama's friends, were standing near the table with their coats still on, chatting with

Tama. Robbie sat across the table, and as I approached, I saw that he was toying with the plastic salt and pepper shakers, stacking them and knocking them over, stacking them and knocking them over. Was he not having a good time?

Wait, no. I wanted this to work. I did.

"Hey, guys. What's up?" I asked upon arrival.

Jenny looked at me like I had a booger sticking out of my nose. Lissa didn't even bother. Robbie lifted a hand and attempted a smile. It was a failed attempt.

"I have to talk to you," Tama said, getting up.

"We'll be at our table," Jenny said, looking at me with irritation.

"I'll stop by and visit in a few," Tama said. Then she grabbed my hand and dragged me toward the bathroom.

"I'll be here!" Robbie called after us with a touch of sarcasm.

The bathroom door swung closed behind us and Tama grabbed my wrists. "Omigod, Robbie is the goods!" she squealed.

I couldn't have been more shocked if she'd shoved me up against the wall and mugged me for my loose change.

"What?"

"He is so sweet, KJ! You have no idea!" Actually, I kind of did, but whatever.

"He's been opening doors for me all night, and he keeps adjusting the heat in his car to make sure I'm comfortable, and he didn't even get mad when I sent back my food at the restaurant," she said, checking her hair in the mirror. "Leo has, like, a meltdown when I do that."

"Well, that's . . . great," I said. "I'm glad you're having fun."

"This is not just fun. It's fate," she said, whirling to face me. "I didn't even know guys like this existed out there. It's like he actually cares what I think and how I feel. I really think I might dump Leo for him."

My stomach churned. This was the best-case scenario, wasn't it? Robbie wanted Tama, and Tama had done exactly as I'd hoped—she'd realized how great Robbie was. I was no longer responsible for the heartbreak of the century, I was responsible for a whole new couple.

"Of course, I'll have to do something about his clothes," Tama said, staring into space. "And those drumsticks have got to go. But he has potential."

My mouth opened slightly, but nothing came out.

"I am so glad I did this," she said, grabbing my wrist. "Come on!"

We stumbled back out into the diner and found Robbie and Cameron sitting across from each other at Tama's table in silence. Cameron jumped up when he saw us.

"There aren't any tables," he said. "We're gonna have to wait. Unless . . ."

"No! Sit with us!" Tama said, sliding in next to Robbie. "It'll be fun."

Robbie sighed and shook his head. He placed the salt shaker atop a rather large condiment pyramid he'd constructed.

"Something wrong?" Tama asked.

"Just wondering if we're going to get five minutes alone tonight," he said flatly, letting the salt shaker crash to the table. Tama's face fell. Okay, tension!

"Maybe we should just go," I said.

There was a commotion by the door and Leo appeared out of nowhere, his face red with fury.

"I knew it!" he blurted, storming toward us.

"Leo?" Tama said, feigning surprise. Badly.

"Oh, you've got to be kidding me," Robbie said.

Leo stopped at the head of the table. "Get up." He flicked his fingers at Robbie.

"Why?" Robbie asked calmly.

"So I can kick your ass, twerp," Leo said.

Tama slid out of the booth. "Leo. Don't make a scene."

"Gimme a break, T. You live for this," Leo snapped. "I'm just giving you what you want, drama girl."

"I'm outta here," Robbie said, standing up. Leo reached right around Tama and grabbed Robbie's shirt. Both Tama and I shrieked. A couple of busboys hovered, waiting to see if they'd have to intervene.

"You're not going anywhere until we do this," Leo said.

"Save your energy, man. I'm not with your girl," Robbie said calmly. He turned and looked right at Tama. "In fact, I have zero interest in being with your girl."

It was so blunt even my heart broke. The kids at the tables around us laughed and oohed. Tama looked like she was about to hurl. Leo, confused, released him. Thank God.

"You set this whole thing up, didn't you?" Robbie said to Tama, grabbing his jacket. "You just wanted to make your man here jealous. I'm so stupid. It's so obvious you had no interest in me. I mean, you talked about yourself seventy-five percent of the night and spent the other twenty-five checking yourself out in every reflective surface you could find. Oh! Or looked around the room to see if there was anyone better to talk to. That was way fun."

That got an even bigger cackle. Even Cameron laughed. I felt like I was witnessing an act of mass destruction.

"Well, you wanted him? Here he is. You got him," Robbie said, thrusting both hands at Leo. "And he can drive you home."

With that, Robbie turned around and walked out of the diner with his head held high. His exit was followed by a smattering of appreciative applause.

ACT TWO, SCENE ELEVEN

In which:

WE KISS

"I CAN'T BELIEVE HE DID THAT, MAN. WHO KNEW ROBBIE DELANO had such balls?" Cameron said gleefully as he turned his car onto my street. "That was classic. I mean, that's gonna go down in Washington High history!"

I stared out the windshield, wishing he would stop talking about it. Ever since Robbie had left, I'd had a hard time concentrating on our date. Tama and Leo had left together, shouting at each other the whole way, and everyone in the diner had spent the rest of the night gossiping about them. Meanwhile, all I could think about was whether or not Robbie was okay. He'd seemed okay, but maybe he was just putting up a front. I knew how much he liked Tama. How much time he'd put into wooing her. He couldn't be totally okay.

"You're up here on the left, right?" Cameron asked.

"Yeah."

My heart skipped a beat. We were almost home, which meant we were almost saying good-bye, which meant . . .

Oh no, did I really eat an onion ring with my burger?

"This is me," I said, pointing at my driveway.

"Oh. Right."

Cameron made a quick, skidding turn and pulled in. My father's car wasn't there. It was past ten o'clock. Suddenly I had a whole new reason to feel nauseated. If my father pulled in behind Cameron, there was going to be hell. He'd have to move his car so that Cameron could get out, and then he'd have to meet Cameron, and if he wasn't home yet, that meant he was going to be in awful condition. Who knew what he would do? What he would say? I had to get Cameron out of here as quickly as possible.

"So," Cameron said.

"Thanks for tonight," I told him, reaching for the door handle. I was just turning my head to go when he swooped in and his lips landed right on my earlobe.

Mortifying. Completely and utterly mortifying. I opened the car door, desperate for a quick escape.

"Wait," Cameron said.

I glanced at him and he grabbed my face between his hands. My eyes widened in surprise and he pressed his lips into mine. My heart seized and I froze up, one foot outside on the ground while the car door pinged uncontrollably. After ten seconds of lip-mashing, it was clear Cameron wasn't going to give up, and I realized that this was it. This was my first kiss. It was actually going to happen this way.

So I tried to kiss him back. I closed my eyes and moved my lips. The second I did, his tongue shot into my mouth and I almost gagged. What was happening here? This was not magical. This was not romantic. There were no fireworks. There was only the strain in my neck from my awkward position, the taste of ketchup in his mouth, and the terror that at any second I'd hear my dad's car pull up and he would drunkenly pummel this guy for mauling his daughter in the middle of his driveway.

And then, he released me. It was over. It was all I could do to keep from running my sleeve across my lips. Cameron grinned at me.

"I guess I'll talk to you tomorrow," he said.

"Okay. 'Night."

I turned away from him, blinking back tears, and slammed the car door behind me.

ACT THREE, SCENE TWELVE

In which:

IT GETS WORSE

I COULDN'T BELIEVE THAT HAD JUST HAPPENED. BEFORE I EVEN realized I'd made the decision, I was walking around the side of my house toward the backyard. I just couldn't go inside right now. Couldn't deal with my mom, who'd be worried about my dad. Couldn't deal with my dad when he did come home. I just wanted to get away.

I was halfway into the woods when I realized what a bad idea this was. I had no idea where I was going and it was pitch-black under the trees. I took a wrong step and my entire foot sank in gooey mud.

"Ugh!" Great. Now I was not only lost, cold and badly kissed, but I had also ruined my only good non-sneaker shoes. As I checked out the damage, a branch snapped nearby and my heart started to pound.

"Is someone there?" A rustle of leaves. My vision went black from fear. I gripped a nearby tree to keep from fainting.

"Hello?" I cried. Whatever you are, please just don't kill me.

"KJ?"

Finally, my ears cleared. My logic cleared. I knew that voice.

"Robbie?"

He emerged out of the darkness like a white knight. Except that he was still wearing black and gray. Just behind him, I saw the bridge. So maybe I wasn't as lost as I'd thought I was.

"What are you doing here?" he asked. He looked down and grimaced. "And what's with the mud foot?"

"I was . . . walking to the bridge," I admitted. "The mud foot was just an added bonus."

Robbie laughed. "C'mere."

He helped me hobble over to the bridge and we sat down. I peeled my shoe off and wiggled my toe inside my tights. "My mom's going to kill me."

"I'm sure you can clean it up. It's never as bad as you think it is," Robbie said.

He was such a good friend, trying to make me feel better even though he'd just had the worst night ever.

"Robbie, I am so sorry about tonight. That must have sucked with everyone in the diner staring at you and laughing. . . ."

"Whatever," Robbie said with a shrug. "I don't care what they think."

"God, I wish I could be like that," I said, awed. "I would have died if everyone had been looking at me like that."

"Yeah, well, I had more important things on my mind," he said. "Like what an idiot I was."

My heart panged. "I'm sorry. I should never have let you go out with her."

"Please. KJ. I asked for your help with her," Robbie said. "This is not your fault."

I bit my lip. "Except that it is."

"How do you figure?" he asked.

"Before you left tonight, she told me . . ."

Understanding lighted his face. "She told you she was just using me?"

"Kind of," I admitted, feeling all sour inside. "And I wanted to tell you, but—"

"Unbelievable," Robbie said. "She is unbelievable."

"I'm sorry. I should have just told you. But I . . . I wanted it to work out."

Sort of.

"Don't worry about it, KJ. If you'd told me, I would have gone anyway," he said.

"You would have?" I asked.

He nodded, but with a grimace. Like he was realizing just how silly he'd been. "I really liked her. I thought she was, like, an original, you know?"

My heart constricted. I stared down at the water beneath our feet.

"But I've been thinking about it and I just realized I barely even knew her. I just sort of made up all this stuff about her that turned out to be totally untrue." He laughed derisively. "Stuff I wanted to be true, I guess. And that sounds completely and irrevocably pathetic," he added, covering his face with his hand.

"No, it doesn't," I said, thinking of Cameron's totally unromantic kiss. "Believe me. It doesn't."

"Thanks," he said, ducking his chin.

We sat there for a moment, listening to the rustling of the leaves overhead. I took a breath. Felt at peace. Like nothing could touch us here.

"Dude, how psycho is Leo?" he said out of nowhere.

I laughed out loud. "I really thought he was going to flatten you."

"Yuh-huh!" Robbie was wide-eyed. "Have you ever actually noticed how big he is?"

I laughed. "He does have an impressive girth."

"You couldn't have pointed that out to me before I went after her?" he joked.

"Hey. You were all 'She deserves better than biker dude,'" I said, lowering my voice. "Who was I to stand in the way?"

Robbie laughed. "You know what, KJ? You're the original," he said. "You totally broke the mold, Grandma would say."

I blushed and looked away, happy for the pitch-blackness so that he couldn't see the full effect his words had on me. When I looked back again, he was still watching me. And was it just my imagination, or was his face closer to mine than before?

My heart expanded, filling my chest with hope. Was Robbie going to kiss me? Oh, please let it be better than that slop-fest with Cameron. Let kissing be way better than that was.

Robbie reached his arm around me and my eyes fluttered closed. This was it. Concentrate, KJ. Don't mess it up this time.

And then, he slapped me on the back.

"So, it seemed like you and Cameron hit it off," he said. "At least something good came out of tonight."

My eyes popped open. My heart dropped like a carnival ride. "Uh, yeah. Totally."

"Good. That's good. If he likes you, then maybe he has more functioning brain cells than I thought," Robbie said.

I forced a smile. Wow. I was really bad at this boy-girl stuff. I had thought there were signals there. Were there not signals?

"We should probably get home," Robbie said, standing, the soles of his good shoes scraping against the bridge. "There's a clearer path a little farther up. I'll show you."

He offered me his hands and hoisted me up. I pushed my foot back into my mud shoe, which was completely and totally disgusting, then trudged after him into the trees. We walked for a few minutes in silence, but I was mentally cursing myself the whole time. How could I have thought Robbie wanted to kiss me? He didn't like me. He asked me to help him get someone else. No one would ask a person they liked to help them get someone else. How stupid could I be? And that kiss with Cameron! Ugh! I was such an amateur. I mean, that had to have been me, right? Cameron must have kissed, like, hundreds of girls, so he couldn't be that bad at it. And now he probably never wanted to come near me again. And, oh God, what if Robbie realized that I had thought he was going to kiss me? Had he read my signals well while I'd completely misread his? He probably thought I was so pathetic! He was probably laughing at me right now up there, while I stared at his back, totally clueless.

I was a complete and total love failure. This was the worst night ever. It just did not get any worse than this.

We stepped out of the woods, and I recognized Fred's backyard with its creaky old swing set and huge barbecue pit. We cut around the side of his house and came out on my street a few houses up from my own. I wanted to say something to Robbie to break the awkward silence. Anything to make this awful burning sensation of shame go away. But when I looked at him, his face was flashing red and his eyes were wide with shock.

"Oh my God," he said.

My blood froze in my veins. I turned around, almost knowing what I was going to see before I saw it. The ambulance. The shattered glass. The flashing lights. The crooked telephone pole. And my father's car. My father's car. My father's car.

Totaled.

END ACT THREE

ACT FOUR, SCENE ONE

In which:

HE'S "OKAY"

I RAN. I RAN PAST THE AMBULANCE. I RAN PAST THE CAR, THE FRONT seat of which was completely collapsed.

No one could survive that. No one. . . .

I ran past the phone pole with its jagged wood shards sticking out in every direction. I ran past the cop, who yelled at me to come back. Past the spot in the driveway where I'd just been kissed. Past my mom's car. The tree my dad taught me to climb. The azalea bush he covered with fake cobwebs every Halloween. The broken step he never fixed. I ran past it all and inside my house, wanting to see him. Wishing to see him. Sitting at the kitchen table cursing the damn telephone company for their ridiculous placement of their poles.

But he wasn't there. My mother was. A policeman was. My brother was. And Fred. Totally incongruently, sitting with my brother at the bottom of the living room stairs wearing a Superman T-shirt. But then, he lived right up the street. He must have seen . . . must have heard. . . .

"Sorry, KJ," he said, standing and hiking up his pants. "I

just came over to see if everyone was all right, but if you want me to go—"

I could not for the life of me focus on what he was saying.

"Mom?" I choked.

"KJ, it's okay."

I'd never seen her so pale. Her eyes were crazy alert. Like pinpoints of nuclear energy. How could anything be okay when she looked like that?

"Mom? What—"

"He's okay," she said, putting her hands on my shoulders. "He's unconscious right now, but the EMTs don't think there are any major injuries."

Robbie reached out and squeezed my hand. It was the first moment I realized he was there. This didn't make sense. None of this made sense.

"But I don't . . . he's unconscious? How can there be no major injuries if he's unconscious?"

My mother stared at me with this look like, *You know this, KJ.* The cop cleared his throat and looked away. Understanding hit me like a hundred bottles of beer falling off the wall and crashing into my head.

He was unconscious because he was drunk. Because he had passed out at the wheel and not even the impact of his car slamming into a telephone pole had woken him.

I snorted a laugh. Anger soured my fear. "My father, ladies and gentlemen!" I announced, throwing my hands up, tearing my fingers from Robbie's. "What a winner!"

"KJ!" my mother gasped.

"What?" I said, tears stinging my eyes. My fingers clenched into fists. I was so angry, I could have pummeled something.

How could he do this to us? Here we all were, scared out of our minds, and for what? Why? Because he just had to get trashed. Because *he* couldn't freaking control himself. And Robbie was here. And Fred. This was so humiliating. *He* was so humiliating. I hated him. I wished he had died. "What!?" I snapped again. "What, Mom?"

I didn't know what I was saying. I just needed to yell. My mother took a deep breath and set her jaw.

"I am going to the hospital with your father," she said, grabbing up her purse all indignant like. As if I had done something wrong. "I would appreciate it if you would stay here and watch your brother."

"Fine," I said through my teeth.

"I'll stay with you," Robbie said quietly.

"Thank you, Robbie. That would be a great help," my mother said. Like they were friends all of a sudden. Compadres. The calm ones who were rising above it all while crazy KJ lost her shit.

"Me, too. If no one minds," Fred said, glancing at me uncertainly. "Maybe Chris can show me his new PlayStation games."

"Okay. Thanks, Fred." My mother turned to me. "I'll call you as soon as I know anything," she said firmly—slowly. Like she was talking to an imbecile.

She walked by, the cop trailing her out, his hip radio crackling and blurting words like *dispatch* and *call in*. I stood there for a second, trying to get control of myself, but it wasn't going to happen. I couldn't just let her walk out of here like some kind of martyr trailing after her fallen husband. This was his fault. All his. This hadn't happened to him. He'd made it happen. I couldn't take it anymore, all the hypocrisy and silence and complacency. I turned around and walked outside, slamming the door behind me. My mother stopped, said a few words to the officer and waited for me to catch up.

"What're you going to do?" I demanded, practically blind with rage.

"What do you mean?" she asked.

"I mean, when he wakes up. *If* he wakes up, what're you going to do?" I said. "You're going to make him quit this time, right? You have to make him quit."

"KJ—"

"You have to do something, Mom! We can't live like this! It's wrong. No one lives like this! Did you even see Christopher? Did you see his face!? How can you not do something? You've got to make him stop!"

I was gasping for breath, tears streaming down my cheeks. I knew I was shouting, but I didn't care. Let the whole neighborhood hear me. They already knew. They'd already seen what he'd done.

"KJ, I can't make your father do anything," she said, exhausted. "You should know that by now."

Then she gave me this look. This look that cut right through my heart. She gave me this look like she was disappointed in me. Like I was the one who had disappointed her tonight. And then she left me there, sobbing alone, to go off and be with my dad.

ACT FOUR, SCENE TWO

In which:

I MAKE A CALL

AFTER A FEW MINUTES I COMPOSED MYSELF. I DRIED MY FACE AND walked back into the house. Walked past Robbie. Past Fred. Christopher careened into me, clinging to my legs. I put one hand on his head as I picked up the phone and dialed without thinking about the numbers.

"Hello?" Stephanie's voice obliterated the dam that was barely holding back my tears. Even if she did sound pissed. Just like that, I started to cry again. A choking, gasping, incoherent sob.

"KJ! What's wrong?" she asked, instantly herself again.

"My father. My father had an accident. He's going to the hospital. Can you come? Steph. I'm so sorry. Can you please come?" I had no idea what I was saying. "Please?"

"I'll be there in five minutes."

The phone line went dead. I crouched down and hugged my brother until we both stopped crying, and couldn't have cared less that both Fred and Robbie were standing there awkwardly, witnessing it all.

ACT FOUR, SCENE THREE

In which:

I HAVE FRIENDS

I WOKE WITH MY HEART IN MY THROAT. FRED WAS CARRYING MY little brother up the living room stairs. He didn't see me see him, and I watched him all the way up. I didn't know why he was there.

"Hey. You okay?"

I looked up. Robbie was rubbing his eyes. My head was in his lap.

That was when it all came rushing back. The crash. Christopher's face. My mother's disappointment. My father . . .

I sat up. The cable box clock read 1:34.

"Sorry," I said, pushing my hair behind my ears. "Sorry."

"Sorry for what?" Robbie asked.

My brain was cloudy, and my eyes felt puffy and dry. When I tried to breathe, my nose was clogged.

"For . . ." I looked down at his lap. His jeans. My face was warm and itchy where my cheek had rested on his thigh. "I fell asleep."

"Yeah. So did I," he said. He reached back and rubbed his neck. Yawned. He'd let me fall asleep in his lap while he sat up straight on my couch. Who did that? What kind of incredible, kind, sweet boy did that?

There was a creak on the stairs and Fred appeared. At the same time, Stephanie stepped to the kitchen door, holding a glass of water. "Hey," they both said.

"Hey," Robbie and I replied.

We all looked at one another. What to say?

"He's asleep." Fred pointed with his thumb up the stairs. He'd stayed, too. He'd just carried my brother to bed. What had I done to deserve any of this? Nothing. Zero. Negative whatever.

"Thanks," I said.

"Yeah, no problem. No problem." Fred knocked one hand against the other. "I guess I'll go now. My mom's probably sitting up."

I pushed myself up from the couch and walked over to him. My arms were clutched around myself, even though I wasn't cold.

"Thank you so much, Fred. For everything," I said. "It was so amazing of you to stay, I mean, especially after everything . . ."

Fred shrugged. "What're friends for?"

Tears stung my eyes. It was so simple for him. So blissfully simple. In that moment I loved that about him. He was my friend. He always had been and it looked like he always would be. No matter what. I reached out and hugged him.

"I'm really sorry, Fred," I mumbled into his shoulder.

He patted me on the back awkwardly. "It's okay. It's cool. We're cool."

Then I heard a jangle of keys and I sprang back. My mother walked in through the kitchen door and closed it quietly behind her. She let out a huge sigh, then froze when she saw all four of us standing there on the other side of the room.

"You're still here," she said.

My heart felt sick. I tried to read her. Tried to get any indication of what was going on without actually asking the question. I couldn't ask the question. There was no way.

"Is he . . . is Mr. Miller okay?" Stephanie asked, looking sideways at me.

"He's going to be just fine."

My mother placed her things down on the table. I took a deep breath. I was surprised at how relieved I was. I wasn't kidding when I said I wished he had died. A very, very big part of me salivated for a life without him. Without this. Without all the pain and embarrassment and fear. And still, I was relieved he wasn't dead. And surprised that I was relieved. What was wrong with me? I was an awful daughter. An awful person.

"Good," Robbie said. "That's . . . good."

My mother rubbed her temples. She came over and put her arm around me. I stiffened. "You kids should be getting home. Your parents will be worried."

"Okay," Fred said, ducking his head. "'Night, KJ. 'Night, Mrs. Miller."

"Thanks again, Fred," I said as he loped toward the door.

"I'll drive you," Stephanie offered to Robbie.

"Okay." He turned to me, his hands in the back pockets of his jeans. "Well . . . uh . . . good night, I guess."

There was this sort of anguished look in his eyes. Like there was something he really wanted to say, but couldn't. Because my mom was there. Because the situation sucked. Whatever the reason. On any other night I would have immediately started obsessing about what it could be, but tonight, I didn't have it in me.

"'Night," I said. "Thanks."

"I'll call you tomorrow," he said. "Or today. Later. You know."

I managed a smile. "I know." I walked them to the door. "Steph?"

She looked at me. I didn't even know where to begin.

"I know," she said. Then she hugged me really, really hard. "I'll talk to you later."

My heart felt ridiculously full, then hollow again when I saw the jagged dent in the pole behind her. "Thanks," I said quietly.

I closed the door. My mother kissed my head and squeezed me. "He's going to be okay."

I slid away from her, annoyed, clutching myself so tightly I could practically touch my fingertips to my fingertips behind my back.

"Did you talk to him?" I said flatly.

My mother took a breath, and shook her head as she gazed at the floor. "I'm exhausted, KJ. I need to sleep right now."

"But Mom—"

"KJ. It's time for bed," she told me, leveling me with a glare.

My face reddened with anger as she walked past me toward her room. I'd take that as a no.

ACT FOUR, SCENE FOUR

In which:

LIES ARE TOLD

MY MOTHER MADE ME GO SEE MY FATHER IN THE HOSPITAL. He looked completely normal, except for the bruises on his arm and the bandage on the side of his head. He smiled ingratiatingly at me when I walked in. I felt like my insides were gnawing on my heart from every direction. He knew. He knew how mad I was.

"Hey, kiddo."

I sat down in the chair next to his bed, and it wheezed as all the air escaped from the vinyl. My phone vibrated in my pocket. I took it out to check the screen and my heart lurched. It was Cameron. Third time today. And the third time I was not going to pick up.

I was psyched he was calling me, of course. Of course I was. But I couldn't even fathom trying to be the chipper, don't-you-want-to-date-me girl. Meanwhile I had tried to call Tama four times to tell her what was going on, but kept getting her machine. She was my friend. I figured she'd want to know. Still, I'd yet to get a call back.

"You're supposed to turn those off inside the hospital," my father said.

The very fact that he was telling me what to do right then made me want to scream. I placed the phone back in my pocket without turning it off.

"KJ, I know you're angry with me," he said.

I scoffed and rolled my eyes. Here it comes. . . .

"And you have every right to be. I haven't been a very good father lately."

I stared at the mattress. The white waffle blanket bunched up near his feet. I'd heard this all before.

"And I know how scared you must have been."

"I wasn't scared," I snapped. *I wanted you to be dead. I wanted it.*

"Well, I was," he said. "I want you to know that things are going to change. This isn't going to happen again."

Yeah. Sure. That lie was so big I was surprised his pajama pants didn't burst into flames.

"I promise you, KJ. This is my wake-up call," he said, tears in his voice. "I'm going to go to those meetings. I'm going to get better."

"Okay, Dad," I said sarcastically.

"You don't believe me."

"I said okay," I replied, looking at him for the first time.

We stared at each other. The pleading-yet-condescending look on his face made me want to cry. Like he was mocking me for thinking he wasn't going to make good on his promise. Like my anger and disbelief were somehow amusing. Like he knew so much more than I did. But I knew I was right. I knew he'd be all squeaky clean for a few days, maybe a month, and then go right back to drinking and making everyone miserable. He'd never done anything to prove me wrong.

"Can I get a hug?" he asked.

I rolled my eyes again, but stood, knowing that this ritual meant the conversation was almost over. His arm was all purple and yellow and brown.

"Won't it hurt?" I hedged, hoping to get out of it.

"It doesn't matter," he said.

So I leaned in and put my hands around his shoulders and closed my eyes and turned my face away from him. He kissed the top of my head and lifted his arms to squeeze me. I held my breath and waited for the hypocrisy to be over. The second his arms fell away, I was out of there without a second glance.

"I love you, KJ."

Yuh-huh.

My mother was waiting for me outside the room, holding Christopher's hand. "How'd it go?"

"If he thinks I'm believing him this time, he's cracked," I said.

"I wish you didn't have so much anger, KJ," my mother said.

"Yeah, well, I didn't ask to be this way," I told her. I reached for Christopher's hand. "Come on, little man. Let's go get some candy."

He grabbed my fingers and we walked off. "Do you think Dad's gonna be okay?" he asked hopefully.

My heart splintered down the center, and I nearly crushed his hand. "Of course he is, Christopher. He always is."

ACT FOUR, SCENE FIVE

In which:

THINGS SETTLE

"So, it's a pact, then?" I said to Stephanie, facing her on the couch in my living room. Some random Adam Sandler movie, part of Stephanie's patented mind-numbing movie marathon, played on the TV. "We never fight again?"

"It's a pact."

She reached over our assortment of snacks to shake my hand. I watched her happily take a handful of popcorn and crunch into it, just hoping she wouldn't renege when she heard what I had to say next.

"There's something I have to tell you," I announced.

"What?" she asked, licking some salt from her fingers.

"I went out on a date with Cameron. An actual date," I said. I still could not believe I had done that without Stephanie knowing.

"You did!? When?" she demanded.

"Friday night. Before . . ." I looked away. Looked out the window at the freakishly sunny day.

"Oh. Whoa. Some night," Stephanie said.

"No lie. And there's something else," I told her.

"What?"

"He kissed me."

"Katie Jean Miller!" She bounced up and down, sending popcorn, pretzels and M&M's everywhere. Then she noticed my cringe and stopped. "Oh. Was it not good?"

"No. Not at all," I told her, hugging a pillow to my chest. "But it was my fault. I mean, it had to be my fault, right?"

"I don't know." She was thoughtful. "Did it feel like your fault?"

"It felt like he was feeling up my esophagus with his tongue," I told her.

"Ew! Oh, God. Gross." She dropped some popcorn back in the bowl. "That does not sound like your fault. Maybe Cameron Richardson is a bad kisser!"

"No! You think?"

"Seems like it."

We looked at each other, wide-eyed, marveling at the very idea that someone as worshipped as Cameron, someone who was good at everything, could possibly be bad at the one thing that was of the utmost importance.

Finally Stephanie sighed. "Not to change the subject, but I have something to tell you, too."

"You kissed Cameron, too?" I joked.

"No. I kind of have a new crush," she said, averting her eyes.

I knew it! "I *knew* it!" I told her. "Who? Who is it?"

"It's Andy Terrero." She looked at me quickly, uncertainly, then covered her face with both hands. "I'm such a loser!"

"What? Why? Andy's a nice guy!" I told her.

In fact, now that I thought about it, Andy and Stephanie made so much sense. They were both mature, they were both into science and they were even of similar, wispy-thin heights. They would look perfect walking into the prom together.

"Oh my God! This is why you asked him for help with your math that day!" I said, shoving her leg. "I knew you didn't actually need help! You're such the vixen."

"It's not like it matters," she said, blushing. "He totally wants you! I want the geek-sloppy seconds of my best friend!" she wailed.

I cracked up laughing. Couldn't help it. "Steph, he's not my sloppy anything. And he can't like me anymore after the way I freaked out on him that night. He hasn't asked me a single survey question since. He's totally over me."

"Really?" she asked, peeking over her fingertips. "You think?"

The doorbell rang at that moment and I pushed myself up. "I'm not even remotely an expert on what boys think, but with that one, I'm pretty sure I'm right."

I whipped open the front door and my heart caught. Standing on my doorstep was Robbie Delano. Just one of the many boys I could never hope to understand. He lifted a Dunkin' Donuts bag.

"I come with sugar," he said.

I could already smell the cinnamon through the bag. "You are a god."

"You know, if you say that too loudly we could both get struck down," he scolded.

"Come in."

I walked ahead of him through the kitchen and suddenly, surprisingly, I couldn't stop smiling. After that emotional nightmare of a night, he'd come back.

"Is your mom home?" he asked.

"She's at the hospital with my brother, and then they're

going to my aunt's for dinner," I told him. "I have pizza money, if you're up for it."

"Perfection," he said with a grin. "How's your dad?"

"He's fine. Whatever. I don't want to talk about it."

Mind-numbing. I was all about the mind-numbing. And holding on to this giddy feeling that was crowding out the gray.

"Works for me."

"Hey," Stephanie said, sitting up in surprise when she saw Robbie in my living room. She quickly picked up the snack tray and moved it to the coffee table, swiping up the mess she'd made while bouncing.

"What're we watching?" Robbie threw his coat on the chair like he owned the place.

"*Mr. Deeds*," Stephanie replied.

"Sweet."

Robbie popped open the doughnut box and offered it to Stephanie, then to me. I took a cinnamon and curled up in the center of the couch, lifting the throw blanket over my legs. Robbie dropped down next to me.

"May I?" He gestured at the blanket.

"Uh . . . sure."

And there we were. Me, Steph and Robbie. Sitting under one blanket on my living room couch on a Sunday afternoon, sharing a box of doughnuts.

It was amazing how everything could be so perfect, even when everything was so not.

ACT FOUR, SCENE SIX

In which:

I MAKE A DATE

MONDAY MORNING, FROM THE MOMENT I STEPPED INTO SCHOOL, people were whispering. I could feel them talking about me, pointing me out to their friends.

She's the one. Her dad got into that accident.

I hear he's still in the hospital.

Who drives their car into a telephone pole?

I so loved living in a small town. Everyone knew everyone else's business within five seconds of said business being conducted. Or in this case, crashed. I was at my locker, trying to ignore the whispers of a few of my classmates, when Cameron's voice cut through the chatter.

"KJ!"

I turned around, and my breath caught. I have to say that if Cameron Richardson was hot on a normal day, on a day of crises he was perfectly beautiful. He was all puffed up and harried, and when he stopped in front of me, his blue eyes were filled with concern.

He shot a look at the girls who were gossiping in my direction. "What?" he snapped.

They instantly scurried away. Wow. I could get used to that.

"Hey! I heard about your dad," he said under his breath. "Why didn't you return any of my calls?"

"I'm sorry. I was just . . ."

Embarrassed. Horrified. Exhausted. Completely unsure of why you were calling me and even more completely incapable of talking about the date, the kiss, the crash.

"I was too busy, you know, visiting him in the hospital and stuff."

Liar. You're going to hell, KJ. Straight to hell.

"Oh. Okay. That makes sense. I was worried though," he said. "Are you okay?"

He was worried about me. Cameron Richardson was sitting around over the weekend, worrying. About me. He was so, *so* sweet.

"Yeah," I told him with a small smile. "Yeah. I'm fine. He's gonna be fine. Everything's fine."

"Good, well . . . let me know if you need anything, all right?" he said. "Like, anything."

Now I was smiling for real. "All right."

"Do you wanna do something? Like, tomorrow night maybe?" he said. "Maybe get your mind off stuff?"

Brain freeze. Did Cameron just ask me out? For real? But I thought my kiss had sucked and he'd thought I was a loser and— What was I waiting for? A solid gold invitation?

"Yeah . . . sure." I only had about ten million things to do and worry about, what with my dad coming home tonight and the musical opening on Wednesday and homework and everything, but sure. Yeah. A Tuesday night date? No problem.

“Cool.” Then he winked and walked into homeroom, leaving me all warm and giddy and happy. Kind of like I’d been yesterday afternoon when Robbie had shown up at my house with doughnuts.

Okay. So my life was still a little complicated.

ACT FOUR, SCENE SEVEN

In which:

I'M THE BITCH

THAT AFTERNOON, TAMA SAT ALONE IN HER PRIVATE DRESSING room, humming "Summer Lovin'" while she worked on her eye makeup. I hadn't talked to her since Friday night, and seeing her made me feel all twisty inside.

"Hey, KJ! Good!" she said when she saw me in the mirror. "So listen, I was wondering if you could put Janice in charge of just my props for the dress rehearsal today. I really need somebody to be on top of things for me."

What she was saying made no sense at that moment. "What?"

She clucked her tongue and turned around, draping her arm on the back of her chair. "How are we supposed to have a decent run-through if our stage manager is half out of it?" she joked with a smile.

"Tama . . . didn't you get any of my messages?" I said under my breath.

"Oh, yeah! That's right! How's your dad?" she asked. Like he'd just stubbed his toe. Like my entire family hadn't just spent the weekend on edge.

"He's in the hospital. Why didn't you call me back?" I asked.

She shrugged and returned to her eyeliner. "I don't know. You said he was going to be fine, right? So I figured, what was the point? Besides, Leo and I were crazy busy all weekend, making up, if you know what I mean."

I was speechless. Completely and utterly speechless. She couldn't come up for air long enough to call me and inquire about my dad's near-death experience? I had thought we were friends. Real friends. How could she be so casual about something like this?

"So . . . what about Janice?" Tama asked again.

And then I knew. I knew in that moment that everything Ashley said was true. Tama *was* using me. She didn't give a crap about me and my family. She was just being nice to me so she could get her way on stage. I was so, *so* stupid!

"So, you've forgotten all about Robbie then," I said.

Her brow knit. "Excuse me?"

"Refresh my memory. Didn't you tell me on Friday night that you were going to dump Leo for Robbie?" I said. "Now, all of a sudden, Leo's your man again."

"Look, KJ. That conversation in the bathroom never happened," she said, standing. "Especially not after the scene he made. He totally humiliated me."

"Well, why not?" I asked. "I saw how excited you were! You really liked Robbie, yet you were totally rude to him. And now you have, like, zero guilt over the way that you used him!"

"Uh, do you need a ladder to get down off that high horse of yours or do you just want me to catch you?" she asked, whipping a poodle skirt off its hanger.

"What? What's that supposed to mean?" I said.

"It means, you're one to talk, princess," Tama spat. "You used me, too. To get to Cameron. Everyone uses everyone else to get what they want. That's just the way the world works. Don't act so innocent when you're just as bad as the rest of us."

My brain was having a seriously hard time catching up with her weaving logic. I blushed and lowered my voice. "Wait a minute. It was your idea to get me together with Cameron. I did not ask for your help."

"Oh, gimme a break. Like you didn't jump at the chance the second I mentioned it," Tama said, stepping into the skirt and yanking it up. "You practically licked my hand, you were so excited."

I was going to be sick. I really was. How could she talk to me like this?

"You got what you wanted and I got what I wanted," Tama said, grabbing a white sweater. "It doesn't matter how you get there, as long as you get there."

"Wow, Tama. With that kind of attitude it's no wonder you're in therapy," I said.

Tama's jaw dropped. I froze. Had I really just said that? I wanted to take it back the moment I heard it, but it was too late. The damage, by the look on her face, was very much done.

"You are *such* a bitch," she spat. She tore her shirt off and jammed the sweater on over her head. "You walk around here like you're all high-and-mighty and angelic and above everyone else, but really, you're nothing but a bitch."

She shoved past me and out the door, grabbing her saddle shoes along the way. She slammed the door, which knocked over a hat rack, which crashed behind me and barred the door. My heart was pounding so hard and fast, I had to lean against the wall to keep from blacking out.

I felt awful. Just awful. Tama had told me about her therapist in confidence and I'd just thrown it right in her face, just to get back at her. What kind of person did that? She was right. I was a bitch. Sweet little KJ Miller had morphed into a bitch.

ACT FOUR, SCENE EIGHT

In which:

GLENN GETS AN EARFUL

I DIDN'T LIKE THE WAY IT FELT. BEING THE BITCH. I DIDN'T LIKE IT at all. It made my insides feel black. Sour. Kind of the way I felt whenever I thought about my dad. I didn't want to feel that way about myself. I couldn't. But I realized that was exactly how I'd been feeling, a little bit more each day, ever since that night I'd first told off Glenn. Sure, it had felt good in the moment—freeing. But it wasn't me. I wasn't going to let it be me.

We had thirty minutes until the dress rehearsal started. There was a ton of stuff I needed to do, but I didn't care. I found Glenn in the AV booth, hunched over the motherboard, drinking his Yoo-hoo. One spill and the system was toast, but that was a conversation for another time.

"Glenn. I need to talk to you."

He turned around in his swivel chair. His expression clouded over. My heart turned, but I screwed up my courage.

"I just wanted to say I'm sorry if I hurt your feelings that night at the diner. That was wrong of me to talk to you that way," I said.

He seemed confused, surprised. Then smug. "Thank you, KJ. I accept your apology."

My hand curled into a fist at his attitude, but I forced my fingers open again. He turned back to his board, but I wasn't finished.

"Glenn. Wait. I'm not finished," I forced myself to say.

He raised his eyebrows and looked at me.

"I *am* sorry. But you owe me an apology, too," I said. "You hurt my feelings all the time," I said quickly, evenly. "You can't just walk around grabbing people the way you're always grabbing me. It's rude and it hurts and it's also very invasive. It makes me very uncomfortable and you do it all the time."

Glenn started to look ill. Like he didn't want to hear this. Well, he was going to.

"And you know what else? Your lewd remarks aren't cute or sexy or remotely attractive. They're just offensive."

Glenn was starting to go green.

"Now, I'm not saying this to be mean or anything, Glenn. You just need to know how you make me feel. I should have told you a long time ago, but I . . . I just couldn't," I told him. "And I know you don't want to talk to me anymore, but if you ever decide that you do, I hope you'll treat me with a little respect and not, you know, constantly be staring at me like you're imagining what I look like naked."

I self-consciously gathered my sweater over my chest and held it there, forcing myself to look down at Glenn. I wanted to give him a chance to say something, after all. To apologize, ideally. Instead he just turned around slowly and lifted a pair of huge headphones over his ears. Then he cranked up the volume on some awful guitar music, pointedly shutting me out.

I took a deep breath. Well, fine. So maybe he hadn't reacted the way I'd hoped, but at least I'd finally told him the truth. And Glenn was just the beginning.

ACT FOUR, SCENE NINE

In which:

THE CHART IS REVEALED

I PRACTICALLY TRIPPED OVER ANDY IN THE TINY BANK OF STAIRS between the auditorium seats and the stage. He was sitting there alone, staring down at his ubiquitous notebook, but he scrambled up the second I arrived.

"Oh, hey, KJ. Sorry. I was just . . . sorry. I'll go." He pocketed his book, shoved his glasses up and grabbed his backpack. I hated that I had made him so nervous.

"Andy! Wait."

He stopped midstep and almost tripped over, but grabbed the handrail at the last second. "You need me to do something?"

"No. It's just . . . listen, I'm sorry about what I said at Fred's party that night," I told him. "You didn't deserve to be yelled at like that, and I'm sorry."

Andy looked at the steps and shifted his weight. "Actually, I'm sorry," he said.

I blinked. "Huh?"

"I feel pretty stupid," he said, hazarding a glance at me. "About that whole survey thing?"

Well. This wasn't going the way I thought it would. Did anything, ever? "Okay. . . ."

"I mean, of course you figured out what I was doing. You're a pretty smart person." He started kicking the wall beneath the lockers.

I chewed my lip. "So you really were trying to see how much we have in common?"

His head bobbed up and down. "Yeah, but no matter how much I crunch the numbers, scientifically speaking, we're just not compatible. I wish we were, but we're just not." He pulled out his notebook again and flipped it open. "I give us only a thirty-two percent probability of success if we were to start going out."

I had to bite back a laugh. "Thirty-two percent. That's not good."

"Nope. Not at all. Not good at all." He turned around and leaned back against the wall, shaking his head as he ran a hand down the page. "I was going to tell you that night that, you know, I was going to stop annoying you, but then you went all ballistic, so . . ."

I blushed. "You didn't have to."

"Yeah," he said with a sheepish smile. "Anyway . . . I have to listen to the chart, you know. The chart doesn't lie."

"The chart? What chart?" Now that I'd been set free of it, I was suddenly very interested in this whole process.

"The compatibility chart," Andy said, turning the notebook toward me. Sketched out on the graph paper page was a chart full of color-coded zigzagging lines. My name was written in a tiny, square print across the horizontal axis, Andy's across the vertical. I had no idea what it meant, but it looked pretty impressive.

"Wow. You really put a lot of time into this," I said.

"I had to. Matters of the heart are very important. You don't want to make any mistakes," Andy said quite seriously. "And in math, there are no mistakes. There's a right answer and a wrong answer. Putting the two together just made sense."

I grinned. "You sound just like Stephanie."

"Do I?" he asked.

Stephanie was going to kill me for what I was about to do, but I was so sure it was going to work out, I had to do it.

"You know what, Andy? I want to answer more survey questions, if you don't mind," I said.

"But I already told you, the numbers don't lie—"

"I know. I know. I'm not going to answer them for me. I'm going to answer them as if I were Stephanie," I said.

His brow creased. "Stephanie Shumer?"

"Yep. You want to talk compatibility?" I said, looping my arm over his bony shoulder. "Let me tell you about my best friend. . . ."

ACT FOUR, SCENE TEN

In which:

WE SHARE

I SAT OUTSIDE THE T-BIRDS' DRESSING ROOM WITH A TWIX BAR from the vending machine in my hand. The guys kept walking in and out, eyeing me curiously. But I didn't move until Fred loped out, his blond hair slicked back with two tons of gel, his belly barely restrained by his T-Bird T-shirt.

"Fred. I got you something."

He paused and looked at me like he'd never seen me before. I couldn't believe how hard my heart was pounding.

"I love Twix," he said finally, glancing from the candy to my face. "Is that really for me?"

"Yeah," I said with a smile.

He took the candy bar and held it with both hands like it was the golden ticket itself. I realized right then that I had never given Fred anything before in my life. He'd given me valentine cards and birthday cards and cupcakes and cookies and all kinds of trinkets and notes, but I'd never given him a thing. He'd even been there on the worst night of my life, even though I had publicly torn him to shreds just days before. Looking at him right then, I felt like crying.

"Fred, I'm really sorry," I said.

He blushed and looked at the ground. "I told you already, KJ. We're okay."

"No. We're not. You need to know something, Fred. I figured it out just now, and I have to tell you now before I lose my nerve," I said.

He stared at me, his blue eyes wide.

"You're one of my best friends, Fred," I said past a lump in my throat. "And I don't want that to ever change, okay?"

His entire face lighted up. Like I'd just given him his own puppy on Christmas morning. "Me neither," he said. "You're one of my best friends, too, KJ."

"Good," I said. "Then it's settled."

"It's settled," he said with a nod, tearing into the candy bar. He slipped out one of the Twix and held it out to me. "Share?"

I laughed and we clicked candy bars. "Share."

ACT FOUR, SCENE ELEVEN

In which:

THERE'S A WALKOUT

"'Oh, don't tell me that's why you're wearing that thing,'" Robbie-as-Danny said. "'Gettin' ready to show your skivvies to a buncha jocks?'"

Tama rolled her eyes. "*Horny* jocks."

I hung my head backstage. What was she doing? She couldn't correct Robbie right in the middle of a scene. This was a dress rehearsal.

"This is why on-set romances should be verboten," Ashley whispered. "They're a total disaster."

Tama had been phoning it in all rehearsal. Especially when she was on stage with Robbie. She barely even looked at him, stepped on all his lines, and now this.

"What?" Robbie said.

"You're supposed to say *horny* jocks," Tama said. "God, get it right."

"Tama! This is a dress rehearsal. You're not to be correcting anyone," Mr. Katz grumbled. "You wouldn't do that the night of the show, would you?"

"*She* probably would," Ashley whispered under her breath.

"Well, if he'd get it right, I wouldn't have to," Tama said, exasperated.

"Sorry, Mr. Katz," Robbie said. Like it was his fault. Please. The line worked just fine without the *horny.*

"It's all right, Robbie. Let's just continue from your line," Mr. Katz said, rolling his hand.

Robbie looked at Tama. She twirled her baton—this was the Sandy-as-cheerleader part of the show—and gazed out at the audience. I saw Robbie steel himself for another try.

"'Oh, don't tell me that's why you're wearing that thing. Gettin' ready to show your skivvies to a—'"

"'Don't tell me you're jealous, Danny,'" Tama interrupted.

Mr. Katz groaned and sank lower in his seat in the audience. Tama had just cut off Robbie's funniest line. My blood boiled.

"Unbelievable," Ashley said.

Ashley was right. One bad date was killing our entire production. Robbie gamely tried to continue, but then Tama stepped on his next line. Then his next. Then she tossed her baton up and, I swear this was on purpose, it came right down on his head.

"Ow!" he shouted, doubling over.

The drama dudes, lounging in the wings, cracked up laughing. Mr. Katz popped a Tums and closed his eyes. Well, fine. If he wasn't going to do anything, I would.

"All right! That's it! Cut!" I shouted, walking out onto the stage.

"KJ. You heard Mr. Katz. This is a dress rehearsal," Tama said, blinking innocently.

"I don't care," I said. "If this is how you play the role, the show's gonna suck anyway, so what difference would it make if the stage manager made an appearance?"

There were a few chuckles around the room, but Mr. Katz just shook his head, his eyes still closed.

"Me? What did I do?" Tama asked.

"Oh, come on! You're stepping on all of his lines. You won't even look at him. We can't put on *Grease* with a Sandy and Danny that have zero chemistry!" I cried.

"Hey, I'm trying!" Tama spat. "It's not my fault if he can't act!"

"Hey!" Robbie protested.

Tama ignored him. "You're just taking his side because you're mad at me. How very professional of you, KJ."

"Well, at least she's doing her job!"

Tama and I both turned around to find Ashley striding across the stage toward us.

"Oh, here we go. Please, oh queen of the theater, tell me what I'm doing wrong!" Tama said sarcastically.

"Well, you're taking out your personal life on our production, for one," Ashley said. "Get over yourself already. Did you know that during the filming of *An Officer and a Gentleman*, Richard Gere and Debra Winger absolutely detested each other? But you can't tell that on film, can you? No! Because they were actors!"

"I don't know who those people are," Tama said blankly.

"She's right, Tama. I mean, it's a totally old reference, but whatever," Cory said, coming in from the opposite wing with her sister.

"Yeah. So what if you don't like the guy?" Carrie added. "That's why it's called acting."

Whoa. Wait a minute. Was I really seeing this? Were the Drama Twins and Ashley Brown really standing up to Tama? How many times could hell freeze over in one calendar year?

"It's not that old of a reference," Ashley moped. "I mean, not if you know great cinema."

"I would have gone with Chad Michael Murray and Sophia Bush," Cory replied. "Much more appropriate since they, you know, were married and broke up and still had to work together," Carrie agreed.

Ashley's eyes lighted up. "Ooh. I didn't think of that!"

"Hello? Mr. Katz! Can you please tell them to get off the stage so that we can get back to rehearsal?" Tama cried.

He opened his eyes briefly, but I spoke before he could.

"Not until you admit what you're doing and fix it," I said. "You're one of the leads. Start acting like one!"

"Nice," Robbie said under his breath.

I bit back a smile.

"I don't believe this!" Tama shouted. "I *am* one of the leads! I *am*! And I've been working my butt off this entire time trying to make this show better than all the crap ass shows they've put on at this school for the past five years."

"Hey!" Ashley protested.

"But do any of you care? No-o-o! Do any of you appreciate me? No-o-o. So you know what? That's it! I've had enough!" Tama shouted. "I don't need you people! I don't need any of this crap! I quit!"

"What?" I gasped.

"Yeah. You heard me. Have fun putting on *Grease* without a Sandy!"

Tama turned around and stormed off the stage, right past the drama dudes, who were now so convulsed with laughter they were literally rolling around on the floor. Suddenly, my knees felt weak. So weak, in fact, that I found myself sitting on the stage with the spotlight blaring down on me.

"She did not just do that," I said.

"Oh yeah, she did," Cory said, sounding almost amused.

"And they call *us* the Drama Twins," Carrie added.

"What?" Mr. Katz was on his feet. Suddenly alert. "What just happened? Did our lead actress actually just quit?"

"Uh, I think she kinda did," Robbie said.

"Well, that is just not acceptable. We can't have that. Opening night is the day after tomorrow. We can't go on without a Sandy," Mr. Katz blabbered. He turned from side to side, looking around at the extras and bit players as if one of them would do him the favor of shape-shifting into Tama Gold.

"Mr. Katz!" Ashley said, stepping upstage and raising her hand. "I'll play Sandy!"

"Ashley, you can't play Sandy," I said, looking up at her. She was one big blur, thanks to all the stage lights over her head. "You're Rizzo."

"So? I can do both. I'm a professional."

I hung my head in my hands and groaned. We were so screwed.

END ACT FOUR

ACT FIVE, SCENE ONE

In which:

DEAR OLD DAD RETURNS

CHRISTOPHER AND I SAT ON OPPOSITE ENDS OF THE COUCH, WITH the TV volume down low, listening for my mother's car. I twisted the fringe on the wool throw around and around my fingertip until it was glowing red. I was so sick of people letting me down. I was nice to everyone. I always tried to do what was right. But everyone just kept letting me down. My dad, my mom, Tama. Couldn't anybody just do what they were supposed to do? Couldn't anyone just be responsible? Couldn't anyone keep a promise?

I mean, it wasn't that hard really. My whole life was being responsible, caring about other people, being there when I was supposed to be there. And maybe some people think that's dorky or something, but it felt good to be those things. Why did no one else seem to get that?

Headlights flashed on the front window. Christopher and I looked at each other and jumped up. We hovered by the door for what felt like forever. I was filled to the brim with bubbly hope and sour dread. Like a fresh cup of coffee lightened with week-old milk. Christopher pushed the curtain aside and glanced out. He grabbed the doorknob with both hands and opened it. I heard my father's shuffling footsteps pause.

"Hey, kiddo."

"Hi, Dad! You look good!" Christopher said, which made my mom and dad chuckle.

My heart pounded with nerves. Was he going to want to "talk"? To sit us down, as he sometimes did, and tell us all about how things were going to change? I didn't think I could deal with that right now. That was so not what I needed. For once I was hoping for the ruse. For the play. *The Miller Family Presents: A Normal Family! A Limited Engagement. One Night Only!*

Christopher stepped back to let them in, and my mother went straight to the bedroom with my dad's bag. Dad was moving slowly, but he made it over the step. Christopher closed the door behind him.

"Hi, sweetie," my dad said, reaching out to touch my cheek with his hand.

I held my breath and forced myself not to flinch away. I was still angry at him, which made it hard, but I didn't want to start anything.

"We got your favorite," he said, producing a bag from behind his back.

"KFC!" Christopher cheered. "Yes!"

"I'll get the plates," I said.

I went to the cabinet and said a silent prayer that we could just get through dinner. If we could just get through this meal without a scene, then I could go to my room and close the door. Shut everything out. I just needed to get through dinner. Just get through this night.

I'd deal with tomorrow, tomorrow.

ACT FIVE, SCENE TWO

In which:

WE UNITE OVER A COMMON CAUSE

"TAMA DIDN'T COME TO SCHOOL TODAY," FRED ANNOUNCED THE moment I walked out of history class. He was sweaty and out of breath, and his bangs were stuck to his forehead.

"How the heck did you get here so fast?" I asked him. The bell had just rung. The reverberations still hung in the air.

"Told Maynard I was gonna ralph. You know how bodily functions skeev him," Fred said proudly.

"Yes. An odd trait for a gym teacher," I said as the rest of the class crowded out behind me. "So, wait, she's not even here?"

I had planned on spending my lunch period talking her down, stroking her ego and convincing her she had to do the musical. If I could just put an end to this particular crisis, then maybe I could go on my date with Cameron tonight and actually not be stressed. But if Tama was home playing sick . . .

"She wasn't in homeroom, and Jonathan said she never showed for Spanish, either." Fred yanked up on his jeans. "She's MIA."

There was no way. There was just no way that Tama was actually doing this to us. All that work. All those rehearsals.

Why would she do all of that and then quit? Didn't she see how insane this was?

"Well, we have to call her," I said, starting to panic. "She can't do this."

We turned the corner and saw Ashley, Robbie, Steph and Andy all waiting for us outside the doors to the cafeteria. Ashley immediately threw her hands up.

"She's not here! What're we gonna do?" she squeaked.

"We are so screwed," Stephanie said. "People have already bought tickets! They're gonna want their money back and—"

"This never would have happened if Mr. Katz had just cast me as Sandy and Stephanie as Rizzo, like we wanted," Ashley pointed out.

I glanced at Stephanie. I hadn't thought she'd admitted her lust for the Rizzo part to anyone but me. She shrugged meekly. "We were just talking about it."

"This is all my fault," Robbie said, shaking his head. "I should've never gone out with her. You don't date your costar. It's Hollywood 101."

"You should've come to me," Andy said. "I could have told you that you guys would never work out."

"Oh, really?" Robbie said defensively.

"He has a system," I told him, touching Robbie's arm. "Just chill." I took a deep breath and tried to think. "Okay, have you tried calling her?"

"I did," Robbie said. "She's not picking up."

"Damn caller ID. Has anyone tried from the pay phone?" I asked, spotting it through the cafeteria doors.

"Good idea!" Stephanie said.

We all rushed through the doors and I grabbed the phone. The dial tone was so deafening I had to hold it away from my ear.

"Who has change?" Ashley asked.

"Fred! Fred always has change!" I said.

Fred reached into his pocket and pulled out a wad of coinage, along with a big white fuzzy and a half-mashed mini Snickers. I grabbed a couple of quarters, fed the phone and quickly dialed her number.

As the line started to ring, everyone huddled in closer to me. When it finally connected, my heart gave a lurch. In all the insanity of the moment, I hadn't thought of a thing to say.

"You've reached Tama. If you don't know what to do at the beep, I can't help you."

"Damn," I said under my breath.

"You know, it might come up as 'Washington School District' or something on the caller ID," Andy said. "She'd know it was us."

"Good point." I hung up. "Now what?"

"Why don't I call her?" Fred suggested, whipping his cell phone out of his backpack. "There's no way she's gonna recognize my number."

"Good plan," I said. I rattled off the number for him and it took him three tries in all his fumbling, but he finally dialed it in.

"It's ringing," Fred announced.

I held my breath. I think everyone else did, too.

"Still ringing," he said.

Please pick up, Tama. Please, please, please. . . .

"Machine," Fred announced.

"Just hang up," Ashley grumbled.

Fred raised a finger.

"Fred. What're you doing?" I asked.

"I'm gonna leave a message," he said.

"What're you gonna say?" Stephanie hissed. But it was too late.

"Tama! Hi! It's Fred Frontz here! We were all just wondering if you'd maybe change your mind about, you know, coming back and doing the show 'cause we'd all really like to have you. The show must go on and all that. So, we hope you change your mind. And when I say we, I mean me, KJ, Robbie, Steph, Ashley and Andy, who are all here. Say hi, guys!"

He held up the phone. We all looked at one another.

"Uh . . . hi!" we chorused lamely.

"So, see!? Are you feeling the love? 'Cause I'm feeling the love," Fred continued. "So I guess that's all. Have a good . . . you know . . . day and—"

"Hang up," Robbie whispered.

"And hope you feel better and—"

It was like watching one of those Oscar speeches that makes no sense and goes on for too long.

"Dude. Hang up," Robbie said.

"And I guess we'll just see you, hopefully, tomorrow at least, and—"

Robbie took the phone from him and hit the off button. Fred pushed his hands into his pockets and stared at it. "Voice mail makes me nervous."

"No, really?" Ashley said.

"So what do we do now?" Steph asked.

"We go to plan B," I said.

"What's plan B?"

I took a deep breath and sighed. "Haven't thought of it yet."

ACT FIVE, SCENE THREE

In which:

AN INSANE SUGGESTION IS MADE

"WE NEED A PLAN B," MR. KATZ ANNOUNCED THAT AFTERNOON.

"That's what I said!" I cried.

All the primary actors, plus myself and Mr. Katz, had gathered in the auditorium seats for an emergency meeting. Andy and I and some of the other set-crew people were supposed to spend the afternoon organizing all the props and costumes and making sure everything was set for opening night on Wednesday. Instead, I had asked Andy to run the crew—which pretty much made him convulse with nervous twitches, but what else could I do—and I now sat with Mr. Katz on the edge of the stage. He had tried calling Tama's house as well, but not even her parents or her maid were picking up. What had Tama done, moved the whole family to Florida overnight or something?

This was so unfair. I should have been home right then, buffing my nails and experimenting with eye makeup and listening to my soothing Mandy Moore CD to chill out before my date with Cameron. (Robbie would die if he knew I bought a Mandy Moore disc, but what he didn't know wouldn't kill him.) But no. I was here. Probably sprouting fresh stress zits with every passing moment.

"I should have cast understudies," Mr. Katz said, shaking his head. His stubble was growing in a wild pattern along his chin, and his skin looked waxy under the lights. "Always cast understudies. Always!"

"But, Mr. Katz, you said yourself there wasn't enough talent for understudies," I said quietly.

"I did?" he asked, raising his head.

"Uh, can I make a suggestion?" Ashley asked, raising her hand.

"Not if it's you playing Sandy," I said.

Her hand fell and she grumbled under her breath as she sank lower in her seat.

"Actually, that might be our only option," Mr. Katz said.

Ashley instantly popped up again.

"Mr. Katz—"

"Ashley knows the part. She did it in camp," Mr. Katz said. "Can you do it if you cram tonight?" he asked her.

"I could do it right now, Mr. Katz," Ashley said, beaming.

"Yeah, but who's gonna play Rizzo?" I asked.

"Stephanie will do it," Ashley replied, looking at Steph. "You said you wanted it, right?"

I watched my friend's face completely crumble as her life passed before her eyes. For a moment I honestly thought she was going to faint.

"I can't do it. I don't know it," she said shakily. "Maybe if I had a few weeks . . ."

"I have a suggestion!" Robbie announced, raising his hand. He was perched on the back of one of the chairs, his feet on the seat. "Why doesn't KJ do it?"

I cracked up laughing. So did Mr. Katz. Is it wrong that I was insulted? But he was right. We both were. The very idea was ridiculous.

"KJ?" Cory snorted. "Why would KJ do it?"

"Because she knows it. She knows all the parts. Plus she's blocked half the scenes herself," Robbie said, getting up and strolling down the aisle. "She's the only one who can do it."

Why was he doing this to me? I thought we were friends. Why, why, *why?*

"I—"

"Can you sing, KJ?" Mr. Katz asked.

"I—"

"She can totally sing," Steph said helpfully.

Et tu, Stephanie?

"What?" she said off my look of death. "You can."

Yeah, and there's a reason you're the only one who's ever heard me do it, I thought. Did none of my friends know me at all? Didn't they know that if I got out on stage in front of all those people I would die?

"KJ, this would save everything," Mr. Katz said hopefully. "Can you do it?"

"I . . ." I looked at Robbie, who just smiled back. If this was his idea of a joke, I was not amused. "Mr. Katz, I'd rather talk to Tama. See if we can get her to come back. If we start switching everyone's parts now, this thing is going to be a disaster. Let's just talk to Tama and—"

"Yeah, but Tama won't talk to us," Ashley pointed out. "We only called her four billion times."

More like four, but whatever.

"So we'll go over there," I said, jumping down from the stage. "We'll go over there and we'll ring the bell and we'll make her talk to us. We won't leave until we convince her that she has to come back."

"And what if that doesn't work?" Ashley asked.

"It has to," I replied firmly. "So, who's coming with me?"

"I'll go," Robbie said. "I can be very persuasive."

"Um, isn't she kind of mad at you both right now?" Stephanie pointed out.

She had a point. But when I looked around the room at our other options, I realized we didn't have any. Robbie and I were pretty much the only people she had ever talked to unless she was forced. What was I going to do, send Ashley over there to get water balloons tossed at her head? No. We were the best people for the job.

"We're just going to have to make her talk to us," I said with a shrug.

"Good," Mr. Katz said, checking his watch as he slid down off the stage. "Call me and let me know how it goes." He grabbed up his bag, slipped his sunglasses on and patted my shoulder as he walked out. "But just in case, KJ, you better start going over Rizzo's lines."

ACT FIVE, SCENE FOUR

In which:

WE STORM THE CASTLE GATES

"How could you do that to me?" I whispered to Robbie as we made our way up the front walk at Tama's house. "I can't play Rizzo! Are you out of your mind?"

Robbie looked around, his hands in his pockets. "Why are you whispering?" he whispered.

I paused in front of the door. "I don't know."

He smirked at me in that annoyingly adorable way of his. Suddenly I was smiling like a goof. "This isn't over," I told him in full voice.

I rang the doorbell. It sounded like the gonging of the Notre Dame cathedral bell. Or what I imagined it might sound like. Very intimidating. Last week when I'd arrived, Tama had met me at the door. If I'd been standing here myself and heard that, I probably would have run. I almost felt like doing just that right now, but my fear of playing Rizzo on opening night was greater than my fear of the Gold mansion.

"Very medieval, no?" Robbie said, rocking from his toes to his heels to his toes.

"It's kinda like it's signaling our doom," I said, swallowing against a dry throat.

The door swung open. Tama's mother was even more *Vogue*-worthy than Tama. High cheekbones, ebony skin, big, beautiful eyes. She wore flowing white pants, a fuzzy cashmere sweater, and a confused expression.

"Yes?" she asked.

"Hi, Mrs. Gold. Is Tama here?" I asked.

"And you are?" she said, crossing her arms over her chest.

"Um, KJ Miller?" I said, gulping on intimidation. "We met the other . . . last week? Here. I was . . . here?"

"We're friends of Tama's from school," Robbie said.

"Oh. Well, I'm sorry. Tama's really not feeling well," she said. "She can't have any visitors."

"What's she got?" Robbie blurted.

She looked at him like he'd just asked her for a fifty. "Excuse me?"

"What's she got?" Robbie asked again. "I mean, she was fine yesterday, so I'm just wondering what she caught that, you know, put her out of commission so fast."

Wow. He was good.

"In case we have to warn the school nurse," Robbie added. "If there's some kind of health crisis threatening to fell the youth of Washington High, I'm sure Nurse Sarah would want to know about it."

Mrs. Gold narrowed her eyes, and in that second she looked exactly like her daughter. "If you don't mind, I was in the middle of something."

Wiseass, her tone implied, but she didn't say it. She stepped back and closed the door without another word.

"Nice woman. I think we could really have something," Robbie joked.

"I don't understand. We all know Tama isn't really sick. How could she let her kid get away with something like this?" I ranted. "It's no wonder Tama's—"

Damn. I'd almost just said it again. Tama's therapy was not something to be gabbing about.

"It's no wonder Tama's what?" Robbie said.

"Nothing." I saw something move out of the corner of my eye. A couple of steps sideways and I could see Tama staring down at us from the front hall window.

"Tama!" I shouted, before I could rethink it.

"Tama! Come on! We just want to talk to you!" Robbie shouted.

Up above, Tama shook her head, like we were such losers, and let the curtain go.

"No! Tama!" I cried. "You can't do this!"

"Maybe she's coming down," Robbie suggested hopefully.

So we waited. And waited. And finally the maid opened the door, scaring the crap out of both of us.

"Mrs. Gold kindly asks you to leave before she calls the police," the woman said curtly.

Robbie looked at me and clapped his hands together. "So I guess we're going."

"No. We can't leave," I said, desperate. "We have to talk to her. We have to—"

"KJ, I don't know about you, but I don't feel like getting arrested today. Tomorrow, maybe, but not today," Robbie joked as he strolled toward my car.

"I don't understand this," I said, angry tears stinging my eyes. "Why is she doing this? What the hell is she trying to prove?"

"KJ, calm down," Robbie said, putting his hand on my arm.

But I couldn't calm down. I couldn't. Once again someone was being a big, fat baby and I was the one who was going to have to deal with it. I was the one who was going to have to fix the mess. By going out on stage with no practice, no talent and zero desire, to play Rizzo. The tough girl. I mean, could I be playing any more against type?

"I can't play Rizzo, Robbie. I just can't," I told him.

He took a deep breath and pulled me toward my car. "You won't have to," he said.

Relief flooded through me. "I won't?"

"No." He glanced up at the house. "You heard what Leo said that night at the diner. Tama lives for drama. She loves to be the center of attention. By coming over here we totally gave her what she wants. And tomorrow she's going to wake up and realize that if she doesn't come to school, she's not going to get to star in the play. She's not going to get the spotlight on her all night, and she's not gonna get the applause. When she realizes that, believe me, she'll show up."

I glanced up at the house. Swore I saw the curtains move again. "Really?"

"Trust me," Robbie said confidently. "You can relax. Everything is going to be fine."

ACT FIVE, SCENE FIVE

In which:

SODA IS FLUNG

"YES! ONE HUNDRED POINTS!" CAMERON CHEERED AS THE Skee-Ball machine spit out twenty tickets. "I rule at this game!" He ripped the tickets off and handed them to me. I stuffed them in the plastic Dave and Buster's cup with all the others. The ones he'd won at basketball, at the horse-racing game, at the football-throwing game, the NASCAR game. "You sure you don't want to play?" he asked me.

"Me? No. I'm fine," I told him.

There was no way I'd let him see how pathetic I was at this stuff. No thanks. Standing here obsessing about the fact that tomorrow night I very well might have to play Rizzo in Washington High School's sold-out production of *Grease* was plenty nerve-splitting enough for me. It didn't matter how confident Robbie was in Tama. I couldn't help feeling petrified. Every time my mind wandered to the musical, I physically cringed. The last thing I needed right now was a spotlight on my stunning lack of coordination.

"Two hundred twenty? That's nothing!" the ten-year-old kid on the lane next to Cameron's taunted. He had spiked hair and gapped teeth and a T-shirt that read "You Smell." "I got three fifty this one time."

"Oh, yeah?" Cameron said, taking off his varsity jacket and handing it to me. "You wanna go?"

The kid crossed his arms over his puny chest. "Whaddaya say we make it interesting?"

"What were you thinking?" Cameron asked.

I smiled as the kid thought it over. Cameron was so sweet, playing with this little kid. Maybe there was something here to distract me after all. Don't get me wrong. Watching Cameron Richardson shoot hoops had been plenty entertaining—for the first thirty or so minutes. But after two hours, standing around playing the role of ticket-keeper got boring, even for the hottest guy in school.

"If I win, I get all your tickets," the kid said, nodding at me.

"What if I win?" Cameron asked.

"Then you get all mine." The kid lifted a bucket from the ground. Red and yellow and blue tickets spat out in every direction.

"You're on," Cameron said.

The two of them shook hands.

"Good luck," I said jokingly to Cameron, folding the bulky jacket over my arm.

"I won't need it, babe," he said.

Babe. Had he just called me babe? How cool was that?

A stool finally opened up and I sank onto it gratefully. Cameron rolled his first ball and it almost popped into the hundred circle, but then bumped down to twenty.

"You suck!" the kid taunted. He threw his ball and got a fifty. "Take that, meathead!"

"I'm just getting started," Cameron replied. He threw

another ball. This time he hit the hundred. "Ha! Who sucks now, midget boy?"

I blinked. What was that?

Another ball rolled. The kid got a ten. He mumbled something under his breath.

"Can't take the heat, can ya?" Cameron teased. He threw another fifty. "Aw yeah! I rock. Better start handing over your tickets now, kid!"

The kid's face grew red and my brow started to furrow. What was Cameron doing? Was he really standing in the middle of Dave and Buster's taunting a ten-year-old?

"I am a Skee-Ball god!" Cameron said, rubbing his hands together.

My skin prickled with heat each time Cameron opened his mouth again. Suddenly I found myself rooting for the competition. The kid started to catch up, but even then, Cameron wouldn't let up. He was trash talking like some dude on ESPN. Like this was the Super Bowl or something. If it were me, I'd let the kid win, but clearly that thought hadn't even crossed Cameron's mind.

"Three hundred to two seventy-five," Cameron said, lifting his last ball. "It all comes down to this roll. You ready, twerp?"

The kid nodded, ball in hand. He looked miserable. "Ready."

They both rolled. Cameron's ball popped up and into the fifty hole. The kid's fell right into the ten.

"Yes! I win! I rule all! I am the Skee-Ball champion of the world!" Cameron threw his hands up, and a few kids from the middle school who had gathered nearby applauded. His sweater rode up and got stuck halfway up his chest, exposing a flat, but very white, stomach.

Oh. My. God.

Suddenly, all I saw was Fred Frontz. Fred Frontz and his dorky awkwardness, his uncontrollable overexcitement. The qualities Cameron and his friends had been taunting him for ever since we were kids. I watched Cameron laughing and pointing at the little boy. Watched him yank his sweater down. Watched him high-five a bunch of strangers, cheering with his mouth open and his wad of gum exposed. Watched him hold his hand out for the poor kid's tickets. And second by second, the truth sank in more and more. Cameron Richardson was a complete and total . . .

Geek.

He was constantly playing with his own hair. He chewed gum while eating popcorn. He taunted fourth graders in the middle of Dave and Buster's and thought it was cool. And he kissed like a dog with a saliva problem!

When I really looked at him, I realized he was no cooler than anyone else. He was just so hot it masked his geeky qualities. Maybe every one of us had a little bit of geek in us. It was just that some of us were better at hiding it than others.

"Here!" Cameron said, his face all red from the celebration. He handed me the bucket of tickets. "We're totally going home with that statue of Derek Jeter."

"Uh, Cameron? You're not really going to take that kid's tickets, are you?" I said, sliding down off the stool.

"Why not? I won them fair and square," he replied.

"No, you didn't. You're older than him and bigger than him,

and you've probably played Skee-Ball four hundred more times than he has," I said. "How is that fair?"

"He made the bet!" Cameron protested.

I rolled my eyes, took the bucket and handed it back to the kid. He ran off without another word, probably suspecting Cameron would track him down.

"Hey!" Cameron shouted. He shot me an annoyed look.

"Sorry," I said with a shrug. "But he's just a little kid."

"Whatever." Cameron rolled his eyes. "You can buy me a Coke to make it up to me." He walked over to the bar and ordered two Cokes.

Okay, was he really going to make me pay for his soda just because he wasn't going home with a plastic statue of some baseball dude?

He passed me a soda. Luckily the bartender hadn't asked for money yet.

"So, what's up with you and Tama?" he asked me, his tone back to normal. "Are you, like, fighting now or something?"

"I guess. Sort of." I put his jacket and the bucket of tickets on an empty bar stool and picked up my soda. The glass was cold and slippery, and I didn't even want it.

"You should make up with her," he said.

My brow creased. "You don't even know what we're fighting about. Maybe she should make up with me."

"Whatever. You guys should make up." Cameron shrugged. "I think it's cool that you guys hang out."

Something was not quite right about this conversation. I felt an eerie thump of foreboding and took a step back. Cameron sipped his Coke, oblivious.

"Why do you care if we keep hanging out?" I asked.

"Because, you know, if you're hanging out with her, then you're hanging out with me. And my friends." He looked around the room, as if assessing which game he was going to play next.

"So why can't I just hang out with you? Why does Tama have to be part of the equation?" I asked.

Cameron blushed a little and shrugged. "I don't know. She just does. It's just better if we're, like, a whole group."

There was a lump of clay where my throat used to be. Was he saying what I thought he was saying?

"So if I'm not in with Tama, I'm not in with your group and you can't hang out with me," I said flatly. "Is that what you're saying?"

Cameron looked at me for the first time in a couple of minutes, anguished. "Come on, KJ. Don't make a big deal out of it. Maybe you should call her. See if she'll talk to you."

And finally, it hit me. Cameron hadn't started to talk to me because I'd lost the geeks and started acting more confident and cool. He'd started to talk to me because of Tama. Because I'd been hanging out with her more, because she'd been seen out in public with me, and if she did it, then it was okay for him to do it. Hanging with Tama had made me acceptable to date. And if I was no longer hanging with Tama . . .

"I'm no longer acceptable," I said aloud.

"What?"

My cheeks were on fire. My eyes burned painfully. I stared into my soda, watched the bubbles popping to the surface, the square ice cubes contorting my reflection.

Cameron Richardson wasn't just a closet geek. He was a total jerk, too. Robbie was right. He'd been right all along. Cameron Richardson was as shallow as a puddle. And as transparent, too.

And it had taken me way too long to see it. I looked up into his eyes. He was all innocence.

"What's the problem? I'm just trying to make it so that we can be together. You should be happy I care."

And that's when he got an entire soda, ice cubes and all, right in his beautiful face.

ACT FIVE, SCENE SIX

In which:

THERE'S LAUGHTER AND TEARS

"UM . . . STEPH? DID I ACTUALLY THROW A DRINK IN CAMERON Richardson's face?" I rambled as Stephanie turned her mom's SUV onto my block. "I mean, did I actually do that?"

"That's what you told me," she replied with glee.

I hid my face in my hands. "Oh my God. What did I do? I'm dead, you know that? Everyone's gonna think I'm a psycho."

"Or that you're insanely cool," Stephanie said. "It'll depend on who you ask."

She turned into my driveway and put the SUV in park. I managed to lift my head, which weighed about a thousand pounds, and look at her. "This has been the worst week ever."

"And it's only Tuesday!" she said happily.

"Why are you so Rachael Ray right now?" I asked. "My life is over."

"No, it's not. You just found out that the guy you like is an ass," she told me. "That happens to people every day."

"That's probably true," I said.

"And if I'm in a good mood, it's just because I find the

image of Cameron Richardson doused in Coke and ice pretty freaking hilarious," she said.

I met her eye. "It was pretty funny. Some of it, like, went up his nose so he had this sneezing fit, and soda was dripping down his back and onto this guy next to him and . . . and . . ."

Suddenly I was laughing so hard I couldn't stop. Stephanie held her stomach, making this wheezing sound that would have been alarming under other circumstances.

"And he . . . he . . . he stormed off like this big . . . big . . . baby!" I cried.

Stephanie shook her head. "Stop! Stop!"

"'Oh my God! My new varsity patch!'" I wailed, imitating him. The splash had, in fact, hit the jacket on the stool and the guy in the suit nearby and myself. But it had all been worth it.

"Stop! Seriously! I can't take it!"

After a couple of minutes of laughing, we finally got control of ourselves and I sighed. "Thanks for coming to get me."

"Anytime," she replied.

"I guess I should go inside and start going over Rizzo's lines," I said mournfully.

"Want some help?"

"No. It's cool. I'm just going to do it once. I'm banking on Tama's lust for stardom getting the better of her," I said, gathering my things. "She'll be back tomorrow."

"Yeah. She will," Stephanie said as I got out of the car.

"Steph! You're thinking positive!" I said, surprised.

"There's a first time for everything," she said. Then she blew me a kiss and I closed the door.

I was halfway up the front walk, laughing and shaking my head, when a car pulled into our driveway. I saw the cab light on the roof, just as the front door of my house flew open. My father came storming toward me. For a quick, terrifying second, I thought he was coming out to yell at me, but then I saw the suitcase in his hand.

"Dad? Where're you going?" I asked.

He blew right by me. "Ask your mother."

My heart pounded a slamming beat. He got in the cab and after idling for a moment, the car was gone. My mother came to the open door. I attempted to breathe.

"What just happened?" I asked.

"Come inside, KJ."

My brother stood near the wall in the kitchen, tears streaking down his face. My mother sat us both down at the table. I felt like everything inside of me was shaking.

"Kids, your father is going to be moving out for a while," my mother said.

"Why?" Christopher shouted through a sob.

My stomach went hollow. This wasn't happening. After all these years of wishing for this . . . it couldn't be happening. My father was moving out. My father, not here. I wasn't sure whether I wanted to laugh or scream or cry.

"Because, honey, he's . . . he's sick. And if he wants to live in this house with us, he has to get better," my mother said, reaching for Christopher's hand. He yanked it away and stuffed both hands under his arms. I saw a flash of pain cross my mother's face.

"Is he . . . Did he say he was going to . . ." I didn't know what to ask first. "Mom, what happened?"

"Your father, he . . . relapsed," she said.

"Already? He just got home!" I blurted.

"What's relapse?" Christopher asked.

"It means he had a drink, honey. And he promised all of us

that he wouldn't," she said, looking at me. "So I told him that until he could keep his promise, he had to go."

"You threw him out!" Christopher shouted, getting up. "This is all your fault!"

"Chris—"

He turned around and ran up the stairs, slamming his bedroom door. My mother heaved a sigh and looked down at the table.

"Mom—"

"It's fine. He's just angry. He'll be okay," she said.

"Mom, are you okay?" I asked.

She managed to look at me. "I'll be fine."

"Are you guys . . ." It was difficult to speak past the rock in my throat. "Are you getting divorced?"

"No one's said anything about divorce," she assured me, pushing herself up from the table. "Not yet, anyway."

She opened the refrigerator and stared into it. I wondered how she could think about eating anything right now, but as she stood there longer, I realized she didn't even know what she was doing.

"Mom?"

She startled and closed the door. "You were right, KJ," she said, leaning back. "We couldn't live like that anymore. You kids deserve some stability in your lives. You deserve not to be . . . not to be afraid of your father. Not to be afraid in your own house. That's not what a family is supposed to be. And he . . . he has to figure that out."

I felt like something warm and soothing was enveloping me. I'd done something right. All this time I'd been wishing for the strength to stand up to my dad, but it was my mother I needed to stand up to. The one who would listen. The one who was able to change.

"So," she said. "How was your date?"

I exhaled a laugh. "It sucked."

"I'm sorry."

"It doesn't matter," I said. I got up, feeling so heavy I could have just pulled myself out of a pool fully clothed. "I think I'll go to bed. Unless you need me."

"I'm gonna do the same. But thanks, hon," she said. She hugged me, and for once I gave into it and hugged her back with my whole body. "I love you, kid."

"Love you, too, Mom," I said.

Then I dragged myself up to my room, lay down on my bed and listened . . . to the silence.

ACT FIVE, SCENE SEVEN

In which:

THE WALLS SHRINK

"SHE'S HERE, RIGHT? I MEAN, SHE HAS TO BE HERE." I HAD GOTTEN in the car a nervous wreck, and by the time I walked into the school lobby, I had all but lost control of my bodily functions. I hadn't gone over a single page of the script last night. Not a single word. How could I be expected to concentrate on lines like "God! What a party poop!" when my father had just moved out of the house? "Just because she skipped school again, that doesn't mean she's not here, right?"

Robbie had been wrong about one thing. Tama had not woken up that morning and realized all the things he'd said she'd realize. At least she hadn't realized it before homeroom, because she hadn't been seen by a soul all day.

"I'm sure she's here," Fred replied, walking sideways next to me, like he was afraid to take his eyes off me in case I . . . what? Fainted? Spontaneously combusted? "Although . . ."

"Although what?" I croaked as we walked down the hall toward the back entrance to the stage. "Although what?"

Fred screwed his mouth up. "Isn't there some rule where if

you don't come to school you can't do extracurriculars that day, either?"

"That's a rule? Is that a rule?" I demanded.

"I think it's a rule."

He opened the door and we walked inside. I held on to the handrail along the five downward steps just so that I wouldn't collapse. "Well, it's a stupid rule. They'd have to ignore it for this, wouldn't they? I mean, she's the star. She's Sandy. She's—"

We walked into the first dressing room and I stopped in my tracks. Ashley Brown stood on the block in the center of the room, wearing a ponytail, a neck scarf and Sandy's blue poodle skirt, which Ms. Lin was quickly hemming. All the air in the room was sucked out and the walls shrank in toward me.

Ashley turned around and grinned. "There's our Rizzo!"

ACT FIVE, SCENE EIGHT

In which:

I CONSIDER MURDER

I STOOD IN THE CENTER OF THE DRESSING ROOM, WITH FIVE minutes to showtime, staring at the reflection that wasn't me. That was not my poofed-out hair. Those were not my eyes under all that blue eye shadow. The fake birthmark painted just above the corner of my mouth? Not mine. And those breasts? Those tremendous bazoongas popping out of the low-cut silk black top that Ms. Lin had squeezed me into? Those could not be mine. My boobs had never seen that much light of day. I had long since vowed that they never would. So there was no way those inflated beach balls were mine.

Behind me, Ashley hummed "It's Raining on Prom Night" as she made sure all her costumes were in order. I wanted to grab her and strangle her. If she went down, there was no one else to play Sandy. They'd have to cancel the show. It would be a small price to pay to get out of this nightmare.

"Hey, KJ! Ready to go?" Fred asked, poking his head in. His hair was slicked back from his face, and he wore a white T-shirt, black leather jacket and way too much rouge.

To his credit, he didn't even glance at the fourteen miles of cleavage glaring him in the face. We'd just done a fast-forward run-through in the music room to make sure I knew what I was doing (which I clearly didn't, though no one was man enough to say so), and we'd all been in costume. The boys had gotten most of their drooling done then. I hoped.

"I'm not doing this," I said, whipping a silk kimono robe off the rack. I covered myself and cinched the belt. Once the lighted runway of cleavage was gone, I felt much more self-assured. "Go tell Mr. Katz there's no way I'm doing this."

Ashley stopped humming. Fred paled under his makeup. "What? KJ, you can't not do this."

"Oh yes I can. Call Tama. Get her ass down here! She has to go on!" I babbled.

"Um, KJ? That's not gonna happen," Ashley said, disturbed. "Tama is 'deathly ill,' remember?" she said with air quotes. "Apparently the girl's never heard of hot tea with lemon and 'the show must go on.'"

"She's lying!" I protested. "I saw Tama yesterday! She's fine!"

I started to hyperventilate. Fred yanked a chair out from the wall for me to sit in. I promptly plopped down, put my head between my knees and gasped.

"Are you okay?" Fred asked. "KJ?"

I couldn't answer. I could hardly even think. I kept trying to suck in air, but nothing was happening. My lungs started to burn. My vision grayed over. I kept seeing myself on stage, frozen. Seeing myself on stage with everyone dancing around me while I stood there like an idiot, doing nothing. Staring. Staring into a sea of gaping faces.

"Omigod. She's having a panic attack," Ashley said.

"She's fine," Fred said. He dropped to his knees in front of me. I could see a roll of skin hanging out over the top of his jeans. "KJ, you can do this. I know you can do this," he said, putting his hands on my shoulders. "You have to do this."

I looked up into his kohl-rimmed eyes, as sincere and hopeful as ever. My heart felt like it was being choked in a fist of granite. I was having a heart attack. I really was.

"You're going to be great," Fred said with a nod.

He was so sure of himself. So sure of me. But I couldn't even feel my toes, or my fingertips. And that, I knew, could not be a good sign.

"I can't do this, Fred," I choked out. "I can't. I can't. I can't."

"This is just like when Carrie Bradshaw tried on the wedding dress in *Sex and the City* and couldn't breathe," Ashley said helpfully, leaning in. "Maybe we should take her clothes off!"

"No!" I blurted.

"Your funeral," Ashley said.

"Shut up, Ashley. And back off!" Fred said, taking charge in a way I'd never seen him take charge before.

"Sorry."

"Okay, now, do you want to help here or what?" Fred said.

"What can I do?" Ashley asked.

"Get Mr. Katz! No. Wait. Get Stephanie. She'll know what to do."

"Stephanie Shumer will know what to do," she said sarcastically.

"Just go!"

Ashley ran out. My feet bounced up and down under the chair and I started to rock back and forth, clutching my stomach.

I can't do this. I can't do this. I can't do this.

In my mind's eye I saw Tama staring down from the window, saw Mr. Katz popping Tums, Tama's mom closing a door in my face, my father storming out, my mother all pissed off, Christopher crying, Stephanie, Andy, Robbie, Glenn, Cameron, Fred, Tama . . . I couldn't take it anymore. It was all too much. Too much, too much, too much.

"What's the problem?" Robbie asked, looking scared out of his mind as he ran in with Stephanie on his heels. They were both in costume, too. Him in slick hair and drag queen eyeliner, her with gray streaks painted into her hair, which was back in a bun. It just made the whole situation all the more disturbing.

"The problem is, I'm not going out there!" I said, standing up. I was shaking from head to toe. "I'm not doing it. For once, just one little teeny tiny time in my whole entire life, I'm being irresponsible, okay? I'm not going out there. End of story. Don't even try to talk me out of it!"

"KJ, calm down," Robbie said, walking over to me. He gripped my upper arms in his hands.

"You did great in the run-through, KJ," Stephanie said. "You're going to be fine. You just have to do your best."

"No! It's not fair! How could Tama do this to me?" I cried, tears suddenly bursting forth. I ripped myself out of Robbie's grasp and paced. "I can't take care of everything! I can't fix everything! I'm tired, okay? I'm tired of thinking about everyone else's feelings and cleaning up after everyone else's messes and keeping everyone else's secrets! Why do I have to be the one to go out there? Why me? Why do I have to do everything!? Did you see how many people are out there right now? This is my worst fear, do you get that? My worst fear!"

Fred, Robbie and Stephanie gave one another a disturbed look like they might have to hit me with a tranq dart. And they were right. I was going psycho. But I couldn't help it. I threw a Coke at my dream guy, my dad had moved out, my mom wasn't even sure she was up to coming tonight, Christopher hadn't spoken to anyone in twenty-four hours, Tama had completely and totally screwed us over, and I was going to go out there and make an idiot out of myself. And now I was having a nervous breakdown in front of Robbie Delano, the guy I was pretty sure I was falling in love with.

"I can't take it anymore. I just can't take it," I rambled.

"KJ. KJ. Shh . . ." Robbie approached me carefully. I stopped moving and let him put his arms around me, pressing my face into his leather-covered shoulder. Gradually the crying slowed and I sucked in a big breath. My vision started to clear. I could see straight again. And I realized that all I wanted to do was stay right there. Right there in Robbie's arms I felt okay. I felt normal. I felt like the whole world wasn't closing in on me.

"What's going on? Is something else wrong?" Robbie asked.

I sniffled and looked at Fred. He immediately closed the door. "My dad, he . . . he moved out."

"Oh my God. When?" Stephanie asked.

"Last night. Right after you dropped me off."

Robbie whistled. "Why didn't you say anything?"

"Because who wants to advertise that?" I moaned.

"You could've told us," Robbie said, glancing at Fred and Steph. And of course, he was right. If there was anyone I could tell, it was them. The guys who had been there for me on the worst night of my life. The friend who had been there for me during every bad night leading up to it.

"I'm sorry." I wiped at my eyes and my fingers came away with huge black streaks. "My mom told him he had to quit drinking and get help, so he left."

"Wow. That's harsh," Fred said.

"But then he called this morning and said he was starting AA," I added.

"Well, that's good, right? That's a good thing," Robbie said.

I scoffed. "Yeah, if he actually does it."

"You don't think he will?" Fred asked tentatively.

"He's said this before," Stephanie clarified for me.

I took a breath and blew it out. "I'm just, I can't get my hopes up. I just can't."

And then I started crying again, more quietly this time, but just as nonstop. Stephanie came over and put her arm around me, and I leaned my head against hers. Why couldn't my family just be normal? If they could just be normal, I could handle other things. Like saving the production my friends and I had worked on for the last two months. But I didn't have the capacity to handle it. Not right now.

Robbie reached out and squeezed my hand. He looked at Fred. "We have to do something. She can't go out there like this."

Fred's foot bounced up and down. "I could pull the fire alarm!"

"Ooh! Or call in a bomb threat!" Robbie suggested.

"You guys. People will freak. There'd be a mob scene," Stephanie said. "Someone could get trampled."

"That would be bad," Fred theorized. "Oh! I've got it! I'll streak the auditorium!"

I snorted a laugh through my tears.

"What's that gonna do?" Robbie said.

"I don't know. Distract people?"

"Yeah, I'd say that would be distracting," Robbie said.

I shook my head, laughing as they concocted insane plan after insane plan. All for me. All because they wanted to protect me. All because they cared about me. And suddenly I realized I wasn't in this alone. I really did have people who would be there for me no matter what. They'd just been hiding in the most unexpected places.

"You guys, no one's streaking anything," I said.

"Okay, fine, but all we need is a plan. One good plan," Robbie said. "Oh! Go find Glenn Marlowe! He's sick and twisted! He'll know what to do."

There was a knock on the door and it opened. Andy, who had taken over as stage manager since I would, in theory, be *on* the stage, stuck his head in.

"Hey, guys, it's almost time for the curtain so if, you know, you could maybe get out to the stage so we could, you know—" He looked up and his jaw dropped. "KJ! What happened?"

I was a mess of makeup streaks. Must've looked like a clown who had just been hit by a bus.

"She's not gonna do it, man," Robbie said. "We have to cancel the show."

"Uh, no," Andy said.

We all stared at him. It was the most definitive sentence Andy had ever said. Was it possible he was drunk with power?

"KJ, listen," Andy said, stepping around Robbie. "You care about this musical more than anyone. And you're the only one who can save it now," he said, looking me in the eye the entire time. "Now, if you tell me that what you really want is for me to go out there and tell everyone to go home, then I'll do it, but I don't think that's what you want."

"Andy—"

"Just think about it, KJ," he said. "Is it really what you want?"

I took a moment to think. I thought of all those people out there. All the parents and friends who had come to see their stars. I thought of Mr. Katz and how humiliating it would be for him. Thought of the musicians in the pit, the guys in the AV booth, the faculty members and set crew who had worked behind the scenes. Everyone would be crushed. And I was the only one who could keep that from happening.

Andy was right. After all his survey questions and spending all this time working with me, he knew me very well. He knew I didn't want all those people to be let down. Not for my own selfish reasons. It just wasn't me.

I didn't want it to be me.

"What do you think, KJ?" Stephanie asked.

Robbie and Fred and Andy all gazed at me hopefully.

"Get Ashley in here to help me with my makeup," I said, lifting my chin. "Let's get this show on the road."

ACT FIVE, SCENE NINE

In which:

I GO DOWN

YOU'RE IN YOUR BEDROOM WITH STEPHANIE, SINGING TO KELLY Clarkson. You're just in your bedroom with Steph. There's no one else here. There aren't a thousand people in the audience salivating to see just how spectacular your next mess-up will be. It's just you and Steph. You and Steph.

The intro to "Look at Me, I'm Sandra Dee" started. My heart no longer wished to be attached to my body. There was no cartilage left in my knees. I was supposed to walk saucily around the park bench and launch into song. Instead, I gripped it with my sweaty palm and sort of stagger-stepped to the front. It was more drunken geriatric than saucy, sexy teen. A few people snickered, but that was fine. I was getting used to it.

So far in the first act, I'd recited three of Cory's lines, totally cutting her off. I'd almost vomited when Jonathan Marsters slipped me the tongue during our kiss, which he was *not* supposed to do—and he'd tasted like cigarettes and Cheetos. I'd totally screwed up the choreography on "Summer Lovin'," tripping Ashley right into Robbie before Sandy and Danny were even supposed to be aware that the other one was at Rydell High. I was a disaster. Complete and total.

And now, it was time to sing. A solo. A solo I had rehearsed once in my life, five minutes before the curtain had lifted on this debacle.

Jeffrey stared at me from his piano. I opened my mouth. Miraculously, sound came out.

"'Look at me, I'm Sandra Dee!

Lousy with virginity!'"

Mr. Katz nodded encouragingly from the wings. I kept singing, doing the twirl I'd seen Ashley execute so many times. No one was laughing now. I was doing okay. Maybe I could redeem myself here. Maybe if I just sang my loudest and really focused, I could go out of the first act with a bang.

Ashley-as-Sandy nodded at me and I remembered. I was supposed to be standing on the bench by now. This was it. The big moment. Bring it home, KJ. Bring it home.

I lifted my foot, midnote, and it caught on the underside of the park bench. My heart swooped as my forward momentum careened ahead and my shin slammed into the corner of the bench. I yelped and crashed to the ground, smacking my temple on something hard on the way down. For a second I think I even blacked out, though from lethal mortification or the blow to the head, I have no idea.

There was a huge communal gasp. The music stopped. I looked up into the spotlight, blinking back humiliated tears.

Let me die now, please. Please just let this be the end.

And then, Jeffrey started playing again. Be-bopping away on his piano. Did he really expect me to get up and keep singing? A million pairs of eyes stared in curious awe, unable to avert their gaze from the rampaging train wreck my performance had become.

I hated Tama. I hated Tama in that moment with a venom so deadly it could have brought down a killer whale. She'd done this to me. She'd brought me to this moment. And now that everyone could see I was conscious, they were starting to laugh.

I didn't know where I was. I had no idea what the words were. I envisioned myself getting up and running off the stage and not stopping until I reached my bedroom, where I would burrow under my covers and await the coming of my death or my eighteenth birthday, whichever came first. The laughter grew louder.

"Come on! Do something!" someone yelled.

Help me, I thought. Somebody just help me!

And then, suddenly, all went dark. I blinked for a second, stunned, and realized someone else was singing. Carrie. It was Carrie's voice. She was continuing the song from right where I'd left off. The spotlight had swung over to her at stage right, where she'd been sitting in shadow. But now . . . now she was front and center, singing my song. Jeffrey and the rest of the orchestra caught up to her and clicked into gear, and suddenly no one was looking at me anymore. They were all focused on Carrie.

I looked up into the far reaches of the auditorium. Glenn stood with his hands on the spotlight. It was him. He had saved me. By turning the spotlight on Carrie, he'd forced her into the act. Even after everything that had happened between us, Glenn Marlowe had saved me.

"Are you okay?" he mouthed to me from afar.

I nodded. *"Thank you,"* I mouthed back, tears in my eyes.

Then I got up and joined Carrie and we finished the song, together.

ACT FIVE, SCENE TEN

In which:

I SAVE MYSELF

THE SECOND THE CURTAIN FELL ON THE FIRST ACT, I RAN INTO the dressing room and locked the door behind me. Looking around wildly, I grabbed someone's fleece robe, bunched it up and screamed into it as loudly as I possibly could. I felt marginally better after that. And someone was pounding on the door.

I opened it, expecting Cory or Carrie to shove me aside so they could get changed. Instead, standing before me in a low hat and sunglasses was Tama Gold.

"Nice work out there. Physical comedy really is your thing."

I grabbed her wrist and yanked her inside. Possibly a little harder than necessary.

"Ow!"

I slammed the door. I turned the lock but it slipped out of my sweaty grasp and bounced back.

"You're *here!?*" I demanded, whirling on her.

"I can't believe you didn't cancel," she said. She moved across the room so that her back was to the mirror, and took her sunglasses off. "What were you thinking?"

"What was *I* thinking? What was *I* thinking?" I blurted.

"You're the one who totally screwed us all over. I'd like to know what you were thinking!"

Tama looked away from me and shrugged. "I was sick."

"Oh, please! You're fine! You just wanted everyone to come crawling to you, begging you to come back! You just wanted to prove that we couldn't do this without you!" I shouted. "Well, guess what? You were right! Goody for you! You've found out that you were, in fact, the star."

"God, KJ. What's your problem?" Tama said, looking at me like she was afraid I might explode and shower her with little KJ parts.

"My problem is you! You are so self-centered you don't even realize how many people you've hurt here! You weren't the only one working on this musical the last couple of months! We all were! We all worked our asses off. But did you ever consider any of us when you staged your little walkout? No-o-o! You only care about yourself! All you think about is how you can get what you want!"

"You have no idea what I think!" Tama spat.

"Oh yes I do. Hate to disappoint you, Tama, but you're not that complicated," I said venomously.

"Shut up, KJ. Stop acting like you know me. You don't know me. We're not even really friends!"

That stung for a split second, but I already knew the answer. "You're wrong. It's your little popular posse who aren't really your friends. I'm the one you've told all about your mom and your problems with Leo and your after-school appointments. I'm the one who's been driving you to the doctor and listening to all your crap." I yanked the Pink Ladies jacket off while I ranted and balled it up. "Whether you know it or not, I'm your only true friend in this school. But if you don't get your butt into costume and get out there and start acting like a human being who cares about this production, I'm done. I mean it. For good."

Tama's mouth hung open slightly. Had I actually gotten through to her? Did she actually realize I was right?

Then her eyes flicked past me and stared. Suddenly I realized that, reflected in the mirror behind her, were Carrie and Cory and Ashley. They were all standing in the doorway, and they'd all heard at least part of what I'd just said. For a long moment, no one moved.

Then, finally, Tama sniffed and lifted her chin. "Fine."

It took the world a moment to stop spinning. "Fine?"

"Yes, fine." She snatched the jacket out of my hand and held it out to Ashley. "Get out of my skirt and into your own costume," she said. "I'll go on for the second act."

Outside, dozens of voices cheered and I sank into the nearest chair, weak with relief. It was over. The nightmare was over. This time, I'd actually saved myself.

ACT FIVE, SCENE ELEVEN

In which:

THERE'S A NEW FIRST KISS

WHEN I STEPPED OUT OF THE DRESSING ROOM MOMENTS LATER, IT was to a round of ecstatic cheers. Maybe I'd been an even worse Rizzo than I thought. The entire cast and crew was as giddy as the crowd on a parade route. But I just didn't care. I was back in my own clothes, makeup free and cleavageless. I had gone out on stage in front of the entire school and I'd survived. And now, I would never have to do it again. I was the happiest I'd ever been. Ever.

"That was incredible!" Robbie cheered, grabbing me up in his arms. He twirled me around and I didn't even notice that my boobs were pressed up to his neck. Well, I noticed, but I didn't care.

"I know, wasn't it?" I said as he replaced me on the ground.

"All right, people! Let's break it up!" Andy shouted, walking through and clapping his hands. "We only have ten minutes to curtain!"

The crowd quickly dispersed, running off to dressing rooms and the wings. I smiled at Andy. "You've really gotten the hang of this."

"I'm ready to give you back the clipboard," Andy said, holding it out.

"You keep it."

His eyes lighted up. "Really?"

"Yeah. Take it home," I told him. "I'll take over tomorrow night."

Andy nodded and hugged the clipboard. "Thank you, KJ, for this opportunity. You won't be disappointed."

I laughed. "As long as I'm not disappointed on that other front," I said with a wink.

Andy blushed. "Oh, I got that covered, too," he said, winking back.

"What was that all about?" Robbie asked as Andy walked off.

"Long story," I told him.

"Does it have anything to do with you and him . . . ?"

It took me a second to figure out what he was saying. "Me and Andy? You mean me *and* Andy? No. Uh . . . no. There's no me and Andy."

"Good."

"Good?"

"Good, I mean . . . it's just . . . there are always so many guys mooning over you—"

"Mooning?" I said with a laugh.

"It's a song in the play." Robbie pointed toward the stage for emphasis.

"Right." I blushed.

Robbie reached out and took my hand. He lifted it so that our palms were touching, then laced his fingers through mine. Slowly, he did the same with the other hand. I looked into his eyes; he gazed back into mine. Suddenly, my heart was pounding, if possible, even harder than it had been when I'd first taken the stage.

"Anyway, there's always so many guys mooning over you it's sometimes hard to tell if you have, you know, a boyfriend or not," he said hopefully. Adorably.

I grinned. "I don't."

"Not even Cameron?" he said.

"Cameron is done," I said.

His eyebrows shot up. "Done?"

I nodded once. "Done."

And with that, he jerked me forward and I tripped into him and he caught me and we kissed. We kissed with our hands clasped and my feet on top of his and our whole bodies touching. His lips were soft and sweet and full and perfect and there was no excess saliva to speak of. We kissed until I was so giddy I started to giggle, and then Robbie finally pulled away.

"Something funny?" he said. He was out of breath. His eyes were closed. Like he was so overwhelmed he couldn't open them yet.

"My first kiss," I murmured.

His eyes widened at that and he grinned. "Really?"

"No. Not really. But it felt like it," I said.

He shook his head, but kept smiling. "KJ Miller. A true original."

I tipped my head back and breathed in the perfection. "You'd better believe it."

ACT FIVE, SCENE TWELVE

In which:

WE CELEBRATE

"I CAN'T BELIEVE IT'S OVER," ROBBIE SAID, SQUEEZING MY HAND AS Cory and Carrie ran out from the wings to take their bows.

"Hey, you've still got three more performances," I reminded him. "Don't get lazy on me now."

"Me? Never!"

Ashley and Jonathan were up next. The crowd jumped to their feet, giving them a standing ovation. Ashley preened and waved. After playing two different roles in one night, she definitely deserved her moment. The second act had gone off without a hitch, and it was mostly her professionalism that had kept the first act from going nuclear. I certainly hadn't helped matters. I was impressed she hadn't shoved me off the stage and started putting on a one-woman show.

"You're up, Robbie!" Andy said, shoving Robbie in the back. "Go, go, go!"

"Okay, Mein Stage Manager," Robbie said. He leaned down to kiss me and whispered in my ear. "Can't wait till you're back in charge."

My heart was full to bursting as he ran out to center stage

and met Tama there to take their bows. I couldn't have been prouder of the two of them. They had done an excellent job in the second act, even managing to look like they were in love. I suppose Tama was imagining that Robbie was Leo and . . . maybe Robbie was imagining Tama was me? I couldn't even fathom the idea that anyone would want to replace that tall, willowy gorgeousness with my squat, freckled self, but it made me giggle.

They clasped hands, and Robbie swept his arm out and down as he bowed, while Tama curtsied. Then she did something I never would have imagined in a million years she would do. She stepped back and thrust her hands out at Robbie so he could take another bow. The crowd went absolutely nuts for him. Then the entire cast came together in one long line and took their bows as a whole. I cheered louder than anyone, proud of all that we'd accomplished. We'd done it. We'd made it through opening night. The curtain dropped, and the celebration began.

ACT FIVE, SCENE THIRTEEN

In which:

EVERYONE COMES TOGETHER

SECONDS LATER, THE BACKSTAGE AREA LOOKED LIKE TIMES Square on New Year's Eve. Parents in dresses and ties hugged kids in full makeup, offering up plastic-wrapped flowers and kisses and congratulations. Ashley's parents gave her the classic two dozen red roses, and Jonathan's mom had helium balloons that took up half the guys' dressing room. Stephanie and I were chatting with her mom when I felt a distinct presence behind me. I whirled around and found Glenn standing there with a small bouquet of daisies.

"Hi, KJ," he said awkwardly. He took a step back, like he was afraid to get too close, and thrust the flowers out. "These are for you."

"Glenn! I should be giving you flowers! You saved my life out there!"

Glenn blushed and shrugged. "All I did was move the spotlight."

"It was *so* much more than that," I said.

"KJ! KJ!" My mother busted through the crowd with a bouquet of roses.

"Mom! You're here!" I cried, hugging her with all my might. I felt like I could cry. It meant so much to me that she was there, considering everything that was going on at home.

"These are for you. For your big debut," she said, handing me the flowers. Then she turned to Stephanie and gave her another bouquet. "And for the fabulous Miss Lynch."

"Oh, Mrs. Miller! You didn't have to do that!" Stephanie said, smelling the roses.

"Well, you were both wonderful," my mother said.

"I second that," Stephanie's mom added.

"And I third it," her dad put in. "If you can third something."

"Please. Stephanie was great, but only a mother could say that about me," I replied, rolling my eyes.

"I thought you were incredible," Glenn replied. "Well, I mean, if you don't count the fall."

"He's right, you know, KJ," Mrs. Frontz added, joining our little group with Fred. "For no rehearsal and no prep time, you did quite well."

"You should try out next year!" Fred said, bending at the knees and thrusting his arms out. "I bet you get the lead!"

I was mid-laugh when Robbie slipped his arm around my shoulders. "I bet you do, too."

"Well, I couldn't have done it without you guys," I said. There were a bunch of "aw's" and protests, but I wasn't having it. "I'm serious. All of you. If it hadn't been for you guys, I never would have gotten it together and gone out there," I said, looking from Fred to Steph to Robbie, and wishing like anything that Andy were there, too. "And if it wasn't for Glenn I might still be prostrate on the stage."

Glenn snorted and ducked his head while Robbie knocked his arm with a fist.

"So, I just wanted to say thanks," I said, a lump rising up in my throat. "I'm really lucky to have friends like you."

Fred and Glenn beamed, and I could tell Stephanie was proud of me. I was proud of myself, too. I felt like at some point tonight I had actually learned something. I had actually grown. And it felt good.

"Good speech," Robbie said, giving me a quick kiss on the cheek.

I blushed as my mother arched her eyebrows. "What's this?"

"Nothing!" I replied.

"It better not be nothing. I don't want boys kissing my daughter if it's nothing," my mom joked.

"Mother! Please!" I said, mortified.

"Watch out, people! Coming through! Coming through! Special delivery!"

A couple of cast members dodged out of the way as a huge gift basket wrapped in cellophane appeared in the center of our small crowd.

"Wow, KJ. You really made out tonight!" Stephanie said.

The basket dropped to the ground, revealing a flushed Andy. "It's not for KJ," he announced. "It's for you!"

Stephanie's jaw dropped, and I cuddled happily into Robbie's side. "For me?" she said. "What is it?"

"It's all your favorite things," Andy said proudly. "I've got cheddar popcorn and green pears and chocolate-covered pretzels and several romantic comedies on DVD. Oh! And I got you the new Texas Instruments scientific calculator!" he said. "It's so good. You have to see—"

He dropped to his knees and started to tear into the cellophane. Stephanie grabbed the back of his sweater to stop him.

"Whoa, whoa, whoa. What's going on here?" she asked.

"I kind of answered all Andy's survey questions pretending I was you," I confessed.

"And we have a ninety-one percent compatibility!" Andy announced. "That's unprecedented."

"Uh, Jill? What's going on here?" Stephanie's mother asked my mom.

My mother shrugged in response.

"Wow. A ninety-one percent, huh?" Stephanie said, mulling it over. "That is pretty high."

"Precisely," Andy said.

"But how about if we hang out a little first, then do massive gifts?" Stephanie suggested.

"Huh." Andy stood up, wiping his palms on the back of his pants. "Sounds like a reasonable plan."

"Good," Stephanie said with a grin.

Andy grinned right back. "Good."

"Hey, Cage."

"Tama!" I said, surprised to see her hovering. I'd thought she'd slunk out the moment the curtain dropped. People were still pretty mad at her. "You're still here!"

"Yeah, well, Mr. Katz felt the need to have a little chat," she said sarcastically. As if she didn't deserve to be scolded for what she'd done. "I'm on my way out now, but he told me to tell you I'll be here for the rest of the performances. You don't have to worry."

"Thanks," I said. "That's good to know. You were really good tonight, Tama."

"Whatever," Tama said, slipping her sunglasses on. "I'm outta here."

She slipped easily through the crowd, everyone still dodging instinctively out of Ms. Popularity's way.

"You believe her?" Robbie asked quietly as we both watched her go. "You really think she's not gonna bail again?"

"Who knows?" I replied. "But I'm not going to think about it right now. Right now, I'm hanging out with my real friends."

ACT FIVE, SCENE FOURTEEN

In which:

I SAY THE WORDS

I TOOK A DEEP BREATH OF THE COOL NIGHT AIR AND WATCHED THE steam rise up toward the stars. It was a perfectly clear night, perfect for starting over. Robbie and I walked hand in hand, a few yards behind my mother and Christopher, who had been playing in the lobby with his friends while we were all backstage. He and my mother were chatting in low tones, so even that freeze-out had ended.

"I can't believe it's actually over," I said with a sigh. I had taken the stage and survived. All that worrying I'd done the past couple of nights and now, it was in the past. I had nothing to worry about. Well, nothing musical related anyway.

"I can't believe we actually have school tomorrow," Robbie grimaced.

I groaned and tipped my head back. "Oh, God. Don't talk about it."

"Okay, we'll talk about something else," Robbie said, pulling me closer to his side. "Like, where are we going right now?"

"Fuddruckers," I said, giving a little skip.

He watched me, amused. "And we're excited about fast food because . . . ?"

"Please! They're the best burgers on earth! My dad always takes us there after we do something good."

The moment the word *dad* was out of my mouth, a lump formed somewhere between my heart and my stomach. I stared at the asphalt.

"Are you okay?" Robbie asked, smoothing my hair back from my face. I smiled slightly. I loved how he kept touching me. Like he couldn't keep his hands off of me. This afternoon, we had been just friends. But for the past few hours, he hadn't left my side except to deliver his lines on stage.

"My dad's actually never missed a musical before. If you can believe it," I said sadly. "I mean, he can't be that bad, can he?"

"I'm sure he's a good dad in some ways," Robbie said.

"God, I'm evil," I told him, covering my face with my gloved hands. "It's not like he's *always* awful. It's just . . ."

"It's complicated," Robbie said simply.

"Yeah, and I hate that," I said. "Why does it have to be so confusing?"

Robbie stopped walking, and after a couple of steps I stopped, too, and turned to face him.

"What?" I asked.

"It's just . . . a lot of things are confusing," he said. "Last week I thought I liked Tama, and you were, like, head-over-heels in love with Richardson, but I still knew I liked you, too. That was confusing."

I smiled. "You knew you liked me, too?"

"Yeah," he said. "Didn't you know you liked me?"

"Well . . . yeah," I admitted.

"And it was confusing, right?" he said.

"Yeah. Definitely."

"But now it's all worked out. We unconfused it. We made it simple," Robbie said.

"So . . . what are you saying?"

Robbie stepped toward me. Behind me, I could hear the bonging of my mother's car door as she and Christopher got in.

"Just that the last few weeks have been sucky and complicated and confusing, but maybe all of that craziness had to happen so that things could get simple," he said. "Maybe, right now, your dad is unconfusing things. Just like we did."

I felt a thump of something in my chest. Hope, maybe? I wasn't sure. I hadn't allowed myself to feel it in a very long time.

"You think?"

"I hope," he said, his brown eyes serious as they gazed into mine.

It took me a long moment to say it. To allow myself, after all this time, to form the words. I'd been afraid of them for so long. But somehow, looking into Robbie's eyes helped me do it.

"I hope so, too."